W9-BUM-675

THE FINAL BEAST

FREDERICK BUECHNER

THE
FINAL BEAST

1817

HARPER & ROW, PUBLISHERS, San Francisco
Cambridge, Hagerstown, New York, Philadelphia
London, Mexico City, São Paulo, Sydney

Library of Congress Cataloging in Publication Data

Buechner, Frederick
  The final beast.

  I. Title.
PS3552.U35F5 1982   813'.54   81-47438
ISBN 0-06-061159-6 (pbk.)   AACR2

82 83 84 85 86 10 9 8 7 6 5 4 3 2 1

For Katherine & Dinah

THE FINAL BEAST

Then from the far caverns
Of dead sins
Came monsters, livid with desire.
They fought,
Wrangled over the world,
A morsel.
But of all the sadness this was sad—
A woman's arms tried to shield
The head of a sleeping man
From the jaws of the final beast.

The Black Riders   Stephen Crane

ONE

BLUEBEARD has gone away. He came in while
you were still asleep, and he kissed your
eyes."

"I was sleeping."

"Irma will take care of us."

"I love Irma."

"Bluebeard will come back. He said so."

"I know it."

"You were asleep."

"Is Bluebeard coming back?"

"Yes."

"I want breakfast."

"Let's go wake up Irma. She won't mind."

"I love Irma," said Lizzie Nicolet, Lizard Boy, who
was three. Her older sister, Cornelia, who was five,
bounced up and down on the bed beside her. Pie Face.
The spring sun was newly risen, and there was no
one else awake on all of Congress Street. They decided to leave Irma alone a while longer and played

records on their tinny little cardboard victrola—*The Parade of the Wooden Soldiers, Old Paint, Raggedy Ann*. Lizzie crawled deep into Cornelia's bed with just her enormous eyes showing above the covers. Cornelia changed the records and was Timmy Martin. This meant that Lizzie had to be Lassie. On the third floor Irma Reinwasser slept fiercely, bandy-legged little woman with grey hair short and thick as steel wool, the face of an Arab. She was dreaming of barbed wire, mile after mile of it. Here and there it blossomed like roses, but there was no break in it anywhere as she hastened up and down looking for a way out of her dream. A way out of her dream into what? Heaven only knew, what with Bluebeard gone now, his unread note propped up against the toaster downstairs.

His wife had been dead just over a year. She was backing out of the supermarket parking lot with the car full of groceries, clothes for the cleaner, a carton of posters announcing Sunday School registration, when an oil truck coming down Newton Avenue hit her broadside. Death was instantaneous and strangely gentle. The car was a shambles, but her sun glasses were still on, and there was an unlit cigarette safe between her fingers. The shopping list in her purse suggested her dying thoughts if you can speak of the dying thoughts of one who was simply, the next moment, dead. It was all crossed off except for two things: *Nick's watch* and the single word *Beauty*. The first was clear enough. A broken mainspring was the jeweler's diagnosis when Nick himself went for it a week later, and although he was advised that it was not worth fixing, he had it fixed anyway as if this established that Franny's trip had somehow not been entirely for nothing. But *Beauty* remained a mystery. Lizzie had a doll by that name—from Guatemala, made of papier maché and painted with the spangled tights of a Victorian soubrette. Or did it mean beauty parlor, or some new detergent, hand cream, floor wax? Or just all that Franny took away with her that morning, or all that she left behind in that New England spring.

Theodore Nicolet did not conduct his wife's funeral himself. He had no fear of being unable to get through it but rather the fear of his congregation's so marking his personal grief—the poor young pastor, it must be such a trial for him—that this would be all they felt, a grief both more and less than what was called for, in either case the wrong grief. So Ralph Denbigh took the funeral with no grief at all in his perspiring face but only the insane suspicion that perhaps he was making the great blunder of his career, that she was not really dead at all, or that it was he, not she, who had died. And it was little Ralph Denbigh who buried her in the new cemetery overlooking the river along whose banks the town of Myron stood.

The Vails took the children for the first week. They had not been particular friends of the Nicolets, but they had a big house on the heights with no children of their own but everything else to keep the little girls diverted—horses, a pig, a pond full of goldfish—and when Rooney Vail arrived to make her offer with her sandy hair skinned back under a yellow band, there seemed no reason to refuse it. At that point she called him Ted, a name that no one used who knew him but rather Nick or Nicko, Bluebeard to the children because even though he shaved twice a day, it was not enough. He was a skinny young man with heavy black hair and a clown's arched eyebrows and deep-set, turquoise eyes. "Cold, prickly little eyes," Rooney called them months later, and his smile too she came to deplore. "Oh boy, it gives you away, I mean really!" she cried. "If you want to pass for a priest, don't ever smile." It was a gay, foolish smile, like a drunk's or a lover's.

Irma Reinwasser came about two months later, and again it was Rooney who managed it through a friend of Clem's who worked at the American Consulate at Munich. "She's fifty-five if she's a day, although forty-five is all she admits to," the friend wrote. "She doesn't know much English, and God knows she's no beauty, but she's dead to get to the States, and I'm sure she'll do anything to make a go of it. She's Jewish, and the story is she had a pretty tough time of it during the war, but you don't need to worry that she'll talk about it. She says she loves children and that her favorite sport is long-distance swimming. I explained that your minister friend could provide her with both." So she arrived in the heat of July on the bus from Boston in worn tweeds the color of lead and carrying as her only luggage two umbrellas and a large dress box tied with brown cord. She brought presents for both of the children—an inflatable black rubber monkey for Lizzie and a glass paper-weight containing a view of the Schwarzwald for Cornelia—and any misgivings the two might still have had were dispelled the first time their father took her with them to the beach and she swam all the way from the long pier to the rich man's point and back without stopping. She wore a one-piece black bathing suit with a gum rubber cap and bathing shoes, and Cornelia said that her legs looked like mashed potatoes. Once, when she was trying to unstick a window in the kitchen, it gave way so suddenly that the pane splintered all over the floor, and her exclamation then seemed to unfurl like a banner under which she had spent a lifetime battling: *Wie man's macht, ist's falsch*, which for Nicolet's sake she translated as "Whatever you are doing, it turns out lousy."

All of this had taken place a year before the morning of Nicolet's departure, and when the clock in his church across the street struck six, the two little girls turned off their victrola and padded up the stairs in their bare feet to awaken her.

"Daddy is gone, Daddy is gone," Cornelia threw out at her dreaming, and Lizzie echoed her older sister unintelligibly, not bothering to remove the thumb from her mouth, her forefinger crooked over her nose, and staring out of a dream of her own at the grey head sunk in the pillows. "Bluebeard."

"He is gone," Cornelia repeated, and then jumped

back in fright as all in a moment with the whirling of sheets and nightdress Irma was on her feet staggering about the room like a mad woman—"Oh my God, oh my God!"—and reaching out with both hands for almost anything, the shade, a child. It was the shade that she found first, and it rolled up with a bang so that the room was shot full of sunlight, and she stood there staring it down in her heavy white gym socks, the room musty with the odor of hair and teeth. "What is this you are saying? It's too early for jokes," and she snatched up Lizard Boy in her arms, hugging her tight as something warm and alive to get her bearings by.

Outside on Congress Street, a boy rode past on a bicycle and tossed a copy of the *Myron Repository* onto the cement walk. A gust of air started the last of the lilacs nodding, then puffed out into a breeze that entered the window where Irma was standing with the children and seemed to catch them up in a swelling cloud of sunlight and freshness that swirled them around, all chattering at once, and down the flight of stairs to Nicolet's bedroom where, receiving no answer to her knock, Irma opened the door to find his bed empty and his pajamas hung up on the open door of his closet.

"Did he tell you where he was going? Why he was going?" Irma shook his pillow vehemently as though to dislodge the answer, then "I want my breakfast," from Lizzie in the gravelly, remote voice of a wind-up toy as the cloud caught them up once more and carried them down the second flight when it burst like a soapbubble, leaving them in the cool, dim kitchen at the rear of the house.

A mouse scudded across the linoleum and under the sink. "Maybe he can tell us something. Mousie, *komm! Aber ganz schnell!*" Irma made little coaxing noises with her tongue. "That mousie knows plenty." Lizzie smiled around her thumb. Cornelia, having found her father's note leaning up against the toaster, had already drawn a face on it with a green crayon when with great delicacy, slipping another piece of scrap paper into the child's hands almost before she could notice the exchange, Irma rescued it from her. Without her glasses, she had to hold it so close to see what it was that it nearly touched her nose.

"Look now, this is from Bluebeard. It's going to tell us everything."

"Bluebeard left a letter, Liz!" Cornelia cried with studied excitement and surprise.

"I know it." It was Lizzie's green crayon and she wanted it back but for the moment not enough to ask for it. Irma read the note in silence.

Dear Irma,

I have to go away for a little while. I looked in on the kids before I left, and I'm sure there won't be any trouble from them. No more than usual anyway. I told them I would be back soon, and I believe that's so. I'm sorry to pull this on you so unexpectedly, but the time has come, that's all. If I had any half-way decent explanation for myself, I'd give it to you. There are sure to be people trying to get hold of me for one thing or another, but you can just tell them I was called away suddenly. If I don't make it back in time for the service Sunday, call Denbigh. Take good care of my kiddos for me. I may call some day. *Auf-wiedersehn,*

T.N.

"He writes here that he will be coming back soon," she said absently, all her attention on the note itself which she re-read several times, pitching her shoulders back toward the kitchen window as if the increased light might add some new dimension to the flat little message. "The time has come . . ." for what? Irma understood the idiom in the sense of a car that comes for a passenger, so this meant that the time had come, of course, for Nicolet, and just at daybreak when there would be no witnesses, time in a uniform, on rubber soles. "To pull this on you" meant nothing, and "decent" in this context was obscure.

"Corn Flakes or Raisin Bran?" She scooped Lizzie up into her high-chair, and when the child began to weep, there was an instant almost of terror in Irma's eyes as though all the motherless and now fatherless kiddos in the world were hers to take care of forever possibly; then Lizzie's trembling finger, pointed accusingly at her sister, reasserted reality.

"That green one is hers, Cornelia," Irma said. "Give

it to her like a good girl. There now." And then promising Cornelia the cup that played music, she restored a
kind of peace. The children began to eat, and Irma
stood at the sink running the cold water hard for no
reason other than to give herself time to think.

The long, clean diagonals of swimming, stroke after
stroke, from this point to that point, then shoreward a
few strokes, and back again: a parallelogram. This was
the joy of water, that the lines could be clean. In the
barbed wire dream, objects, creatures, kept menac-
ing her off her course so that it was not the side of a
square that she traveled up and down but a worm's
trail; waking or sleeping, this was the way of earth.
The deep chill of the tap water numbed her fingers
now, and she withdrew them, the slender, braided
stream drumming down again on the old copper sink
bottom.

"No more sugar now, Lizard Boy. Your teeth all will
come spilling out."

Spring, summer, fall, winter rotated in a slow circle;
the numbers one to one hundred ascended a gentle hy-
potenuse. Irma thought geometrically, trying always to
shape experience into forms that she could manage.
The young wife died, then time came at dawn for the
young husband, and these were two points marking
the base of a triangle whose apex chance had yet to
provide, two points hungry for a third. But whatever
or whenever the third was to be, Irma thought, the
result would inevitably be a triangle so that if not the
substance, she knew at least the shape of what lay

ahead, and there was some reassurance in that. Only let the lines be clean.

"How would you like it if we go this morning to the beach and swim?"

"We're not afraid of the water, are we, Lizzie?"

"Not any more."

"Good." Irma turned to look at the children really for the first time that day, and suddenly the question "Why would Bluebeard go away like this?" became for her instead the question "Why would Bluebeard stay?" Only for these two, she thought: to keep them safe and, because there is a wildness in men that children can sometimes cage, to be kept safe by them. He might choose to stay for Pie Face and Lizard Boy, but she discarded every other reason.

His church was old ladies, and another could do for them as well. He must know that. She had seen him come back haggard from their dying, his stomach in knots. The doctor told him that there was nothing wrong with him but just that he had sat out too many terminal cancers—a simple stroke, a heart failure, and he would be back on his feet again. An old woman in a hospital, her legs wrapped up in elastic stockings, her eyes half closed and her teeth out; she whimpered as the fluid went drip-dripping through the rubber tube down into the jar clipped to the bed springs. Or watery-eyed in her own front parlor, she might hold him over a cup of cold tea until whole great reels of the past had come jerking and flickering out like a home movie in which no one explains who the old gentleman with the beard is who keeps running through the dusk or why there should be such endless shots of just that particular section of empty beach. Any other could sit there as well as Bluebeard and ask questions as politely. Why should he stay?

There was God, of course, but God made Irma Reinwasser very angry. He asked so much of His servants and rendered so little: marry and bury, christen and counsel, joke with, solicit from, try somehow to live by Him, live with Him. It emptied a man. Yet skinny and bright-eyed in his black robe, he still had to stand up in the pulpit Sunday after Sunday and speak to Him and about Him to that big, white, half-filled meeting-house of a church with the turkey-red carpet, "And when they tell me he looks like Abe Lincoln," Irma said, "I tell them after Abe Lincoln got shot is what he looks like. If you got God for a friend, you don't need any enemies." What did God give in return? A dead wife, knots in the stomach. She plucked up the bacon with a cooking fork and flipped it over. It spat at her. Why should Bluebeard stay for the sake of God?

Or was it maybe for the sake of God that he had gone? Sobered by this possibility, she sucked her wrist gravely where the hot fat had scalded her. You could never be sure about Bluebeard and God. There were times when she felt that each must take the other as a kind of joke, and when every night just after her light was turned out Cornelia began with "Our Father who aren't in Heaven" instead of "Our Father who

art," you could imagine both God and Nicolet laughing
as in fact sometimes Bluebeard actually did laugh,
so soft you could hardly hear it as he sat there on the
child's bed with his eyes closed. But his eyes were
closed; that was just it. That was why you could never
be sure what Bluebeard felt about God or what his
lightheartedness meant. It might not be a joke at all.

"Maybe Mrs. Vail will go too," Cornelia said.

"She has red hair," Lizzie said, her upper lip white
with milk.

"Lizzie, we don't like Raisin Bran, do we?" Cornelia
pushed her bowl aside and placed the spoon in her
orange juice glass.

"Sometimes I like it."

"What are you saying about Mrs. Vail?" Forgetting
the burn on her wrist, Irma slipped on the kitchen
linoleum in her haste to reach their table. She took
Cornelia's face between her thumb and forefinger and
raised it to her.

"I said maybe she will go too."

Irma kept hold of the round little face unnecessarily
because Cornelia now tendered it, expressionless, to
that voracious scrutiny. Irma shook her head slowly
from side to side. It was not believable that the gossip
should have reached the children; it was not believable
that it should have occurred to them first instead of to
her. "You mustn't say that. People are going to listen."

"But you promised we could go," Lizzie protested,
"and she could go with us."

"Go *where?*"

Cornelia pushed away Irma's hand irritably. "To the beach!"

"You ask Mrs. Vail to go too, Irma!" Lizzie's tone was recriminatory.

"Oh my God!" She had not had time to put on her bathrobe or tidy herself up before the chase downstairs to search for Nicolet, and now as she clapped her hands together and did half of a queer little thunderstruck pirouette there in her gym socks, she looked for the second time that morning like a madwoman.

"Children, be good to Reinwasser, please. Today maybe she is losing her mind." She gave them both their toast and bacon, and finally sat down herself to drink her black coffee. Sun came through the window above the breakfast table now and floodlit her face: the small brown eyes, great wedge of a nose, and zany, grizzled hair. She leaned over her cup like a gargoyle.

"Will you call her, Irma? Will you call her?" Cornelia persisted.

"We love her, don't we, Cornelia. She has red hair and freckles just like Raggedy Ann."

"Oh anything, anything . . ." Irma said. The hot coffee lulled her, the sunlight. It was not even seven yet; ordinarily, she would still be asleep. "Why not?" she said. "After breakfast when we are all dressed and cleaned up nice and the kitchen's put away, I am going to call up Mrs. Rooney Vail, and then we see."

"We call her Raggedy Ann," said Lizzie.

It was shortly after nine that Irma called, and she

let the telephone ring a dozen times, but there was no answer. By now, all ready in their bathing suits and carrying pails and shovels, a dustpan and an eggbeater, the children were eager to be on their way with or without their friend, but now it was Irma who insisted. If Rooney Vail was not at home this hour of a warm June morning, then she was determined to discover where she was instead.

The seed that Pie Face had planted in innocence sent out deep roots; the soil had been well prepared. Grogan, the taxi driver, taking her to the Boston bus one snowy afternoon on her day out, had been the first to approach her with the subject. "That Reverend of yours, he's turning into quite the young fella now the Missus has passed on," and Grogan craned around toward the back seat to see her reaction. She told him that he had better watch where he was going and that no man with a cast in his eye should be driving a taxi anyway. He named no names, but his meaning was clear enough. Others had been less guarded. Hilda, the Bavarian girl who waited on tables at The Old Myron, had asked her point blank if it was true that Rooney was getting a divorce to marry Mr. Nicolet. Perhaps because they were speaking German, Irma let herself reply with somewhat greater freedom, at least acknowledging the subject as not entirely implausible. She did not know anything about the Vails' marriage, she said, but she knew that they had never had any children of their own and that it seemed to make Mrs. Vail happy to be around with the little Nicolets and that

the Reverend Nicolet was happy to have the help of a
lady like Mrs. Vail with some of the things that poor
Mrs. Nicolet had once done for him: errands, calls,
pouring tea, . . . *"Ist dass alles?"* Hilda had asked,
cocking a bold eye at her across the table where they
were sitting. *"Gewiss, dass ist alles,"* Irma said, meaning it.

"Forget about Raggedy Ann," Cornelia said. "Let's
go!" And she tugged at the striped beach towel that
Irma carried over her shoulder.

"Now I am just going to try Mr. Vail at the shop,"
she said. "Then I call the taxi, and we go."

Clem Vail answered almost immediately. Although
normally his manner was agreeable and easy, over the
telephone his voice had a way of coming through
sullen and deep as though he was about to lose his
temper. "She's gone off somewhere," he told Irma,
"and to tell you the truth, I don't know when the Hell
she's coming back." Irma could not quite bring herself
to ask where she had gone, but she did ask if Mrs.
Vail would be coming back that day, and to this Clem
answered only that he would ask her to call when she
returned. And his tone was so final that Irma let the
matter rest there, thanked him, and hung up.

Grogan attempted no conversation as he drove them
to the beach. Irma sat in back with the little girls and
gazed out of the window, seeing nothing, while Cornelia sang one of the songs that she had played on
the victrola just after their father's departure that
morning. It was a song about Raggedy Ann with her

shoe-button eyes shining bright and about how lovely
and soft it was to cuddle her.

But when I'm asleep, then my Raggedy Ann
Goes out with the fairies to play,
For she thinks I don't know it, my Raggedy Ann,
But she cannot fool me that way.

TWO

———◆———

CLEM VAIL had started his Something Shop within a few months of their moving to Myron eight years before, and although the last thing that he needed or expected was to make money, it was a financial success from the start. Originally he bought a run-down old store front at the far end of McKinley Street where the river curved in close to the backs of the shops, but as business increased and his stock grew, he spread out into the building that adjoined it. This was little more than a shed that had been a blacksmith's, then a bicycle repair agency, but he painted the floor bright yellow, restored the Franklin stove to working order, had the smoke-blackened walls shored up, and then it was not long before he could easily have found use for as much space again.

"We sell Things," the sign pasted on the inside of the glass door read. He had begun with what he found in the attic of the Victorian farmhouse that they had bought on the heights: bound copies of old magazines—*Harper's Weekly, Galaxy, St Nicholas*—several humpbacked steamer trunks, shoe boxes full of stereopticon slides, china-headed dolls, some palm-leaf fans, harness bells, a wastepaper basket made from an elephant's foot; but neither antiques nor junk was what he wanted to specialize in, so he expanded in other directions. There was an esoteric assortment of kitchen hardware: rotary cheese-graters, garlic presses, apple corers, little odd-shaped knives for a variety of culinary uses. There was a miscellany of small camping and sports equipment: fishing flies, hand-warmers, crow calls, air rifles, things made of leather and stainless steel, things made of straw, of wood, and an extraordinary collection of bells—donkey bells, goat bells, cow bells, camel bells—all of it set out with little order on long, low tables and the shelves that lined the walls to ceiling height. "It's a damned pack-rat's paradise," Clem said, and he spent hours puttering around in the midst of it, always in khaki—khaki slacks in the winter, and in the summer his brown, hairy legs protruding from khaki shorts. There was a boy's tense toughness about his face except in repose when some kind of dimness blurred it, troubled it. Although in his late thirties, he could have passed for a college senior. He was a sportsman without any particular sport, a businessman without any real business.

"I'm really my own first cousin," was his little joke. "That's why I look like each other. Let me tell you about my family. It's a real bitch," and then, after two or three martinis, he would tell his tale of two New

York brothers marrying two Philadelphia Main Line sisters, then both couples getting divorced and each brother marrying the other sister after which there were further divorces and remarriages; "But anyway, my mother is really my aunt," he would say, "and my uncle's my father, and I'm really my grandmother's niece except that she always calls me Dad. Alcoholism, nymphomania, necrophilia. You name it, in my family we've got it." The only one of them all whom he spoke of as anything more, or less, than a joke, was an unmarried aunt who had brought him up, or at least to whose large house in Connecticut he had returned for vacations from Fessenden, Andover, Princeton. His mother had died in a sanitarium, and after a scandal involving some fraudulent real estate transactions his father had taken his third wife to South America, where presumably he still lived although there had been no word from him since a cablegram at the time of Clem's wedding. His aunt was the only relative of his whom Rooney had ever met, and she died while they were still in Austria on their honeymoon, leaving Clem as her sole beneficiary. Rooney also had a substantial trust fund under her father's will so that together, although few were aware of it, they were the richest couple in town. For the first two years of their marriage they lived in New York, where Clem had worked without interest, ability, or financial incentive in a brokerage office, and then they moved to Myron where they bought their big house and settled down to raise a family.

But children never came. For the first few years
they tried doctor after doctor; for months Rooney kept
a daily chart of her temperature, she spent a week in a
Boston hospital under the most thorough observation,
eventually she underwent a minor operation, but the
result of it all was at last to be told that there seemed to
be no biological reason whatever why she could not
conceive. Then of course the question of Clem arose,
the possibility which all along he had refused to face,
and Rooney with him, because if the fault lay with her,
they both of them felt, it was tragic, but if it lay with
him, it was a bad joke. For over a year he refused any
kind of examination, convinced by now that the out-
come could only be the denial of his manhood, the final
humiliation, and then finally, unexpectedly, he con-
sented. He arose early one morning while Rooney was
still asleep and after grimly reenacting the habit of
his boyhood drove down to the Myron Hospital where a
poker-faced technician immediately placed under a microscope what he had brought in his raincoat pocket
and Clem stood there in the cluttered basement laboratory waiting for the heavens themselves to crack apart
with raucous laughter. "Here, take a look," and the
technician had pushed the microscope toward him,
and with the sweat cold on his forehead he gazed down
at the twitching constellation of human life, the puls-
ing, tadpole bearers of unimaginable generations. "If
this was Coney Island," the technician said, "they'd
give you a kewpie doll," and before he had any idea
what he was doing, Clem Vail had found himself

weeping like a child.

The discovery that their childlessness was the fault of neither, or of both, gave them a sense of release that for a time at least outweighed the conviction that, since the trouble apparently defied medical science, there was nothing that anyone could ever do to remedy it. Physical desire replaced once more what for all the months of their trying had become a kind of clinical desperation, and after five years of marriage, they found themselves in love again, the absence of children binding them together more perhaps than even a child could have bound them. And because of their wealth there was nothing—with this one exception—that they could not have. They were not extravagant in any obvious way—the car that they drove, the clothes that they wore, the trips that they took in no measure set them apart from their friends—but they spent large sums on their house, renovating room after room which for years had stood unused, filling them with books, pictures, antiques, installing a new furnace, a new hot water system; and they gave the impression that there was no limit to the placid abundance that they enjoyed, that whether they entertained six or sixty for dinner, there would always be more than enough good food, good liquor, good silver and china to go around. If there was nothing ostentatious about their bounty, there was also nothing self-conscious or apologetic about it; it was as naturally theirs as poverty was the poor's, and for that reason no one seemed to hold it against them or even to envy it

overly because there was always, too, their barrenness
to pity as if, open-handed young pair that they were,
they offered this as well for the comfort of their friends.

Raggedy Ann. She had a freckly, keen face as
though looking to windward from the deck of a summer sloop, her shoebutton eyes a little narrowed against
the sun, her sandy hair swept back under a bright
band, a wide and gaudy mouth. Clem had met her first
during the spring of his senior year at Princeton when
she had arrived for a houseparty weekend with some
other boy, and somewhere in the course of a fragrant
and labyrinthine evening of wandering from club to
club down Prospect Street, he had come across her sitting alone and a little drunk on the wall in front of
Cottage. Through a sequence of events that neither
of them could ever well remember afterwards, they
had ended up spending most of that Saturday night together on an Army blanket by Lake Carnegie, then a
chance meeting the next afternoon at the railroad station where she was waiting alone for the New York
train, deserted by the angry boy who had brought her.
She wore a black linen dress with a dark kerchief tied
around her hair and looked pale and unapproachable
as a nun; but when, with a pang of dread and longing in
his stomach, Clem had gone up to her, she smiled and
recited, "I did but see you passing by, yet I shall love
you till I die," and standing there in the rumpled seersucker suit that he had been wearing since the evening
before and with a night's growth of beard on his chin,
Clem asked her to marry him. Her widowed mother,

who knew something of the Vails and their history, was fearful of the match, but Rooney prevailed, and the wedding took place after graduation that August in a weathered shingle house on Martha's Vineyard overlooking the sea.

She ran away from him on their honeymoon. They were staying at an inn in the Pinzgau valley in Austria, and there was no warning, no quarrel or blunder to explain it. He had left her taking a nap after lunch to drive up to Kitzbühel to buy a pair of ski boots, and when he returned, she was gone, leaving no message for him, no note. He spent the rest of the day searching the mountain trails with their little colored markers, not even hearing the occasional *Grüss Gott* of a villager; he looked in the church with its life-size wooden Christ painted with terrible wounds; in desperate, guide-book German he made what inquiries he could. It was not until the evening of the next day that he traced her to Innsbruck and finally found her eating veal paprikash at the Goldener Adler. She seemed quite glad to see him as though he was the one who had gone away and now returned. "Oh Lord," she said, "I felt so hemmed in by all those mountains. And for two people that bed they gave us just isn't big enough. I had to get off by myself," and when he asked her at last if she would have eventually come back to him, her only reply was, "I don't know, I don't know," kissing the palm of his hand, so quiet and puzzled that it was clear that she really did not know, and neither, of course, did he.

He never came to know. After his moment at the

hospital laboratory, there had been the relief, the resignation to childlessness that reunited them in a way that
for a while made the idea of her running off again unthinkable; but this did not last for long, and often after
a few months when he would come back from the
Something Shop to find her unexpectedly gone, he wondered whether she had not perhaps felt herself hemmed
in once more. It was not the love that bound her to
him that he doubted so much as simply whatever it was
that did or did not bind her to precisely this house, this
bed, to Myron, the geography of their life together.
Rooney seemed to remain on the surface here, uncom-
mitted, while Clem went out of his way to hem himself
in wherever he could, surrounding himself with his
knives and his bells, his decoys, ski wax, fishing reels,
standing guard there among them day after day in
his khakis, this potent and somberly handsome young
soldier without any particular battle to fight or any
enemy that he could clearly see. While Rooney came
and went, it was Clem who joined the field club, became a member of the zoning committee, the hospital
board, and it was through Clem's decision to look
around for a church to join that they had first met
Nicolet the winter before his wife was killed.

Clem was furry-chested, blunt-fingered, a little in-
distinct; Nicolet was a skinny, dark blade. Clem
joined; Nicolet belonged. Clem brooded, and Nicolet
had his clown's eyebrows, his giddy, sudden smile.
As Nicolet moved along, he left markers behind to
trace his passage—new blackboards in the Sunday

school rooms, an old woman delivered of some garbled memory, a benediction at the highschool graduation, the two little yellow-haired girls—whereas looking back on his own past, Clem saw only places where he had rested between the laps of a race whose purpose seemed not so much to get anywhere or to win anything as just to keep himself in condition, for something.

"Why do you want to join a church? You believe in God or something?" Nicolet asked once as they stood in his office, a wet snow falling past the window with flakes as big as flapjacks, and as at the crack of a starter's pistol, Clem had the sense of another lap's beginning.

"Do you?" He was surprised at his own question since he had no real reason for asking it.

"Sometimes I believe in the hot breath down my neck."

"I suppose if somebody was breathing down my neck," Clem said, "I'd believe in that too."

"Somebody probably is."

"I've never gone in too much for the Holy Ghost."

"Well, I'm sure the feeling's mutual."

Clem both liked him for not urging him to join, and felt menaced by it, as though Nicolet left it to him to prove his seriousness. Clem persisted, and in the end he both joined Nicolet's church by confession of faith—faith in Nicolet, as much as anything, in the wisdom just of joining, of hemming yourself in, the goblins out—and persuaded Rooney to join with him. She showed little enthusiasm for the move. "If I were

God," she said, "I'm damned if I'd be so interested in religion and churches. I'd be interested in making things. I'd always be making marvelous new worlds, and marvelous new kinds of people to put in them . . . babies." But as time went by, it was more apt to be she than Clem who went to the Sunday services where she always sat in the next to last pew, usually in black with her red hair in a bun tucked under her broad-brimmed black hat, a witch or a nun. She told Nicolet that she was no good at praying and the hymns were too high for her and she could never remember what his sermons were about. "So I add up the hymn numbers. Somebody's got to do it. And if they come out even, that's good."

"She watches your eyes too," Clem said. "She says they're the color of a swimming pool."

"Clem's are like caramels," she answered. They had been sitting there, the three of them—just a week before Franny Nicolet's death—underneath the great elm in front of the Vails' barn, and it was such an easy, defined moment with the lilacs still out and the minister come to call that it was some minutes before either of the men realized how angry Rooney was. "There's just one reason, you know, why I come dragging in there every Sunday. I want to find out if the whole thing's true. Just *true*," she said. "That's all. Either it is or it isn't, and that's the one question you avoid like death."

Poor Nicolet. It was her sudden, quiet rage rather than her question that he was unprepared for, and instead of trying to answer, he tried to placate, to divert, throwing his arms up in the air like a scarecrow and making some idiotic noise, a cry for help. The complete failure of his gesture—Rooney ignored him and hastened across the lawn into her house—brought a dim smile to Clem's lips, and as Nicolet got up to follow her, he stopped him. "It's this not having kids," he said, a kind of veteran for once. "Sometimes she just blows up. It's nobody's fault."

"I'd hate to lose her."

"Yes," Clem said.

But nothing was lost. Franny Nicolet died, and it was at Rooney's suggestion that they took in Cornelia and Lizzie, and day after day she spent leading them around on the broad back of Bunny, the old Morgan mare, showing them the goldfish pond, the pig, the hidden staircase that led up from the back of the linen closet to the attic above. As often as he could, Nicolet came to watch them eat their supper of sandwiches and broth and put them to bed, and Rooney was always nearby, as inept as she was fascinated at the ceremony of it: the teddy-bear went here, the octopus there, and without the stained and ragged strip of blanket Cornelia could not go to sleep at all. Our Father who aren't in Heaven. Clem would watch her watching them. And then once they were returned to their father's house, she did the marketing for a while, helped sort out and dispose of Franny's clothes, took the children to the beach or out for a walk while Nicolet paid his calls, and became at last Raggedy Ann with her shoebutton eyes burning bright and full of nursery talk, disheveled and gay. Nicolet himself she left to his old ladies, who seemed to find a kind of self-forgetfulness under the shadow of his bereavement, and she never even alluded to the question that she had accused him of avoiding like death perhaps just because it was like death that he avoided it. Yet Sunday after Sunday she kept returning to her accustomed place in his church to add up the numbers of the hymns or whatever it was that she did there, and after the service she would stop with the others where he stood in his black robe at the door and shake his hand like a stranger.

It was not until late that fall that Myron took any notice of the situation. By then Irma had long since had both the children and the housekeeping well in hand, and yet Rooney's red station wagon was still to be often seen in front of the Nicolet house. Will Poteat in his column for the *Myron Repository* made his first, oblique reference to it—"Folks say things are brightening up on Congress Street"—but no one at that time seemed to make much of it. Certainly Clem did not. The errands that she ran, the odd jobs for the church office, helping with Lizzie and Cornelia, marked for him the first real step that she had taken toward allowing Myron to hem her in, and this greatly pleased him. It struck him that in many ways she was more his than she had been for months, and far from thinking of Nicolet as a rival in all this, Clem considered him a kind of collaborator.

Then, on the day before Nicolet's departure at dawn,

Clem returned around five o'clock from the Something Shop and found Rooney gone. Thinking that she would be back in time for supper, he sat out on the terrace drinking gin and tonic until almost nine and only then ate alone. She had not returned by the time that he went to bed, and she was still not there when he awoke the next day. It was while he was driving to work that spring morning that he decided all in a moment not only that he had lost her forever but that all along these last few months he had known in some deep and hidden way that he was losing her.

THREE

— ◆ —

FRANNY, FRANNY, poor little animal. . . ."
His shoes still wet with dew from the lawn, he
left quickly drying footprints on the cement
path as he left. The birds sang like a jungle, but almost
everyone was asleep on Congress Street.

"What did you dream about?" he had asked Pie Face.

"Angels."

"What were they doing?"

"They were dancing." It was what she always said
that she dreamed about. He had tried often to find
out what angels looked like. "They're black and little,"
Lizard Boy once said. "Like flies." Nicolet wondered
whether children really had dreams.

He had taken nothing with him, not even a razor or a
toothbrush. Over his arm he carried the jacket of his
baggy grey suit, and he had fifteen dollars in his wallet.
He had thought for a time of taking the car, but although Irma did not know how to drive, she might find
someone to drive it for her, and so he left it. His plan

was to take the bus to Harmon Falls and from there to continue however he could to Muscadine.

The new sun dazzled him from the white façade of the church across the street. The bulletin board read, "Pentecost: the Birthday of the Church. 11 A.M. Sunday. Mr. Nicolet." *Maybe Mr. Nicolet, and maybe not and I shouldn't have waited till the fourth Sunday after Pentecost to preach about Pentecost anyway.* He was talking to Franny now, or to God. But Denbigh would always pinch-hit, and there was no need to worry about the kids, he said, because he would be keeping in touch whatever happened, and Irma was the salvation of them all. Everything they did killed him—brushing hair, snaking out of bathing suits, underpants, Pie Face's confidential "Bluebeard, I think you're going to die soon." "Why? Why?" Because his face was so bony, she told him, and there was gold in his teeth. Daily he died. *I'm Bluebeard now*, he explained. Before that, it was all Indians, and that was how Pie Face and Lizard Boy had happened: Indian names. *Can you remember, wherever you are? Any of it?* He squinted up at the sound of a jet. Remembering would be Heaven and Hell both. At one end the long arc of vapor began to drift away. *Our Father who aren't in Heaven, hallowed be Thy name.* Cornelia had thought that it was *Harold*, not *hallowed*, and logically, then, it became the Harold angels that you hearkened to at Christmastime. *Oh, Harold, be merciful and keep them safe*, he thought. *Franny, my dear . . . .*

*   *   *

"How far you going, Reverend?" The bus driver had climbed out to leave a stack of newspapers in front of Belcher's Drug Store, where Nicolet waited.

"How far will you take me?"

"As far as you want to go."

"Oh well, to the end of the line then. The sky's the limit." Nicolet waved one arm in the air expansively. "I'll take one to Harmon Falls."

"It's nice to get company this early," the driver said, squeezing in under the wheel. "Anything special going on over at Harmon Falls?"

"Not that I know of. I'm just passing through."

"Business trip, Reverend?"

"In my business, everything's business."

"Can't ever leave it behind, can you?"

"You can try like Hell." Nicolet caught sight of the driver's quick glance in the mirror. "When a parson says Hell, it's not like cussing. It's theology." When he smiled, his eyebrows rose absurdly as though he were asking a question or some kind of permission. "Hell's like what it is to try to leave my business behind. Hopeless." Then suddenly he closed his eyes. The empty bus went rattling over the railroad tracks and turned up Newton Avenue past the supermarket where the accident had taken place. It was not to blot out the sight that he closed his eyes, but to draw it closer, touch it.

"Now that was an awful shame, and it hadn't ever

ought to have happened. Those crazy truckers . . ."

"It was her fault too. She shouldn't have been backing."

"Well, the way I look at it, when your time comes to go, you're going to go no matter what you do. Of course, maybe that's not how you're supposed to think about it. I don't know."

"Harold's the only one who really knows."

"Harold?"

"He runs a dancing school." Opening his eyes, Nicolet glanced through the dusty window at a stray gull who had flown up the river from the sea. "For angels."

Listen to me, Franny. It was a way he had of praying: unspoken conversations with the Christ in people, he said, with the compassionate and the canny in them, with the unforeseeable and the jagged. *I'm on my way.* A kind of agonized excitement shot through him, and yet as he let his head sink back against the plush head-rest, his face turned toward the window, he could have been an invalid, deep-eyed and immobile in the early morning light. *What will you do when you get there?*

It is better to journey joyously than to arrive. It was a saying of his father's, poor old Roy, who had never arrived anywhere, and Nicolet saw him sitting now in his boarding-house bedroom, also looking out of a window, the futile and embarrassing old man.

Has she called you to her?

No.

Why has she gone there herself?

I don't know.

They need you so at home.

Franny, tell me what to do.

Don't make a fool of yourself, my dearest. It's what Poteat has been living for.

That was it, of course. He sat upright and loosened his tie.

"If it's too warm back there for you, you can open that window." The driver's eyes watched him in the mirror.

"How far to the next stop?"

"This hour I don't stop till somebody flags me." They were passing a farm now where square black Angus grazed. From his pocket Nicolet took Rooney's card. She had evidently mailed it in Myron before leaving, and it had come enclosed in an envelope—a turn of the century souvenir postcard, from the Something Shop probably, that showed a dapper young man in a straw hat smoking a Cheroot against the background of what must have seemed at the time a skyscraper. Printed above his head were the words, "Thinking of you in—" and then a blank where she had filled in the name Muscadine: On the reverse she had written only, "No one is to know. No one is to come," and, in place of a signature, "Nobody."

Do you love her, Nicko?

Rooney crouched down until the seawater lapped against her freckled shoulders, then ducked under for a second to emerge with her hair plastered dark russet against her forehead and neck. "Now one hand under the tummy and the other under the chin, and you kick like a wild woman." Lizzie squealed, exultant, "Raggedy, Raggedy, Raggedy!" and bobbed around in her orange life preserver with her legs and arms flailing. "Now I'll take them away just for a second—they're right underneath there in case. You can't sink," and all in a moment then, choking and terrified, Lizzie grabbed out and seized her around the neck, clinging like a monkey with her lips blue and chattering as Rooney carried her out—"Oh, my poor drowned rat!"—one of her hands cupped under the defeated little backside, the water dripping down her face like tears. Nicolet, his body milk-white in his bathing suit, and his salt-stiff hair sticking out in all directions, wrapped a towel about them both and stood there with his arm around them to give this shelter too from the suddenly cold, grey breeze that whipped the stinging sand against their calves. "Give me your poor, your huddled masses," she shuddered, and a gull, clumsily flapping, mounted the wind up and up, then dropped his clam down to the grey rocks.

She's the thorn in my flesh, the cross I bear. Once I pushed her out a window.

"The medicos give me little longer stop come my son." They had telephoned Roy Nicolet's telegram to him in the middle of the night, and he showed it to Rooney late the next morning. "Do you mean to say you're still here? You call yourself a priest?" He had just returned from the hospital so that he still wore the clerical collar that he hated because he said that it made him feel like *The Song of Bernadette*. She had come by to leave a bundle of old dresses for the autumn rummage sale.

"I have dozens of these," he flapped the yellow paper at her. "He's been on the point of death for thirty years, maybe longer—a specialist," he said, "a specialist in dying, an artist when it comes to the death-bed summons, and they're always remarkable for this same fine literary flavor. Medicos! Medicos! Where does he get it? He runs a boarding-house, you know—strong as a horse. Dying just a hobby for him." Then he held perfectly still and silent for a moment before staggering slightly backwards with one hand on his heart and the other outstretched toward Rooney. "Come, my son."

"But how can you mock him, I don't care what he's done! Of course you've got to go."

She was sitting downstairs on the sill of an open window with the bundle of clothes in her lap, and "Of course you do, of course you have to go," he said in preposterous parody, coming toward her all hunched over in his black suit, grimacing and waggling his finger. "Of course you do, of course you must," and then as he thrust the finger at her, she lost her balance and fell backwards into the pile of dead leaves just beneath the window which he leaned out of then to look down at her there with her hair the color of the leaves, and "Of course," he said, "of course it's the only thing to do."

But in the end she made him go, and when he arrived, it was all as he had predicted. Roy Nicolet sat by the window in his bedroom, old and heavy-faced beneath his unkempt mounds of candy-white hair, and murmured something vague and shamefaced about alarmist doctors, wonderful new drugs. Having broken appointments and left all kinds of work undone in order to make the half day trip, Nicolet departed in anger within less than an hour of his arrival, and when Rooney heard this, she did not see him again for two weeks and for both of those Sundays was also not to be seen in church. It was during this period that Poteat's column included the words, "The shining red wagon is missed on Congress Street, where winter seems to have come early, and not even for jolly Saint Nick will the sweet birds sing."

At a crossroads the bus stopped to take on several passengers, and Nicolet half rose from his seat, Rooney's postcard falling from his knee to the floor, but then, retrieving it, he sat down again. He removed his necktie and placed it together with the card in the pocket of his jacket. *Amen.*

One of the passengers was a girl of nineteen or twenty who wore toreador pants. Her hair was done up in fat curlers with a scarf tied around to cover them, she wore no make-up, and in one hand she carried a small suitcase. "You better mind your manners, Betty," the driver said. "There's a Reverend back there." There was sleep still in her unopened, morning face, and she took a seat across the aisle from Nicolet while the three workmen carrying their lunch pails walked all the way to the back and sat down on the last seat in a row.

"Off to work?" Nicolet asked.

"I sure am," she said. "I almost missed the bus."

"I would have made it wait for you."

"This one never waits."

"Where do you work?"

"I'm a waitress up the road," she said. "They make us keep our own uniforms laundered, so I carry mine in this." She laid her hands flat, the fingers spread apart, on top of the suitcase on her lap. She could have been a young whore, Nicolet thought, coming back clumsy and dreaming from her love's labors, and yet she would have spoken in the same humdrum, flat-foot way of one who had nothing at all to fear from him and nothing at all to gain.

"You're a Reverend?"

"That's right." He thought no, I am captain of a vice ring with pictures in my pockets that would set your breakfast burning. "I have a church in Myron."

"I come from Muscadine."

"Oh, Muscadine, Muscadine . . ." He felt a pang like homesickness. "Tell me about Muscadine," he said. "I've never been to Muscadine."

"It's not very big," she said. "Just an old hotel and a couple of stores. It's in the woods."

"Hick town!" One of the workmen spoke out loudly from the back of the bus, and his two friends guffawed.

"Muscadine is Noplace," one of them said. "Hickville."

"You tell him, Betts."

Nicolet turned around in his seat to look at them, his expression amused, inquiring. They gazed ostentatiously out of the window, at their lunch pails, their hands.

"How do you get to Muscadine?" Nicolet asked them.

"Ask Betts," the first one said with stifled hilarity.

"They run a stagecoach in about once a month, don't they, Betts?" asked one of the others. The girl had taken a magazine out of her suitcase and gave the impression of being lost in the perusal of it. Again the bus stopped, and the entrance of several more passengers seemed to end the episode as suddenly as it had begun.

Nicolet reached across the aisle and touched the girl's sleeve. "Don't mind them," he said. "The joke was that there really wasn't any joke."

"They're the ones that are the hicks," she said, not looking up from her magazine. "That's the joke."

"But tell me," he was half whispering, and he could feel the silliness of his face as though it were something ill-fitting that he wore, "how do you go to Muscadine really? Is there another bus or something? I have to get there."

"I wouldn't know," she said. "I never heard of the place," and she moved as far over toward the window as she could and turned her back on him. He settled back in his seat again and pulled the shade down far enough to take the sun out of his face, then stretched his arms up over his head and yawned tears into his eyes. *Harold, forgive us, watch over us and keep us safe*, and then as the bus jounced softly along over the dusty road, he thought of the name Muscadine, Muscadine, until it was no longer a name but an intuition, an echo. He thought of the sermon that he had to write for Sunday, Pentecost—the sound as of a rushing, mighty wind and cloven tongues of fire. They could not be drunk, Peter said, because after all it was only the third hour of the day. Then an invalid again with his eyes glittering, his beard blue, he glanced almost languorously across at the sullen and nubile young waitress, whore, hick, whatever she was, and fell asleep.

The bus driver awoke him. "Rise and shine, Reverend. This is Harmon Falls." The other passengers had all left, and the air of the empty bus was stale. On a map the driver showed him Muscadine some forty miles to the northwest at the end of a tortuous thin line that marked the unimproved roads. It was midmorning, and the sun was still bright and hot, but there were dark clouds on the horizon. Nicolet's head ached lightly as he stepped out onto the pavement.

It was a disheveled, glaring town with too many automobiles, and Nicolet crossed the street to the grass common where he sat down on a bench near a squat pyramid of cannon balls and a pigeon-stained cenotaph. He had gone to sleep thinking of Pentecost, and it returned to him now, just coming awake in the shade—a moment not unlike this, he imagined. There were all the accustomed sounds of morning—the traffic, the pneumatic drill at work on the parking lot by the bank, footsteps and voices—and then just the first unaccustomed intensification or distortion of it so that the man unloading vegetables from his pick-up stopped with a crate of tomatoes in his arms and shook his head vigorously sideways as though he had water in his ear. The hum of blood in the head of someone about to faint: the sound began to drift and spread like a cloud swelling in the slow wind. A horn honked and kept up a steady blast that began to reverberate like a bell, a noise within a noise. Nicolet drew his feet together and leaned forward with his chin in his hands, his shirt tail coming out in back. The fire began unspectacularly: whispering flames from hair and fingertips. Then it spread to the shoulders, a conflagration swept high by the hastening wind, and upturned faces burst into flame with everyone getting out of cars at once and yelling, and only then did the big man raise his voice: "Men of Judea, and all who dwell in Jerusalem, let this be known to you . . ." Nicolet watched a butterfly open and close its wings on a cannon ball. "The birthday of the church took place in the midst of terrible fire." That might be a way to begin. He got up with his jacket hooked over his shoulder on one finger and walked away.

At the drugstore where he drank a cup of coffee he found out that there was no bus or train to Muscadine and that a taxi would cost more money than he had, so there was nothing to do but hitchhike. The druggist, on his way to deliver some prescriptions, gave him a ride as far as an intersection at the edge of town where there was a road that he said would take him to the road that led to Muscadine. The druggist also advised him that he would have a better chance of being picked up if he wore his jacket and tie so Nicolet put them on again, smoothed down his hair with his hands, and took up his stand by the curb.

Leaving behind him his children, his church, and begging a ride to a town that he had never heard of to find a young woman who had written that she would be thinking of him in Muscadine but not to follow her there—he wondered whether, if he reflected carefully enough, he would find a moment after which it had become inevitable that he should finally end up on this particular point of this particular road. But Nicolet had a memory for incidents rather than for events, for glimpses rather than for panoramas, and no one such moment occurred to him—only a miscellany of them like bits of moving picture film cut out because there was too little light or too much or because the focus was wrong. He found that he could not even remember clearly what Rooney looked like but only a few snapshots of her, especially one that showed her standing somewhere in the snow with her hair blowing and her face trying to smile but braced against the cold. As a car went by going the wrong way and two children waved at him through the back window, he could not even remember for sure when he had decided to leave that morning. He waved back at them in a doubtful and tentative way as though perhaps it was a mistake and he should be in the car with them. He was not really sure why he was going to Muscadine or why Rooney herself had gone.

But instead of disturbing him, this made him feel suddenly stupid and gay, and as the next car approached, he went down into a burlesque half crouch to thumb it extravagantly, a long, slow sweep of his hand as his whole body swung to the arc of it. It was good to be going and not to know why; if you waited until you knew why, you would never go anywhere. It was faith, after all: simply to go—to have as having not, to grasp nothing but always to hold in the open palm of your hand. He had stayed there crouching at the end of the arc with his thumb still out as he watched the car disappear around the bend in the road with the result that he did not notice the next car speeding up from behind until with a great roar it shot past and sent him spinning back up the curb where wildly, pointlessly, he spun around once more because he could not help himself but had to do this ungainly little dance with the dark clouds gathering and his arms and legs flying out. He ended by catching hold of the telephone pole in the crook of his arm and swinging once around it to a stop with his cheek pressed against the rough, dry wood and his eyes for a moment closed.

Oh, and she was in some sad, queer mess, he knew, the barren young wife, Raggedy Ann with money to burn and the wide, bright mouth that trembled at the corners when she smiled, so of course he must go and seek her out, the one lost sheep of his flock, strayed there to Muscadine. And to escape the old ladies and their dying, to court some lilting death of his own while his youth was still on him and he could still make a gift of it somewhere—these too were a part of his going, he thought, and Harold. . . . Nicolet stood there with his cheek to the pole and his eyes closed beneath the raised brows when he opened them to the touch of the first, big drops of rain. Silken and warm, they came faster, a cloudburst, and with his head down and clutching his jacket tight at his chin, he started to run along beside the road as the cars sped by him with their tires sizzling on the wet macadam. The rain beat against his clenched face, unbelievably sweet to the taste, and Harold, Harold, be at the end of all our journeying, he thought, as with the sickness of something like joy at the pit of his stomach he loped along through the fragrance of it.

FOUR

—◆—

"I N BETWEEN retreats, I retreat," Lillian Flagg
said. "I crawl into a hole and read whodunits
and play bridge or watch television." She was
sitting deep in an armchair with a book open on her
lap and her feet in incongruously stylish shoes resting
on a lopsided hassock. Her small eyes looked tired, almost hurt, but for all of this, there was a freshness, a
kind of capable vigor about her. "There's some sort of
balance wheel down in our natures, thank God, that
tells us when we've had enough religion. It's what
keeps me from flying off in all directions and getting
even funnier than I am already. Funny-peculiar," she
said. "You know." She had a puffy little chipmunk-
cheeked laugh.

"Do you feel like talking?"

Without turning around, Rooney shook her head.
She was sitting on the windowseat watching the raindrops trickle, combine, slide crazily down the windowpane. Lillian Flagg went back to her reading. The

room smelled faintly of wood smoke and coffee. The pine walls were hung with mounted fish and the silhouettes of fish cut out of birch bark. There was a wide engraving of General Washington addressing the Continental Congress, a dusty peacock feather stuck under one corner of the frame, and behind Mrs. Flagg's chair a Mexican serape with part of the fringe missing. The floor was covered with hooked rugs, and there seemed to be pillows everywhere, faded reds, greens, yellows.

"Of all the places you've ever been, which is the one where you were happiest?" Lillian Flagg had asked that morning. "The one where you'd most like to be now."

"Oh God," Rooney said, "I've been so many places. I'm so old, old."

"Just think of one."

"Is it true you're a witch?"

"I'm a good witch."

"I'm rotten at games," Rooney said, but she had done the best that she could, trying to think of some one place while Lillian Flagg repeated dreamily, "A game. A game. A game." There was her mother's house on the Vineyard set up on the dunes overlooking the sea where the muslin curtains flapped and billowed out into the bedrooms and naked between damp sheets you went to sleep to the rumble and hiss of the surf, awoke to the glassy and blinding shimmer of it in the morning sun. "I've been happy plenty of places, but never happiest."

"Then just a place where you've been happy will do." In that tidy and practical voice she could have been giving a recipe for sponge cake, but wide apart under plucked eyebrows, her eyes continued their search.

"When I was sixteen, we spent a few months in Bermuda," Rooney said. "I especially remember the smell. It was marvelous—cedar wood and kerosene stoves and sun-tan oil and horse. I've never smelled such a gorgeous smell. It was terrifically exciting for some reason, maybe just because I was sixteen. You'd bicycle places at night along the coral roads, and it was like a bird flying. In those days there was some kind of narrow-gauge railroad, and if you paid for a first class ticket, you got to sit in a car where the seats were regular wicker armchairs and you could move them around anyplace you wanted. Like a porch. I'd love to be there again." With both hands she brushed her hair back from the temples, the silver bracelets falling down on one arm. "Is that what you want?"

"What is there about it?" Lillian Flagg asked. "Some word. Can you give some one word for the power of that place, whatever draws you back to it?"

"Oh Lord—life," Rooney said abruptly, impatiently, as if to get rid of a word that she did not want. "That's the first word that hits me. It had the smell of life to me."

"That's a good word. Now," she said with a little intake of breath and opening her eyes wider as she drew her clasped hands up to her chin, "now just think

of that power you call life—it's not a bad word for it—
and try to see it, feel it. Oh, it's fantastic, you
know . . ." Her smile was almost laughter, quick
and trustworthy. "Like electricity. It's the great cur-
rent that keeps everything going—the whole show."
The little gesture of unclasping her hands and holding them up for a moment as though to catch a balloon was wooden and incomplete, but it was clear
enough what she intended by it: the earth itself, the
solar system.

"Try this game," she went on. "Imagine that power
flooding into you now like light—just spilling all
through you, making everything sweet and clean. A
house is shut up for a long, long time—that happens—
and you open one window, then another and another,
and the fresh air and the sun come streaming in, and
the cobwebs blow away and the shadows disappear.
There's life in the house again. You've got to try to
see this happening, and after a while you may even be
able to feel it. It's like the needles and pins when your
foot's been asleep. All that life coming back. There
now!" With a brisk sigh she stood up, her hands
clasped at her waist like a singer. "You play that
game for a while now. I'll see about lunch."

As she walked away, her legs looked too thin for
the portly little corseted body, and her hair needed
combing. Left by herself then, Rooney tried to think
as she had been told, but it was not a success. With
her eyes open, she could not force her mind to leave
the room—all the pillows that needed shaking, the

dried flowers, wondering who had caught the fish; and facing the window with her eyes closed, she saw grainy red-orange, in places bruised a darker red with here and there a tiny worm of light; color replaced thought. "It's no use. I don't have the mind for it," she had said as she joined Lillian Flagg in the kitchen where she helped her make them each a sandwich which they ate on the porch steps outside.

But after they had eaten and the thunderstorm came, she tried again, sitting there on the window seat with her hands in her lap. Or, rather, this time she did not try but just leaned drowsily back against the pillows and stared out at the weather, at the flicker and drip of the leaves, the pool gathering in the sag of the canvas deck chair. Because she had never been there before, the things that she saw called up no associations for her, and she saw them as things pure and simple—a grey squirrel sat up on his delicate haunches and licked his paw at her—until with a kind of glazed inertia she gave way beneath the weight of her own history, her name, whatever purpose she had in being there, and they spilled off like raindrops to leave her part of the landscape that held her, a thing among things.

She became what she saw through the window's weeping: the stubbly lawn, earth and grass pelted by rain. It was what the good witch had meant—inundated by life. Less than half waking, Rooney played this game. Dandelions became her eyes, her mouth the ragged, glistening leaf, and from her stomach, cupped between brown hands, a white birch grew. Touching her cheek to the pane, she felt the wet soak deeper and deeper down so that when Lillian Flagg said, "Do you feel like talking?" she had nodded no, tongueless and sodden beneath the fertile rain. Then for a moment in the mended silence she thought that deep inside of her something moved. Perhaps it was life—cedar and horse smell, thunderstorm. Terrified, she turned from the window.

"Who caught all those fish?"

"Flagg." Lillian Flagg closed the book on her hand to keep her place. "My husband was the fisherman of the family."

"My husband fishes too." Rooney smiled down at the window seat as she spoke. "Though in some ways he's really more of a fish—he's terribly careful not to get hooked."

"Who by?"

"I don't know. Life," she said. "That word again. He just never swims far from his hole in the rocks, that's all. He's always ready to flip back in under at the drop of a hat."

"What did he think about your coming up here to see me?"

"I didn't tell him I was coming." For the first time Rooney met her glance directly. "I didn't tell anybody."

"Why not?" Lillian Flagg held her there.

"Why should I?"

"Oh my dear girl, it makes no difference to me whether you told anybody or not." She released her now, her tone suddenly breezy, a little bored. "No differ-," she paused, "-ence - at - all." She became the *grande dame* for a moment, wagging an impatient hand to dismiss any misunderstanding and, flutily, "No, no," she repeated. "No. It's just that you put me in mind of King Saul going to visit the witch of Endor."

"I don't know about King Saul."

"You should. He disguised himself and went by night. He was afraid he might lose his reputation."

"I suppose there was something of that," Rooney said. "Except for me it was more being afraid I'd get a reputation I didn't deserve."

"What kind of reputation is that?"

"For believing in something enough to come here. I don't really believe very much in anything."

"Well, that doesn't matter a bit, at least not at first. At first," Lillian Flagg said, "believing . . . praying . . . it's all just playing a game. Quite ridiculous really, and why not? We are all quite ridiculous." She gave a little laugh. " 'Lord, I believe. Help Thou mine unbelief.' That's it, you see. The man who said that didn't really believe very much in anything either, and it made no difference. His boy was healed. You believe in spite of not believing . . ." As a gust of wind splattered the rain against the window, she paused as though aware for the first time of the storm. "It's the best any of us can do at first, and it's enough."

"Believe in what? You keep talking about believing.

I wish you'd make it very clear," her fingers trembled as she traced circles on the cushion, "what a person has to believe in."

"Miracles. Miracles. Miracles." Lillian Flagg dealt the words out briskly, neatly, like a bridge hand. "That's all. Believe in life . . . believe in the stars . . . believe in whatever you think has the power to heal and give it any name you want. If it's just your body that's out of whack, anything will do that you have enough faith in. Christianity doesn't have any corner on the healing market, you know. Witch doctors with rings in their noses can do it. Television quacks. Medicine men. I've seen these miracles worked by people you wouldn't touch with a ten foot pole. It's faith that heals—any faith. When it comes to healing the body, the Lord doesn't ask questions. Thank you," she added suddenly, opening and slapping her book shut again with a little bang and the weary-eyed smile puffing out her cheeks. "Thank you, Lord. Hallelujah!"

Rooney paused for a moment. "Well, but suppose . . ."

"I get mighty peculiar sometimes."

"Suppose that there's nothing wrong with your body. That it's not your body at all. What do you look for then?"

"At last, at last." Lillian Flagg leaned her head back against the chair and closed her eyes. "I've been on the go since the middle of April, you know. How many weeks is that? All over the East. Retreats with groups of ministers—old ones and young ones, fat ones and thin ones. I've lectured them on the laying on of hands. On prayer. It's enough to give you the jim-willies the way most of them pray. I always picture Jesus standing there with his hands tied behind his back so he can't do a thing. You know why? Because they will never ask him to do a thing—at least not a thing they really want. Because in their hearts they refuse to believe that he really can do a thing. Oh, bang it into their heads!" Opening her eyes, she thumped the cover of her book with her fist. 'Ask and it shall be given you.' You know. But first *ask*. You don't have to be very bright to see that. Keep on asking and believing the best way you can and don't worry about the little voice inside that says, 'I don't believe.' Just pray it down. The Lord will hear you above it.

"Since April I've been hammering at all this, and then I'd just gotten back all set for a quiet little nervous breakdown in Muscadine," Lillian Flagg said, "—that's what Muscadine was made for—when you pulled in from nowhere. Everything was red. Your car was red. Your hair was red. Your eyes and your nose were a little red. I expected it all to go up in flames any minute, and I thought 'There goes my quiet little Muscadine breakdown,' but now at last you ask a question that means maybe we can settle our business and both just collapse. How did your question go again?"

"I want a baby," Rooney said, and at once the air

seemed decked with bells—monkey bells, donkey bells, camel and temple bells, all of them ringing as if the air about her was a curtain of bells and if she moved a muscle, she would set still more of them jangling. "If nothing's wrong with my body or my husband's body, then what is wrong, Mrs. Flagg?"

"People get hurt." Only the two women's mouths moved—nothing else in the room. The bells were still. "They hurt other people, and other people hurt them, things that happen hurt them. It locks doors inside a person—rooms and passages are shut off—and nothing in the world, nobody, can get in the darkness of those closed up places. No light and air, no life. Then it's not the healing of the body that has to happen. It's the healing of the memories. My dear, it's the forgiveness of sin."

"I don't believe in sin."

"Then maybe you believe in the darkness—in the locked up rooms."

"I don't have to believe in them. I live in them— weekends and holidays especially. Mother's Day."

"Then open them. Let them be blessed."

"By the stars again? Or the local witch doctor?"

"When it comes to sin, I'm afraid only God can stand the stench."

"He has a strong stomach, doesn't he?" Rooney stood up, smoothing down her skirt with her hands. "It wasn't forgiveness I came for, I can tell you that. I thought maybe you'd give me a little bag of fingernail clippings and hair I could hang around my neck."

She glanced at the window. "The rain's stopped. I think I'll go out for a while."

"Then I'll just go to pieces right here. Comfortably." Lillian Flagg took off her white button earrings and dropped them into the ash tray at her side. "Go in peace, my dear."

As Rooney picked her way through the puddles, the rutted dirt road became a corridor splashed with sun. Birds sounded the alarm, and children ran out of the woods to join her, swarmed about her corduroy skirts, then flocked along in front, threading in and out of the trees—the shadows of children among the damp leaves, damp smell of leaf-mold. Overhead the drifts of cloud bared ragged patches of watery blue. A wind-blown old man in a jeep rattled to a stop at her side. "Is this the road to Muscadine?"

"All roads lead to Muscadine. I'm a stranger here." His eyes were the watery blue of the sky. He cleared his throat and roared down on the accelerator all at once, jolted cumbersomely off through the dappled children, plowing them down. Room after room lined the green corridor of the road, and lighting her cigarette, Rooney squinted at them warily over the cupped match.

If where she stood at this moment on the road was the present, with the future at her back, then the stretch that she faced was the past. It was her day for games, Rooney thought, and Lillian Flagg the high-

waisted, spindle-legged games mistress urging her on
so that she herself could return to the bridge games
and detective stories where she gathered her forces
for the next bout with the priests she coached in
prayer—blowing her whistle and then, in a reedy con-
tralto, "All right, boys. Now one, two, three. Believe!" It would kill Nicko, she thought, making one
of his terrible faces and barking like a dog; yet in any
game the stakes were finally yourself. She peered
down the road through the skein of smoke from her
cigarette. That would be girlhood, the stretch from
the humped white stone to the bend, beyond it the
snaking slope of childhood, infancy and birth in the
valley somewhere. Loose-limbed, one hand on her
hip, she advanced a step or two: Rooney Vail, Rooney
Jessup, Clem's girl, Roo—ferret-faced and wiry, clam-
bering up the dunes on all fours, a pony.

She peopled the woods with faces, filling the endless, rustling rooms, but in whichever she looked,
however unpromising, there seemed light and air
enough; nobody choked for breath. Neighing, she
cantered out of the dining room with her tawny mane
flying just as they were helping her father in through
the French windows, grey-faced and speaking as
though his mouth was full of marbles: "Don't let
them take my teeth, God damn it. I'm going to die
with them in," her mother following just behind in a
white tennis dress and not a hair out of place. No
doors were locked there, no passageways closed off.
In a puddle the sun swayed, and she let her cigarette

fall into the sun. The two house mothers cornered her on the edge of the hockey field where she was taping her ankle—Mike and Ike, one of them had a moustache and could quote Dostoyevski in Russian. They told her—"I mean they were positively slavering," she described it later—that young ladies did not run around the dormitory halls in just panties and bra, and less in shame she wept than in anger, bewilderment, relief even, that this was so, that the fetlock was an ankle after all, the thunder of hooves only the patter of a girl's bare feet. Ike wept too, though more of a whinny, confusing her, and like three leaves trembling on a single stem, their heads bowed closer and closer.

Nicko said that sin meant moving farther and farther apart . . . from other men, God; and leaning over the pulpit, he drew his hands slowly away from each other until his arms were stretched wide like black wings. Then he straightened up, only his Adam's apple agog. "Like points on the surface of a balloon you blow up, the distances grow greater and greater until distance is all there is wherever you look . . . landscapes of air. . . ." But faces dipped and shimmered here among the leaves as she walked, and there seemed to be none so distant that she could not reach out and touch it.

When she came to the turtle-shaped white rock, at the side of the road, she sat down on it and poked the mud off her shoes with a stick. Then something shook the branch above her, sprinkling her with rain, and she looked up, narrow-eyed, at the heaving sky, the enormous cavalry of cloud.

It was not that she suddenly remembered the one room that she had forgotten but rather as if she could no longer avoid acknowledging the one room where she had been all along, craning out from it at the others. She held tight to the sides of the rock as though it had risen in the air with her and was teetering along crazily after the clouds. Clem drove into Boston one October afternoon leaving her in charge of the shop, where she sat at the back near the unlit Franklin stove in a yellow cardigan and wearing horn-rimmed glasses, leafing through some of the old bound copies of *Harper's* and barely even glancing up at the occasional entrance of customers who seemed less strangers there than she among the racks of fishing flies, hardware, Victorian debris. She disliked the place for its clutter, disliked them for liking it, and the breeze came off the tidal river smelling of mud. Her hands felt like ice. "We don't make love any more. We make attempts," she told Clem when he left her—he had lifted her chin to press his mouth into the pit of her throat—and after that first year in Myron their attempts had all failed: every day, dutifully, to catch the moment by surprise, then every week only, with a kind of dogged passion—mare and stud, no fee unless there was a standing colt, the lonely jokes that failed at last even to bore them.

It was just at closing time and she had let down the rattan curtain at the front window and was putting

away the cash when he came in with his thin hair
blown into a cock's comb, his indoor face flushed from
the wind. She reached around and turned the key
noisily in the lock behind him to indicate that he was
to be the last one to enter that day, to be quick about
it, and for a moment before speaking he shot a glance
almost of panic at the curtained window, the bolted
door. She caught his panic easily, dropped the key-
ring to the counter-top with a clatter to make clear that
either of them was free to pick it up and run the
moment the pressure grew unendurable, then laughed
too loudly when he stated his unfrightening purpose
not to buy at all but to ask, if she had time, a few professional questions—a quite unfrightening man, she
thought, older than she but not as much older as he
looked.

He stared at her appraisingly, choosing his words
with slow care, and with so much the air of a professor made all the little silences his own to break or
prolong that she found herself caricaturing the college girl for him as with arms akimbo, tossing back
her hair, she led him to the badly sprung sofa at the
rear of the shop where she pushed aside the pile of
green rubber ponchos and invited him to sit down.
Where had they lived before coming to Myron, how
many children did they have, had they ever run a shop
before? His questions made them strangers all over
again, and she felt a kind of wanton license to
create whatever biography she thought might interest
a stranger most—with their three sets of twins they

had left the ancestral acreage in Virginia to be near the sea for the sake of Clem, who had only a few months to live—but even were she to do so, she felt sure that no more than the plain recital of fact that she gave him could it shake the unblinking stillness of the man who sat there as though made of wax with his pale hair, pale eyes, the heavy, pale smile encouraging her, she thought, to take as much rope as she needed to hang herself.

After a time, abruptly, the questions came to an end, there was a terrible silence with the rattan at the window glowing red from the late sun, and then because she had answers that fitted none of his questions, because there was nothing in the whole foolish place that he wanted to buy, because it was a way to make something there her own if only the silence, she reached out with her thumbs and like a sculptor working in clay shaped away his smile, closed his eyes, and leaned back with him into the cold and slippery pile of green rubber.

FIVE

——◆——

I RMA walks funny." Lizzie Nicolet stood on the bottom rung of their slide and addressed her sister, who had reached the top and was crouching there for a moment before making her descent. She craned around to look down at Lizzie behind her.

"That's because her feet got hurt."

"Probber—prob—prob . . ." Holding the guard-rails to support herself, Lizzie arched back as far as she could go to stare upside down at the sky, then continued pensively, righting herself. "Probably it was a —probably a giant hurt them."

"Probably it was a bad giant."

"Irma's feet look awful." She climbed up a rung. "She let us see them once."

"Probably they got mashed," Cornelia said, and lying flat on her stomach, she eased herself half way down, feet first, before letting go of the sides and sliding the rest of the way. Lizzie stepped down off the ladder and went to the swings. She twisted one of them around and around as far as its chains would permit. Then she stood back with her thumb in her mouth and watched it unwind noisily, clanging against the metal legs. Cornelia continued to lie where she had stopped, half on, half off, the slide, and with one finger traced from behind the laborious passage of an ant up the slope of hot tin.

"He's still watching us," Lizzie said. Across the yard from them, a man stood on the sidewalk leaning with one hip against the picket fence and reading a newspaper which he had folded down the middle lengthwise and held in one hand like a subway rider. Without apparently interrupting his reading, he waved his free hand at them lazily. Cornelia tried to help the ant by flicking it forward but succeeded only in maiming it.

Irma Reinwasser was making their beds on the second floor where through the window she could watch them play. The slide with its ladder made a triangle, the crossbar from which the swings hung and the two legs at either end made a rectangle and two smaller isosceles triangles. The geometry of it reassured her against the hodgepodge of lilac plumes, colossal depth of sky; no matter if the whole thing trembled as the two little girls swung back and forth, their blond heads turned toward the street which Irma could not see. The floor of their room was littered with crayons and a miscellany of their father's shoes which they had dragged out of his closet while she still slept—a pair of sneakers with holes worn through over the little toes, bedroom slippers, one of the black Oxfords that he wore only to preach in so that they showed no signs of use. The sneakers and slippers she tossed into the hall to pick up later, but the black shoe she dusted off and cradled for a moment.

It was a day and a night since his departure, and there had been no message from him, no clue. When his secretary telephoned from the church the afternoon before, Irma had told her only what his note had directed her—"called away suddenly"—but although she tried to make it sound as routine and plausible as she could, the secretary was not satisfied. There was a trustees' meeting scheduled for that evening, she said; had he left no indication when he would be back or at least where he could be reached? What could she say to them? "Say to them he doesn't tell Reinwasser all his secrets. Say to them he needs a rest maybe, you blame him?" and she had hung up as abruptly as now she shied the black shoe out toward the others. Say to them he left behind his motherless children. Say to them Mrs. Rooney Vail has also left. And then she relented about the shoe that lay defenseless and bereft where it had struck the doorjamb and fallen back into the room. She took it away to his closet where she paused among the mystery of his clothes, remembering a face that was not his face but enough like it so that she could not easily separate them—a younger face, dark like his, with a stupid, dazed smile. Screwing her eyes shut, she shook her head involuntarily. *Wie man's macht, ist's falsch.*

* * *

"Have one." The man had taken a small brown paper bag from his pocket and extended it over the fence toward Lizzie, who had slowly traveled half the distance from the swings, dragging Raggedy Ann by one foot.

"It's licorice," he said.

Lizzie gazed at him, saying nothing. He had a pale face, heavy about the jaws, with deep dimples on either side of his mouth when he smiled. His thinning, grey-blond hair had receded on either side of his forehead, and his seersucker suit looked too small for him. He jostled the bag toward her on the palm of his outstretched hand.

"See, they're good," and he stuck out his tongue on which sat a piece of licorice the size of a button. The bag fell to the grass. "Oh dear, what am I going to do now?"

Cornelia ran over from the swings, picked up the bag, and held it out to him.

"Take one," he said. Cornelia sucked in her upper lip and shook her head.

"Are you Cornelia?"

She nodded.

"Why don't you run in and ask your daddy if it's all right?"

"Candy makes your teeth fall out." Lizzie had joined her sister at the fence, and they stood there side by side looking up at him.

"Does Daddy say that?" the man asked, taking back

the bag and replacing it in his pocket.

"Daddy's gone," Cornelia said, her voice hushed and constricted with the effort of speaking to a stranger.

"Then we can just go across the street to the church and ask him."

"He's not there," Cornelia said, sucking in her lip so far that her words were barely audible, her face still tilted up at him stiffly as though held in a vise. The creases on either side of the man's mouth deepened and darkened; you could see his gums when he smiled.

"Where is he then?"

"Probably," Lizzie said, taking her thumb out of her mouth. "Probably he isn't anywhere."

"Everybody's somewhere. I'm here talking to you, and you're there talking to me. Right at this very minute," he said, tapping the crystal of his wrist watch with his fingernail, "your daddy's somewhere too."

"He said he was coming back soon," Cornelia said.

"You've got a black tongue," Lizzie said, pointing up at him, her great eyes brimming with fascination.

"You and Cornelia have white moustaches," he said.

"That's just milk." Lizzie retreated a step.

"How come you know our names?" Almost paralyzed by the boldness of her question, Cornelia awaited with hunched shoulders whatever the consequences might be.

"I think I must have heard them from a friend of

yours once." Grasping a picket in each hand, he crouched down on his haunches and peered at them through the fence. His eyes were amber colored, their blond lashes and eyebrows almost invisible. "I think it must have been Rooney Vail."

"She didn't go to the beach with us." Cornelia relaxed. At eye-level, he looked less formidable to her —a big white animal in a cage.

"Why didn't she?"

"She's gone too."

"We call her Raggedy Ann, don't we, Cornelia?"

"You mean she and Daddy went somewhere together?" the man asked.

"Probably," Lizzie said. "Probably they didn't."

They ran after the cat, which suffered itself to be patted and then disappeared around the back of the house with the little girls after it.

As he rose too quickly from his crouch, dizziness almost felled him, and holding on to the fence, he leaned forward heavily on his arms. Little burning discs of light floated up and down in front of him like fireflies while somewhere nearby a power-mower started up, then choked, backfiring. With a handkerchief he wiped his forehead and dabbed under his chin. A whiff of lilac in the air made him close his eyes, and when he opened them, he felt well again. Tucking the newspaper under his arm, he crossed to the other side of Congress Street. In full sun, the white façade of the church blinded him, and he put on dark glasses. *Pentecost: the Birthday of the Church.*

Sunday, 11 A.M. *Mr. Nicolet.* Through his glasses, everything became the blue of moonlight, of ice.

"You're wasting your time, Padre," he said.

Ralph Denbigh had come up from behind, clapping him on the shoulder, but he had seen his reflection in the glass of the bulletin board and spoke without turning. Denbigh was a short, dapper man in black clericals and steel-rimmed glasses with a handsome little wedge of a smile.

"How is Willy Poteat, the poor man's Pegler?"

"You're looking for jolly Saint Nick?"

"Himself," Denbigh said. "But don't misquote me."

"Well, jolly Saint Nick has flown the coop." Next to Denbigh, Poteat looked larger and heavier than he was, everything about him unwieldy. "He has been translated," he said, drawing the word out to twice its full length.

"And I hear he's taken the funds for the new hymnals with him and the organist's wife. Let's go face him with it together." Denbigh took Poteat's arm and started to lead him to the door.

"You go, little father." Poteat smiled as he disengaged himself. "He's not there."

Denbigh cocked his head to one side and regarded him for a moment in quizzical silence. "You wait here then," he said, "and if he's not, I'll be back in a second and buy you a cup of coffee. I'd like a word with you, friend."

Poteat nodded. Out of his pocket he took the stub of a pencil and some pieces of notepaper fastened with a pin as Denbigh hurried up the steps and into the church. "The busy little Fauntleroy of God," he wrote, then crossed it out. "The busy little bee of God disappears into the temple-shaped hive with honey on his tongue and feet and in his eyes. He is in search of the vicar who is said to be in rut. The perfidious queen of the hive, she of the flaming locks, has also flown away into the dung-smelling world. *O altitudo!*" For a few moments he studied what he had written, then tore off the sheet and, crumpling it into a ball, stuffed it into his pocket.

He stretched his arms wide in the sunlight, flexing them at the elbows, and gave a great grimace of a yawn as he watched the two little girls across the street try to spread a beach towel on the grass. "Hi!" He mouthed the greeting silently and tossed a single, languid wave in their direction where they squatted with their backs to him.

"The infernal loveliness of it. . . ." He brought his arm down and let it rest across the shoulders of Denbigh, who had reappeared beside him. "Just see. . . ." and with a sweep of his other hand he commended to him the whole length of Congress Street with all its trees and lawns, the children tilting their towel into the sun. Then playfully he drew his arm tighter about Denbigh's shoulders, forcing him to lean sideways, and with his dimples darkening, looked down at him. "Was I right?"

Denbigh's glasses glittered as he turned his head. "It's apparently his father."

Giving his shoulders one last squeeze before releasing him, Poteat laughed. "You certainly stick together, you boys."

"Look, everybody's not as bursting with youthful vigor as you are," Denbigh said, pulling his jacket straight. "The old boy's in his eighties, and he hasn't been well for years. Nick's had to run up there like this before on the spur of the moment."

"I'm a large, sloppy man," Poteat said, "and you're a small, tidy man. Life's queer as Hell, isn't it?"

Denbigh gave his rapid, jaunty smile. "How about that cup of coffee I promised you?"

"It keeps me awake," Poteat said. "Plus there's a paper to put to bed. Thanks just the same."

"Then tell me one thing, Will." With his hands deep in his trouser pockets, Denbigh faced Poteat squarely now, his feet wide apart. "Why do you have it in for Nick anyhow?"

During the long pause, Denbigh rose on his toes and sank back again, jingling coins. Then Poteat took out his brown paper bag and held it forward. "It'll make your tongue black," he said. "Have one."

"You never miss a chance to take a dig." Closing his eyes, Denbigh shook his head at the bag. "In a small town like this everything gets blown up way out of proportion anyway."

"In a small town like this, Padre, where news is scarce as ice-cream in Hell, a man in my trade has to dig wherever the dirt looks interesting."

"Look, friend, where do you get this dirt business?"

"Soil then. You dig where the soil looks most promising." Poteat took a piece of licorice and placed it in his mouth. "And the soil looks most promising where they've put on a little dressing." He shifted the licorice into one cheek where it made his face look lopsided. "Where you can smell a little of the old stuff—the genuine, bonded article."

"Hey, Will, old man . . ." Denbigh reached out and plucked a stray thread off Poteat's seersucker jacket, then with his thumb and forefinger ran slowly down the edge of the lapel. "This is a nice guy we're talking about. A pastor."

"Who isn't nice?" Poteat said. "Everybody's nice."

"So be nice, will you? You've been dead wrong about Nick."

"You're nice, and I'm nice," Poteat said. "This is a nice little town."

"I won't keep you." Denbigh's even, white teeth glistened as he smiled and extended his hand. "Thanks much."

"It's been nice." Poteat shook his hand. "You're a sturdy little man of God."

Denbigh drew his fist back to his ear, then punched Poteat lightly on the upper chest. "Thanks much," he said, and took off down the sidewalk at a trot.

Irma Reinwasser took hold of the towel by two corners, and Lizzie and Cornelia each held one of the other two.

"*Eins, zwei, drei!*" Irma bent over deep from the waist as the two little girls sank all the way down until they were crouched on their heels in the grass where at last the towel lay flat.

"There he is!" Lizzie cried, pointing across the street.

Still leaning forward, with one hand at the small of her back, Irma squinted into the sunlight.

"Never talk with a stranger," she said, vaguely, watching him walk into the shadow of the big catalpa tree.

"He's not a stranger. He knew our names." Cornelia spoke with exasperation.

"Probably he loved us," Lizzie said, and then with a sudden dreaming look in her eyes, and as if from a great distance, "I've got something in my pants."

"*Schwein!*" Irma picked her up around the waist and carried her at arm's length into the house.

When Poteat reached the Something Shop, he stopped for a while to look at the contents of the window. There was an ancient Victrola with its speaker gaping like a great tin lily, next to it a cast-iron easel supporting a mirror whose glass was held in place by a Revolutionary War soldier and an Indian brave, both bearing American flags. Thrown over the back of a child's rocker and fanned out like a wedding train was a patchwork quilt bound with claret-colored velvet, its patches of old damask and brocade stitched here and there with figures—a spray of goldenrod, in spidery letters of blue thread the words

Go To Sleep. On one side hung a water-stained photograph of an old man with a walrus moustache and a straw hat with Our Pop written in black ink across his shirt-front with a heavy pen. At first glance, Poteat took the shop itself to be empty, but as he studied the cluttered interior more carefully through the glass, he made out the figure of Clem Vail stretched out on a sofa in the back reading a newspaper. He wore khaki shorts with one fuzzy leg pitched out over the arm of the sofa, the other sprawled off to the side so that his bare foot rested on the floor. As Poteat entered, he noticed a Help Wanted placard thumbtacked to the door. Over his head a bell jangled, but Clem did not turn from his reading.

Poteat reached up to a shelf and, without looking to see what it was, picked off the first object that his fingers touched—a pepper mill—and held it out at arm's length in front of him.

"How much?"

Clem craned around to look over his shoulder, his forehead wrinkling. "Take it," he said. "No charge to the press."

"I don't want it."

"What do you want then?" Clem pulled himself straight on the sofa, crossing his legs and resting the open paper on one knee. Poteat noticed that he had not shaved that morning and wondered if he had spent the night in the shop.

"Social notes," Poteat said. "The comings and goings of Myron's young bloods. That sort of jazz."

He picked up a donkey bell and rang it. "Have you had any major routs up there on the heights recently? Planning any little trips anywhere? Your wife?"

"Nothing."

Poteat replaced the bell on the counter and drew several circles around it with his finger. "What does a man do with these things? Rings them, I suppose."

"God knows."

"Do you need help?" With his hand on the counter, he had leaned slightly to one side as he spoke, bringing his face into a shaft of sun. He had pushed his bottle-blue glasses back on his forehead when he first entered, and in the dazzle of light his eyes looked almost golden.

"Come again?" Clem was quick and unsure, frowning as he rubbed his stubbly chin with the flat of his hand.

The silence belonged to Poteat, and golden-eyed, dimpling, he prolonged it. "Help," he said. "You've got a sign out there."

"Oh God . . ." Clem laughed. "Just somebody to sit on things here when I go off to Boston or something. Know of anybody?"

"Your wife's on strike?"

"She's not here." He reached down and started to pull on one sneaker.

"Social notes, social notes." Poteat took the notepaper out of his pocket and cushioned it in the palm of his hand, pinning it there with his pencil stub.

"It's just her mother," Clem said, poking back under the sofa for his other shoe. "Nothing very social."

"Be gone long?"

"Look, buddy." Clem lurched up off the sofa and stood there with one foot still bare. He was slightly taller than Poteat. "I'm a shopkeeper. I work. Here," he said, grabbing a broom from the corner and shoving it toward Poteat. "Here," he reached into the pocket of his shorts and took out a key-ring which he slid across the counter toward Poteat's hand. "If you want to help, unlock those cases, sweep Hell out of the floor. Otherwise, old buddy . . ." He smiled expectantly.

"Drones don't work," Poteat said. "They just wait on the queen's pleasure." When he reached the door, he paused to breathe on his blue glasses and wipe them before putting them on again. "Thanks much," he said.

SIX

YOU don't want to buy a hotel cheap, do you? I ask everybody that question." The thin man with the eyeshade pushed the pen forward and turned the register around. "Muscadine. . . ." He swiveled the wire rack of picture postcards slowly as he spoke—*Moonlight over Muscadine, Autumn Glory.* "It's the end of the line. It's the jumping off place." His amusement was noiseless, a mouthful of neglected teeth. "I'll make you a good price."

"How much?" Nicolet took the pen and scratched it at the edge of the blank to start the ink flowing.

"Make me an offer."

"I'll have to sleep on it."

Leaning forward to scrutinize what Nicolet had written, he got in his own light. He reached up and held off to one side the bulb and shade that hung down on a long cord above his head. "Canuck?" he asked.

"Just French."

"Well, I can't say it, but I can tell you what it means. My wife's Canuck. La lib," he began, tracing with his finger the name which Nicolet had put down. "La liberty. Means liberty."

"They should get you working on the Dead Sea scrolls."

"Turn to the left at the top of those stairs. It's the third door on your left. That's two lefts." He closed the register and replaced the pen in its holder. "Bath at the end of the hall. If you want to go into the hotel business, you can let me know in the morning."

Nicolet tripped on the first step, catching hold of the bannister. "In the morning there may not be any hotel," he said.

There was an iron bed, a bureau with a paper doily under the glass, a straight chair, and no light except for the one fixture in the middle of the ceiling which Nicolet switched off as soon as he had undressed so that he was no longer enclosed in a room but at large in the young night, sitting there in his underwear with his feet up on the cool radiator and looking out at Muscadine. The rain had stopped, but a fine mist hung in the air and blurred the street light across from the hotel. He had decided to make no inquiries until morning so she might be lying asleep on the other side of the wall for all he knew, but this was so little of all that the night was rich with that it failed to stir him as he leaned back into the darkness that seemed without walls, the whole world gathering one by one on the open fields of dreaming, the living and the dead.

René Laliberté, for one. Only as his pen touched the paper downstairs, had the name come back to him— the recurring plain-song of Roy's reminiscence: "My tragic young dad, the grandfather you never saw, who to free his black brother left behind his native France and gave his arm . . ." soft and expectant through the Gregorian dusk of his memory, then the little catch of breath and ". . . in the rifle pits at Petersburg." Roy's style was consistently elegiac— *The medicos give me little longer. Come my son*— and on the table by his bed he had enshrined the Brady photograph that showed the sad eyes and curly beard of his father in his Union uniform, over one shoulder a cape to cover the ruined arm. Léon Nicolet. In the rifle pits at Petersburg. Why the alias, Laliberté, Nicolet had never understood until now, suddenly adopting it himself: a grand new name to match a grand new destiny, liberated from your native France, or from a parish of old ladies, to set at liberty your black brother, or your red-headed sister. It was all the same: to liberate yourself. Nicolet reached out and closed his fingers on the shadow of his grandfather's cape. *Well met in Muscadine. You and I, Léon, we understand.*

For liberation, the loss of an arm might not be too high a price, not even the begetting of Roy, the old and impossible child asleep now in a room like this, Nicolet thought, with a crescent of white hair across his eyes like a plover's wing. If that was the price they had asked of the grandfather, what was the price they would ask of him? He fretted the hair on the back of his neck, looking out at the wet, dark street. Would they ask of him Harold, or was it Harold himself who would ask something else?

That afternoon rain had soaked him until you could see the flesh through his shirt. A silent truck driver with a mouthful of popcorn had taken him part of the way, letting him off at a crook in the road by a gravel pit where he took shelter under a lean-to until a boy in chinos and T-shirt stopped and beckoned him in; by then he no longer cringed through the downpour but sauntered out, grinning. "Christ, you been swimming the channel?" The boy's smooth jaws were working at something as he spoke. Nicolet bent double to squeeze rain from his trouser cuffs, and almost cracked his head against the dashboard when the boy started off with a splatter of tires on gravel. "I don't go in for hitchhikers much. Sometimes they're sex fiends or something," and Nicolet, his face still dripping, replied, "I'm a minister." Then the boy had flushed, swallowing whatever it was, and for a mile there was nothing but the tick-tock of the windshield wiper until at last the boy said, "No sweat, what makes a guy decide to be a thing like that?"

"Well, there are three steps," Nicolet had said distractedly, digging into the inside pocket of his jacket to see if Rooney's postcard was still there, his wallet with the dog-eared photograph of the two little girls hugging a snowman that had Franny crouching behind it with her face where the head should have been. "The first step is to be a beer drinker or at least the friend of beer drinkers. It helps anyway." He laid the postcard on his knee and tried to dab it dry with his handkerchief. The ink had run, but the message was still legible: "No one is to know. No one is to come."

"It was a muggy spring evening after exams," he said, "and I was tossing off a few with some of these beer-drinking friends of mine when the subject got around to religion as it usually does in such cases. I wasn't much interested—not even the first step had happened yet, you see. But I stuck around and listened anyway. Nothing to lose. There was one character there who had pimples all over his chin like jam. You kept wanting to wipe it off for him." Nicolet suddenly remembered whom he was talking to and noticed gratefully that the complexion of the boy was clear and fresh as he frowned ahead at the road through the gouts of rain that quivered against the windshield. "Anyway," he went on, "he'd been getting sloppier and sloppier, this pimply one. Everything was four letter words. It was really quite funny for a while in a dismal kind of way. Especially when he got into one particular rut. Eats it. You know army slang? Everything was eats it. His girl friend. His roommate. The faculty. They all ate it. It. It." He thought of poor Denbigh. "I hope you don't think I'm

talking this way just to sound like one of the fellers."
For the first time, the boy smiled faintly.

"Eats it," Nicolet said. "The great fecal indict-
ment. It's all he could say. I suppose I should have
been able to see what was coming next, but I didn't.
We'd gotten on religion, I told you. Well, he suddenly
said a memorable thing, an epic thing—at least it was
to me. In fact it was step one right there except that
like steps two and three I didn't know it was till later.
What he said was very simple. He just put together
two things I'd never heard put together before. One
of them was eats it." Nicolet turned the postcard over
on his knee and examined the dapper young blade
with his cheroot and his boater, thinking of him in
Muscadine. "And Jesus Christ," he said, with some
effort drawing himself back to what he had been telling the boy. "That was the other thing he said. According to him, Christ eats it too."

Nicolet found himself shivering in his damp clothes
so that when he began again, he stammered with cold.
The car seemed to be going at somewhat less speed,
but otherwise the boy showed no reaction. Nicolet was
sorry that he had begun, but he was beyond stopping now. "At the time it knocked me for a loop even
though I must have been half tight myself. But it was
step one, the voice in the burning bush all right
whether it sounded much like it then or not. Much
later I realized my drinking companion had spoken
the truth. Christ does eat it, of course. You know
why?"

The boy shook his head.

"Because it's all this world has ever given him to eat. And yet he keeps coming back for more."

In the dark of his hotel room, Nicolet clenched his face into a terrible grimace and rapped hard on the side of his head to cast out the memory of the bored and disgusted boy who had said only "Christ Almighty!" as he sat there trapped in his car with this man growing drunk as a child in a tent might grow drunk on the snugness and peace of the rain coming down, this absconded, bluebeard priest babbling out his apologia until he lost all track of his audience. At best the boy must have thought that he was crazy, a sick man; he had turned on the heater to still his rider's chattering teeth, but the gush of warm air had only made him drunker, loosening his tongue for step two. Nicolet called out in his dingy room at the memory now—"Holy God, I'm an ass . . . my father's son!" his oath and his prayer—and stalked up and down in the dark with both fists clamped tight to his scalp and the wreck of a smile.

He had gone on to tell the boy, or whomever by then he thought that he was telling, how when Father Ferris spoke, it was like water leaking out of a tap, a rapid drip-drop of word after word until suddenly the words came too many and too fast, mingling and tumbling out in a stream of incoherence; Father Ferris was the Guest Master and thus the only monk permitted to speak to visitors although, because of his stroke, it was a rare visitor who came away much the wiser. This second step toward becoming a minister, Nicolet explained, was a step into silence.

He spared the boy an account of why he had gone. On the grounds of rapidly failing health, old Roy had persuaded him to stay at home that last summer before his graduation from college, promising to teach him the hotel business, but Nicolet had been able to endure it only until August. Roy's hotel was a house of peeling gingerbread where he lived with his several more or less permanent boarders and where in an improvised barber shop on the first floor he gave an occasional haircut dressed in his felt slippers and the green and black lumberjack shirt that summer and winter alike he wore as a jacket. Redolent with talcum powder from his barbering, or perched, round-shouldered, on the high stool where he sat by the stove to stir up the breakfasts that he served to the paying guests, he would soliloquize disjointedly to his son about the difficulties that he had digesting, about making out menus, about defeat and death, sometimes about Léon, until finally Nicolet said goodbye one afternoon and left. Why he had sought out the monastery then, he had no clear recollection, he said, except that it was not far away, and he was curious, and he must have had questions that he thought might be answered there. Heaven only knew why he had gone, Nicolet told the trapped boy; Heaven only knew why he was going where he was going now, he said, and bent down to warm his hands where the heat flowed in under the dashboard.

"None of them spoke except to God. Imagine it!"
He smiled at the memory. He had thought that they
would speak to him, the interesting, bony young man,
that they would cluster around in their oatmeal-col-
ored cowls to ply him with answers, marvel at his coming, encourage him to join them in their vows. But
instead they rapped wood: rapped on the door of his
cell at dawn with a muffled "Christ is risen!"—
rapped on the refectory table as they finished their
food—the abbot clapped his hands to signal the end
of their silent meals, and they would file off to the
chapel, chanting psalms. At matins and lauds, ves-
pers and compline, he squirmed like an eavesdropper
to the sound of lover's talk; and when he met them
in corridors, not even good morning, good night. They
would only nod and smile as though it was some joke
too rich for telling. Round-eyed and quick as a bird,
Father Ferris did what he could to make amends, but
then his words would start to run together again like
raindrops on a windowpane. "So on the third day, I
rose from the dead and went home," Nicolet said. "All
the time I spent there smarting under the silence—
the Great Silence they called it—I never thought of
speaking to the only one who might have listened and
might even have said something worth hearing. Although what he said, of course, was the silence itself."
His eyes brimming with his drunkenness, Nicolet
placed his finger to his lips. "The second step," he
whispered.

There had been no time for the third because they

reached the narrow tar turn-off to Muscadine and the boy let him out, lingering for a moment to watch him cross the highway, then shaking his head or waving or crossing himself—it was hard to be sure through the misted window—as his car leapt forward and away. The rain had stopped by then, and Nicolet completed the remaining five miles or so on foot.

He pulled only the sheet over him now and lay back with the one limp pillow doubled up under his head and watched headlights drift across the ceiling. Would Irma remember their prayers, he wondered, not that it much mattered: Lizard Boy stopping in the middle of hers to squeal up from the nest of fur animals as her feet found his face bent over her in the dark, "Bluebeard's whiskering me!" Then Cornelia's "Our Father who aren't . . ."—"Who art, little Pie Face . . ."—"Aren't, aren't!"—hilariously, and after all, that was the secret, he thought: the laughter. And that was also the third step which he found that he had to finish off now as he rolled over on his stomach, pressing his lips to the hot pillow. Whenever in their fashion the old ladies asked him the boy's question— "No sweat, what makes a guy decide?" —he had spoken always gravely of a process rather than any one event, of a slow pursuit rather than the sudden blaze of capture, and the one event that there was he censored out because they expected this gravity from him, and he saved all his terrible faces, his dancings in the rain, for the children and Franny, for Rooney. But there had been an event, and he assembled the old girls now in his bedroom to hear it—with little whimpers they leapt like cats to the bureau top, radiator, foot of his bed.

In a pulpit with a top like an orange press, the college preacher had plucked uneasily at the dead air as the oaken hood seemed to drop lower and lower, pressing out of him nothing that you could not have expected: like Caesar, the Lord had refused a crown when the Tempter offered it—"all the kingdoms of the world in a moment of time"—yet again and again in the hoping heart of the believer he was crowned, yes, of course, "crowned amidst confession and tears," the preacher said, yes, his tone so sepulchral that it could have been Roy's except for the faint Scottish whirring of the r's—then suddenly, "crowned amidst *great laughter.*"

The preacher had barely paused at the phrase, but it was the end and the beginning of Nicolet: the great laughter at the heart of silence, the incredulous laughter and rain dance of faith. It was his third step, the most that he had in the way of event, and he smoothed it out now in the dark and let his head sink down heavy on it. *Dear Harold, who art and aren't, neither and both—who takest to eat what the world gives . . . show us thy hand.* The old cats scattered when without warning he tripped and fell backwards into sleep.

With the razor he borrowed the next morning from the man at the desk, he cut himself just below the cheekbone. He tasted the blood at the corner of his mouth before he saw it in the narrow strip of mirror above the basin, and he did not staunch it until he had finished shaving the other cheek so that by then it had become a gaudy sight—René Laliberté in the rifle pits of Petersburg, he thought, remembering for the first time his new identity. He had woken to the thought again that Rooney might be asleep on the other side of the wall from him, and as soon as he got downstairs, he asked if she was staying there only to be told that except for himself there was nobody staying there. "I tell you, you can have this place cheap," his friend said.

"Is there an antique shop, an oracle in a cave— any kind of famous landmark?" Nicolet asked, looking through the picture postcards. "Why would a person come to Muscadine?"

"Most of them come to die." His noiseless amusement cracked his mouth open so wide that Nicolet was not prepared for the sudden sharpness of his question. "Why did you come yourself? Are you a cop with all these questions?"

"I'm just a tragic young dad." Even as he spoke, he caught sight through the front window of the figure of a woman hurrying by with a bundle in her arms, and by the glint of sun on her hair, the pitch of her shoulders, he was sure that he recognized Rooney.

By the time that he reached the hotel porch, she had disappeared, and he stood there with his hand on the railing scanning the street as the morning breeze teetered the empty rocking chairs. Then he saw her again. She had crossed to the other side and was walking rapidly away, not turning to the sound of her name as he called it out. He clattered down the wooden steps and along the sidewalk to the corner, then crossed the street at a run with a dog at his heels now, barking, and finally overtook her at the entrance to a drug store where he caught her by the elbow from behind. "Raggedy Ann!"

The face that the woman turned to him was a stranger's face, leathery and coarse-featured, starkly alien. "Are you crazy?" She held her groceries between them like a shield.

Or a cop, a sex fiend, his own Grandfather's ghost —there had been so many theories since Myron that it was hard to be sure as she entered the store and pushed the glass door shut on his apologies so that he was left with his own reflection: his grey suit wrinkled and shapeless from yesterday's rain, his hair uncombed and a shred of toilet paper marking the cut on his cheek. The pharmacist in a white jacket appeared at the door to stare out at him through the glass, and protesting his innocence with a shrug, a foolishly smiling shake of his head, Nicolet turned and continued back down the sidewalk. He tried to smooth down his hair with the flat of his hands, then plucked off the piece of paper and started again the slow trickle of blood that he dabbed at with his handkerchief as he walked. The dog that had joined him in his chase across the street trotted along at his side and licked his fingers when he paused across from the hotel.

Suddenly then as he patted the dog's warm head,

the day engulfed him—the fathoms of blue sky, the
sunlit combers of wind that kept the rockers nodding
and himself now Laliberté with the bright world opening before him like a hand, a flower. He wondered
idly what had been so tragic about the other Laliberté. Certainly not his wound which had been little
enough to pay for the cape and the sad eyes—Nicolet
glanced wryly at the handkerchief stained with the
mystery of his own blood—yet Roy had always insisted on the tragedy as of course he would, and so
Nicolet had never more than half listened—some
cruel disillusionment, some forgotten scandal. Poor
Léon, but in its terrible beauty the world itself was a
scandal, and the lightness of his own heart. He
thought of the word 'beauty' that Franny had not
scratched off her shopping list and of how not even
her death had been able to scratch it off for him because the world was as beautiful still without her.
Forgive me, my dear, and he smelled breakfast on the
air, gave the dog a slap on the rump that sent it
sidling off with its ears pinned back.

It was after he had eaten and was wandering from
shop to shop down the one real street in Muscadine
that he saw Rooney again, and this time there could
be no doubt. He had discovered that there was no
other hotel in town where she could be staying—
he had searched through the telephone directory to
see if there was any name that he might recognize as
a relative or friend—and finally there seemed nothing
left to do but wait around there in as many places as

possible, keeping watch. It might take hours, of course, days—she might have left Muscadine or never come at all—and he entertained himself with the absurdity of finally buying the hotel after all and settling down to run it for no other reason than that someday years later, unfrocked and dishonored, he might shuffle downstairs in his slippers to find that at last she had arrived. Then Roy again—the old man's wires reached him even in his dreaming. God knew what Roy Nicolet waited for in his hotel. For a father, a son. And then Nicolet saw her.

He had raised a little souvenir cushion to his nose—I Pine for you and Balsam—and was breathing in the fragrance of the needles when he looked out of the shop door and saw her coming down the street long before she saw him. She had the walk of someone going nowhere in particular, a face so unguarded, so flagrantly itself in this place where she could have expected no one so much as to notice her that he felt that his own long glance was a kind of betrayal. And then she saw him. "My God, you look like the last bloody rose of summer."

"I've been thinking of you in Muscadine," he said, and puffing out his chest, he crooked one knee and took a long drag on his invisible cigar, then let the smoke escape as he flicked off the ashes fastidiously.

SEVEN

C LEM called me the day after you left," Nicolet said. "You didn't even tell him where you were going."

"You knew. Did you tell him?"

"I didn't get your card till after he'd called."

"Did you call him back then and tell him?"

Nicolet shook his head.

"Why did you come, Nick?"

"I came to bring you back."

"I would have come back anyway."

"Clem didn't think so. I didn't either. I wanted you back."

"Do you say that to all your lost sheep?"

"You're my first. It's the break I've been waiting for."

Through the same woods where Rooney had wandered alone the afternoon before, they had followed an old logging road as far as a partial clearing knee-deep in ferns. Rooney sat between the roots of a bully oak, leaning against the great, baffled trunk with its little jutting shelves of fungus. Some distance away, Nicolet sat on a fallen branch, and between them the ferns trembled more gold than green in the morning sun.

"I said that he said that you said that . . ." Nicolet plucked a spear of grass and placed it between his two thumbs, cupping his hands together. ". . . that she said that . . ." and he blew a long, hoarse note.

"I wrote you not to come."

"In a pig's sweet eye."

She smiled. "Did he cry?"

"Clem?" He glanced up at her inquiringly over his hands. "Not a drop."

"I've seen him cry. Men don't have the faces for it."

"Don't tell me about it."

"Why did you want me back, Nick?" He looked to her as though he was paying no attention, shielding his eyes from the sun as he glanced up into the branches of the tree that rose above her. His thin lips were slightly parted, and the shadow of his hand blackened the upper part of his face like a mask.

"That's my job," he said. "Bringing people back."

"Kicking and screaming, digging in their heels?"

"The ones I deal with mostly don't even know they've gone away. How do you bring back a respectable old body who thinks she's never left?"

"Back where? A respectable young body . . ."

"Back to Myron," he said, "to Clem."

"But it's so pathetic!" For a moment she held her

hands out to him. "You come all this way, scratched and bleeding, to get me to do what I would have done anyhow. You're such a clown, Nick."

With a clown's face, dark among the ferns on his branch, he smiled at her. "If the boys at headquarters get wind of it, I'm through, of course. My one big chance, and I flub it."

"Then it was just for Clem you came?"

"Maybe I'm in the wrong line of work."

"It must have been unnerving for you, though, when you thought I'd run out for good. 'Found near Muscadine: a runaway red bitch with circles under her eyes.' Then what? 'Rightful owner,'" Rooney said, "'please claim.' Poor old Nick, wondering who the rightful owner might really be at this point. At least wondering if Myron might wonder once word got around that I'd gone. Didn't you think you'd sleep easier yourself—not just Clem—if you got me back to him quick?"

Speaking slowly, his expression half puzzled, half amused, he struck her as feeling his way to something that would suddenly light up everything. "You know, I think I really came because I loved the name of Muscadine. If you'd gone to a place named anything else, I mightn't have budged an inch."

"You're a runaway too, aren't you, Nicko?"

"My father was, and his father before him."

"Where are we running?"

"You can never be sure." He broke a piece of bark off his branch and tossed it out between them.

"A clearing in the woods for the moment. It gives you a chance to get your bearings." He squinted up at what there was of the sky. "Home would be behind us. That way." He pointed. "We have to go home, don't we, Rooney?"

"You came all this way just to say so."

"I want to hear you say so."

"Listen, I was a horse till I was eighteen. I could keep going for miles."

"Denbigh," Nicolet said. "My little brother in the Lord."

"Little Ralph?"

"I'm trying it out on him now, just a game."

"You mean if we kept on running?"

With his eyes shut tight, Nicolet nodded. "I'm trying to see what it would do to his face. It's a brave little eager face. No," he shook his head. "It's not too good what it would do to it."

"That's a ghastly game," Rooney said. "I see Clem's."

"Don't." Nicolet held up one hand, his eyes still closed. "All I can get of Poteat are those heavy-duty dimples and a mouthful of teeth. Chomp, chomp." He opened his eyes then to her silence and gazed at her through the green air. Her face looked white against the dark tree. "It's home for us, Raggedy Ann."

"All I wanted was somebody to hold my hand in Muscadine. That's not so much." Through her frowning, she smiled at him. "I couldn't bring Clem

because I didn't even want him to know where I was
going ."

"Afraid he'd laugh?"

"Dear God, I was afraid he'd cry. You can't guess
what it means to him, Nicko—having a child. It
got to be that every month when the time came
around, if I was a day or so late for some reason, he'd
make some wild excuse for not going to work just so
he'd be there to find out as soon as I did whether this
time . . . it had worked. And of course it was always
the same bloody business. Bloody," she said with a
terrible little laugh. "Now he won't even talk about
it. I didn't want to get him excited about Mrs. Flagg,
and God knows I've lied to him enough already, so
I just took off the way I did."

"Has she worked a miracle for you, your Lillian
Flagg?"

"The miracle was really her taking me in at all.
I just arrived without warning. You know who told me
about her? Franny. Just that she was supposed to be
the real thing . . . if there is a real thing. Her name
always stuck in my mind."

"I'd never connected her with Muscadine," Nicolet
said. "Come to Muscadine and be healed." He spoke
absently. "Come to Muscadine and die. Maybe the
dying comes first."

"She's tried to teach me how to pray, and I'm lousy
at it. She's prayed for me. I thought I'd die when
she started except she's so matter-of-fact—like the
president of a woman's club. But it would kill you,

Nick. They're so corny, the prayers. She admits it. She always says them to Jesus, and she says it's important to call him that—not Christ or Lord or anything—because Jesus is the part of his name that embarrasses people to death when they use it alone, just Jesus. She says that underneath that embarrassment is the part of us that's revolted by him. It's so damned queer. So you say Jesus to get that part out in the open where he can get at it."

"Cornelia says Harold."

"You'd die, you'd die." She shook her head.

"I've been dying."

"I've got to tell you about it because you're the first person I've seen since I got here. It's been so queer, Nick. I don't believe anything much, God knows, but sometimes I thought I could feel something happening. Once in the rain. She lays her hands on your head, and the prayer is really just her talking about you to him. She could be talking to anybody, nothing fancy. Once she even laughed because he already seemed to be doing what she was asking him to do, not a creepy laugh, but the way if a child does something especially clever. She said it was amazing what God could do on his own sometimes. What she asked him to do for me was to walk back through my memory, as though it was a long hall. She asked him to open all the closed doors, and to bless whatever he found inside. Is it just mumbo-jumbo, Nick?"

She lit a cigarette when she had finished, tossing back her hair, and he saw that she was listening still to the echo of her own words rather than for whatever he might find to say in reply. For the moment he could find nothing; yes and no alike were only grammar, rhetoric. As Nicolet, he felt that he could have managed one or the other, but as Laliberté he could only marvel at a face made for braving the sight of an ocean, a child, the disorder of her garden, as it gazed now instead through the smoke from her cigarette into the silences that as a runaway he was himself running away from or towards.

"I'm not a mystic," he said. "I'm a cop. A firm but friendly guardian of the moral order. I bring wives back to husbands and husbands back to wives."

"You look like a mystic," Rooney said. "You look like St. Francis about to start preaching to the birds."

With his face tilted up to watch the shimmering canopy of leaves above her head, with his hands clasped between his knees where he squatted on the rotting branch, the position of his body had already made him a supplicant so that at the suggestion from her it was a matter only of sinking the few inches left to the earth. He spread out his arms in a gesture half beseeching, half exhorting. "Feathery ladies, little sisters, break the silence with your glad evangels. . . ."

In the interval of their saying nothing, the sounds of the clearing drifted to the surface—crickets, a thrush, the distant barking of a dog. His arms began to ache, and the sun was hot; down his narrow, blue jaw he felt a ripple of flame as all about him beating wings descended. "Twitter, twitter, cheep, cheep, cheep," he said in a tiny voice. "I'm famous for my imitations of saints. You should see me do the martyrdom of Polycarp."

Rooney smiled uncertainly, as if she had noticed nothing. "I've got memories that need blessing, Nicko. There's that much for sure."

"Oh Lord, I'm an ass!" He sprang to his feet and scrambled to her through the ferns, crouching down beside her. She was Sarah and Hannah and Elizabeth, the barren wife all freckled and damp-eyed among the shadows as he clowned in the sun; she was the sheep of his pasture, Raggedy Ann, his beloved, his child.

"I've got to spew it out at somebody. Be good to me, Nick." Slowly with her fingertips she traced vague circles on the little patch of earth between them as if to conjure him into not hearing what she had to tell him, glancing away from him into the woods as she spoke.

In a room stained crimson with sunset she had cuckolded Clem in his own junkshop with the wind off the river smelling of mud. The fall of their first year at Myron she had clung to a stranger without a name and drowned with him in the crimson depths of her boredom; she had ruined his smile with her thumbs, with her absence of either love for him or lust, and all of this she translated now for Nicolet into a language so remote and muted that he was tempted to pass it over as only a troubling dream until she glanced up at him suddenly with a face that even now was drowning.

To save her, he knew, would be somehow to save himself; and as if in search of something that would set them both free he studied that face which seemed to float there in the sunlight so close to his own that he saw it magnified out of perspective: a single, still eye, the shadow dividing her lips, a wisp of hair the color of autumn. Only her face seemed real to him, the delicate flesh and muscle of it, the tanned cheek which his fingers touched for a moment as he might have touched a fern or the bark of the tree. That was perhaps the truth that he looked for: that only what you could touch was real, and the corridor of the past with all its rooms—his own no less than hers—was a dream. Rooney's betrayal of Clem, his own betrayal of Roy, of Franny by slowly forgetting her— it was all just smoke that one sweep of a living hand could brush from his eyes. The outrageous simplicity of the solution tempted him to smile, and only her one tear stopped him. It trembled, glistening, down the side of her nose.

"You could have done so much worse, you know," and then he had to smile, the whole fullness of her grief hanging to her nostril like a ranee's pearl. "Cruelty, bitterness, self-pity—they take root in the soul and keep growing. But this, six years ago. . . . It exists only by being remembered. So much better just to forget it now, and better for Clem too. Better for God."

Even as he spoke, he saw the hopelessness of what he told her—forgetting was a state of grace, after all, not an act of the will—but he went on with it anyway because the melody if not the meaning of the words seemed right as she touched away the tear with her knuckle. He knew that it was not the language of Nicolet or of Mrs. Flagg that he spoke—no call to repentance, no prayer for the memory's healing—but the language of Laliberté: Forget it, forget it. You bade farewell to your native France, you left the old man in his lumberjack shirt to stir up breakfast for the paying guests, in the morning loveliness of Muscadine you put behind you once and for all the sunset and the stranger. You liberated yourself.

"This afternoon or tomorrow," Nicolet said, "I'll take you back to Myron, to Clem. No more brooding. Right now is all that matters. The rest is nothing . . . noplace . . . and the way the world goes, what happened was so little. God knows. In my line of work, you get to be an expert. And it's never happened again, has it?"

"Sometimes I've wondered if it ever happened at all," Rooney said. "I've seen him again off and on— just by accident, on the street somewhere. We never speak even. Maybe that's the worst of it. I don't know why I can't tell you his name." She shook her head. "Honor among thieves."

Nicolet got to his feet and offered his hand to help her up. "Starting now," he said, "don't think of anything in Muscadine. Just think of Muscadine in Mus-

cadine. And as for the baby . . ." With a pang of
homesickness, he remembered kissing Lizzie's sleeping eyelids when he had left at daybreak the morning
before, and for an instant he could not think what he
had been about to say. "I'm sure Mrs. Flagg's word
carries great weight in high places."

She stood beside him brushing off her skirt, un-
conscious for the moment of anything else as with her
bare head bowed she picked off a burr. *Harold*, he
thought, *have mercy on the stranger. Have mercy on
me for hating the stranger.*

"You make an awfully queer minister," she said.
"But thank you for coming, Nicko."

For envying the stranger.

"It all seems so easy," Rooney said as they walked
through the rustling ferns.

And for several hours after that it continued to
seem easy—as if they had reached the summit of a
hill above the battle, their view of the turbulence into
which they would have to descend soon enough only
deepening the momentary sense of reprieve. Nicolet
remembered that he had never paid for his room at
the hotel so Rooney drove him back and, while he
paid, bought sandwiches and milk for their lunch
which they ate in the car as they drove slowly through
the countryside, not stopping anywhere on the road
because it was only as long as they kept moving from
landscape to landscape that they felt safe from whatever it was that menaced them, safe from any necessity to talk, safe from each other. With all the win-

dows wide open and the red station wagon filled with
summer, they drove for miles of easy silence through
the woods around Muscadine with Rooney at the
wheel and Nicolet leaning back in the seat beside her,
his face turned toward the rush of soft air. It was not
until mid-afternoon that they decided to stop back at
Lillian Flagg's for Rooney's belongings and return to
Myron that day.

It was Lillian Flagg who persuaded them to wait.
What Rooney had told him about her and what he already knew of her as a healer, a guardian of Christian mysteries, had not prepared Nicolet for the portly
little figure in overalls and a coolie hat who appeared
out of the garden where she had been weeding, a
smudge of dirt on her chin and the weary-eyed, puff-
cheeked smile as she shook his hand when Rooney
introduced them and announced their plan to leave.
"Your parish can stagger along without you another
few hours, I expect," she said almost as soon as they
met, her smile still there but as though she had entirely forgotten it in the intensity of perusing a new
face. "I'd like you to stay here this evening. You can
go home tomorrow any time you please. Both of you.
Don't be frightened, Mr. Nicolet. Oh dear no . . ."
She sounded a little out of breath, opening her eyes
wider for a moment, like turning up a lamp, and
then, as if she had seen all that she needed, complet-
ing her smile. "I've been known to eat two or three
little pastors like you for my breakfast, but as Mrs.
Vail knows, I've just recently had my fill, so don't be

nervous. We'll have a sherry before supper."

Then, taking Rooney by the hand, she disappeared back to the weeds, and Nicolet, having been pressed into staying, found himself abandoned by the sagging porch steps of the bungalow. Was she a great warrior of the faith, or a deluder of the credulous, a deluder of herself? Could the line be drawn neatly at all? The best that you could do was to look into her eyes and place your bet, but when he had tried to do so, he had found her looking so much more masterfully into his that he had glanced away. Was she asking herself the same question about him, he wondered: a warrior of the faith, or jolly Saint Nick, as Poteat had written of him, off on a spree.

Nicolet had seen, of course, the references to himself and to Rooney in Poteat's column in the *Repository*, but they had troubled him little and Rooney even less, apparently, because she had never mentioned them to him. Yet at the thought of Poteat now, he winced—at the recognition that somewhere in the shadows of his thoughts, largely nameless and faceless, Poteat had been lurking all along. The man himself Nicolet scarcely knew: he had appeared at church a few Sundays, always arriving just in time for the sermon and leaving before the final hymn, but apart from that he had seen him only in passing as he shambled down Main Street asking questions for his column where the most florid exaltations of the New England landscape were scattered among ironic sketches of life in Myron and cumbersome innuendo directed against whatever had happened that week to catch his pale and simmering eye. "He's got it in for you, old man," Denbigh had said to him once. "You better go heap some coals of fire on his head by being nice," and surely if Poteat were to see him now, Nicolet thought, he would find all his hostilities justified —jolly Saint Nick, the philandering padre, idling away a late June afternoon with his red-headed doxy and her conjure-woman while his old ladies teetered unshriven towards death, his trustees snarled at their canceled meeting, and even his own children did not know his whereabouts.

It would be almost time for their supper. Irma called them in toward the end of the afternoon to clean up, and they ate in the kitchen at five—sometimes in silence so sleepy and drunk on warm food and summer that they would forget to chew, just sitting there blankly with their mouths half full and their spoons flopping; sometimes hilarious and wicked, talking bathroom talk and bubbling their milk, playing their endless games of You be Bluebeard and I'll be Raggedy Ann—I see something yellow and it's not on the table, not on the wall. Nicolet climbed the porch steps and entered the living room. The breeze through the window had upset a jelly-glass of wildflowers—pearly everlasting, tansy and yarrow—and he set it up again, mopping the water with his blood-stained handkerchief. A fly buzzed across the low ceiling. It took him some time to find the telephone which stood on a wicker table half hidden by a pile of books—*The Late Mrs. Null, The Cloud of Unknow-ing*—and when the operator asked him for his name, he faltered through the spelling of Nicolet, then waited in silence with the receiver pressed into his cheek so that one corner of his mouth was drawn back in a lopsided smile.

"Wie geht's, Irma? Hier ist dein Freund, Til Eulenspiegel."

Her indignation soothed him, and he held the receiver a little away from his ear, listening with his eyes closed. He could hear first her muffled cry of "Bluebeard!" to the children, followed by the clatter of their feet, some German expletive. "At last you are letting us know you are alive!" she said. "The children keep asking, 'Irma, has he gone to Heaven?' and all I can say is, 'It's your father who knows about Heaven, you ask him when he comes back if that's where he was.' How do I know what to tell them? Everybody is asking me where you have gone, so I tell them nothing like you said, and the church woman, she thinks I'm crazy. I'm going crazy here. Mr. Vail called—I know nothing. Mr. Denbigh left just a few minutes ago. He brought shovels for the children—very nice. Now I throw away all the rusty ones, today they took your shoes out and filled them with sand. You want I should be the one who asks him to preach your sermon Sunday? I'm not even a Christian, and you've got me running a church. Stop it, stop it Lizzie!" It was like a cageful of birds, the fierce whispers, the clinking of china in the background. *Rules and Exercises for Holy Dying, The*

Scandal of Father Brown—he ran his fingers along their spines until he could hear her back and breathing again.

"As of now, you can consider yourself an honorary Christian," he said. He spoke quietly, pinching his eyes shut again with his thumb and forefinger. "I'll be driving back tomorrow with Mrs. Vail."

"*Also*, she is with you then. . . . So now what do I say?" The excitement was gone, her voice hushed now and breathy, and in the pause that followed he had a clear vision of her standing there in the kitchen with the receiver touching her mouth—the frizzled grey hair, the goblin face—as her question trembled across the miles between them, conspiratorial, as if in speaking of Rooney's presence with him he had betrayed his guiltiest secret. She was prepared to say whatever he told her to say, to protect him at whatever cost even as a wife, he thought, would have tried to protect him, and for a moment Irma Reinwasser became a wife, and he answered her in the accents of melodrama, sighing deeply with his hand on his heart. "Say that to the end I have resisted her every wile and kept myself faithful to you . . . my own true love." He could hear the children calling, "Irma, Irma!" but from her no sound. "Irma?" he said.

"I am still here."

"I was worried about her. I came to bring her back, that's all."

"Everywhere now people are worrying . . . all the world."

"Don't you worry, Irma. I'm coming back."

"That's don't worry?"

The fly had found its way to the window and kept hurling itself against the screen. "That's don't worry," Nicolet said. "Can I talk to my babies now?"

"First Lizzie . . ."

"Is this my old Liz? How's my wiggler?"

There was a long silence, then as if from far away the husky little voice. "Fine."

"Have you been a good baby?"

"Fine."

"What did you do today?"

"I don't want to talk any more." She said this to Irma, speaking around her thumb; her enormous eyes were dazed, Nicolet knew. Her hair needed cutting.

"Hi."

"Is this my Pie Face?"

"Yes." Her voice was deep and tremulous. "Where are you?"

"I'm in Muscadine. I'm coming home tomorrow."

"We thought you were in Heaven."

"Talk louder, little one. Do you miss me?"

"We saw a man with a black tongue."

"That must have been nice. I saw a lady with red hair. Have you been having a good time with Irma?"

"Yes."

"Did you have fun putting sand in your old Dad's shoes?"

"Just some of them. That's all right. I have to go now."

"Hey, wait a sec. Can I talk to Irma again?"

"She went upstairs."

"What did Lizzie just say?"

"She said Irma was crying."

"Of course she wasn't crying. What is there to cry about?"

"Lizzie said it."

"You and Lizzie go up and say goodbye to her for me. I'll be home tomorrow."

"Goodbye."

"Goodbye, little ones."

The whole room where he sat was transformed by her tears, if tears they were, if Lizzie was to be believed—the saddest room, suddenly, that he had ever seen: the faded pillows and the peacock feather, the sprawling square of saffron light from the late sun, the birch-bark silhouettes of trout curling away from the wall where they were nailed. He had never seen Irma cry. Rooney's had been a single tear, crystalline, an adornment; Irma's would be rivulets streaking the large-pored cheeks and tracing the great baroque curves of flaring nostril—Savonarola retching at the stake. From such a sight you hid your eyes, and Nicolet leaned forward with his face in his hands, humming tunelessly.

He had a strong sense of waiting for something more than just the return of the two women, more even than his own return to his parish, his children, yet what it was he could not have said. But for whatever it was, Lillian Flagg set the stage with remarkable speed. She had come in from the garden chat-

tering to Rooney about aphids and the ladybugs that
you could get from California to devour them; she
had plumped the pillows, swatted the flies, lit the
lamp, as he and Rooney had stood by awkwardly,
avoiding each other's eyes, and then the two of them
had disappeared upstairs to change their clothes before supper, leaving Nicolet to prepare himself as best
he could at the mirror above the kitchen sink where
he recoiled, grimacing, from the reflection of the cut
on his cheek, the blue stubble of beard and his wild
hair. In less time then than he would have thought
possible, Lillian Flagg had come down again in a
flame blue dress with a little cape and a brooch at her
throat, her face startlingly pale but fresh and quick as
she brought in the tray of sherry and glasses. "Mrs.
Vail is going to have a little snooze till supper so we'll
have to kill this all by ourselves." She motioned him
to the couch and sitting down in the wing chair facing
him, raised her glass to him in silence, drank a third
of it, and wiped her mouth with a tiny handkerchief.
"Have you ever received the gift of the Spirit, Mr.
Nicolet?"

For a moment he could not think what she was talking about, the vivid little woman in pearl earrings,
peering at him with a look of faint amusement.

"The Holy Spirit," she said, and at this positively
smiled.

"Oh, oh . . ." He raised his hand to her to wait a
moment, swallowing the sherry hard. "If I remember rightly, aren't there lots of different kinds of
gifts?"

"Yes, I know, I know. First Corinthians twelve. Healing. Tongues. Prophecy." She brushed them all away. "I don't mean the frills. I mean the real business. 'The spirit that resurrected Jesus from the dead shall also give life to your mortal bodies.' The life," she said. "That's what I mean."

Nicolet shook his head.

"I didn't think so," she said. "You get so you can tell. Pray for it, Nicolet. Nothing else really matters, you know."

"Have you received it?" He watched her closely, his eyebrows raised, for some betrayal of quackery—a wave of her hand and the table would start rapping, the birch-bark fish would peel off the wall and float shimmering through the dusk on silken threads.

"Oh dear, yes." With a tidy little sigh she took another sip from her glass. "Otherwise I wouldn't be here now. I'd have dried up and blown away long ago." She repeated the trick with her eyes: when you thought that they were wide open, they would open wider still for a moment, apparently quite independent of the rest of her face or of what she was saying.

"How was it?" Nicolet asked. "All it's cracked up to be?" It surprised him to find suddenly that he disliked her. Who, looking at them, would take her for the professional, he wondered, and himself for the fumbling dilettante, or was this part of the divine absurdity, part of the great laughter? In any event, he was unable now to laugh, much as he wished that he could, unable even to return her owlish smile with his

face stiff and unmanageable as he sat there at her bid-
ding, drinking her sherry, with the knowledge that,
whatever the justice of her claims, it was to her and
not to him that Rooney had gone for some kind of
rescue.

"It was in the days when I was much more mixed
up with individual healings than I am now, and I'd
come to the end of my rope. I was all out of juice. So
I came back to Muscadine to ask for help. I prayed
for a shot in the arm, for more strength to heal. And
you know what I was given?"

Nicolet shrugged.

"Absolutely nothing. I was afraid I was through,
all right. I'd thought I was pretty hot stuff. And I
was, you know. But then I had enough sense to pray
for guidance. I said, 'Lord, what do you want me to
pray for now?' And the answer came through quite
clearly. 'Pray for the Holy Ghost.' Which was quite a
surprise, I assure you, because I'd always assumed
with the healings and all that I already had it—whatever it was. Right in this room I prayed," she said,
"and right in this room I received."

"Amid tongues of fire?" Nicolet asked. "A mighty
rushing wind?"

"If you'd been here, you wouldn't have seen a
thing. I didn't. It was all inside—an intense burning
in the middle of the head. You can't work that up on
your own—there's so much you can, but not that. I've
tried. Some kind of change in the air of the room, a
fragrance. And joy, Nicolet. Joy. Joy." She pelted him

with the word, the brooch at her throat glittering as she leaned forward to set her empty glass on the table. "Joy splashing like a fountain and spilling out over the sides. The certainty of it, Nicolet. Truer than you'd ever believed—all of it, and more. Hallelujah! Praise the Lord! Revival talk, little man. And nothing, nothing, is ever the same again."

He knew that for the first time now he had her at his mercy, that to laugh if he could, to make a face, to be Saint Francis again and preach to the fish, to the dead fly, would be to destroy her unless—and his face trembled with the effort of holding it still—unless she were to laugh out with him, throw back her head and drown his laughter in hers.

"Just like that," he said, snapping his fingers. "Never a doubt again? Never the impulse to run?"

"Oh, there are still the ups and downs—life moves. And the downs can be deep and dark. But underneath, always, the joy. Like an underground spring. There now," she said. "Those are my credentials, such as they are. They're what you wanted to see, aren't they?"

"All I wanted was to go home," Nicolet said. "You told me to stay, for some occult reason."

Lillian Flagg leaned back tiredly in her chair, resting her chin on her fingertips. "Don't hate me, Mr. Nicolet. You're the one who can help her, not I."

"I hope I've helped her already. I don't hate you."

"Then prepare to," she said. "Because you've done nothing for her. Somebody's got to tell you that."

There was the sound of Rooney's footsteps crossing the floor above their heads, the closing of a door, and in the silence that followed, their eyes met with such a depth of complicity that for a few moments Nicolet could not disengage himself enough to address her.

"I think that was a human being that just passed by . . . on her way to the john." There was a rumble of water in the pipes as he managed at last a smile that failed to mock Lillian Flagg, as for an instant he had intended, but held her there at arm's length with a kind of bemused affection. "Not really ours at all, Mrs. Flagg, to help much or harm much—whoever in Hell we think we are. She'll ride our advice like her horse, wherever she wants."

"Nicolet, I may adopt you." She ran her hands briskly up and down her bare arms, never taking her eyes from him. "Oh Lord, how advice bores me, especially when it's good. And yours was good enough. 'Go back to your husband.' That probably didn't come so easy, did it? 'Forget your infidelity.' She told me, you see. It's so modern, and it's so sane, and it's just the advice she'd want if she wanted advice. Only give her what she really wants, Nicolet."

"Give her what, for Christ's sake?"

"For Christ's sake . . ." Lillian Flagg took a deep breath, then let it out slowly, shaking her head. "The only thing you have to give." And then she almost shouted at him. "Forgive her for Christ's sake, little priest!"

"But she knows I forgive her."

"She doesn't know God forgives her. That's the only power you have—to tell her that. Not just that he forgives her the poor little adultery. But the faces she can't bear to look at now. The man's. Her husband's. Her own, half the time. Tell her he forgives her for being lonely and bored, for not being full of joy with a houseful of children. That's what sin really is. You know—not being full of joy. Tell her that sin is forgiven because whether she knows it or not, that's what she wants more than anything else—what all of us want. What on earth do you think you were ordained for?"

What on earth did he think about anything, Nicolet wondered, and when Rooney came downstairs smelling faintly of soap from her bath, and the conversation turned entirely to objects—what there was in the refrigerator for supper, the best road back to Myron—he wondered even if his talk with Lillian Flagg had taken place anywhere but in his head. Nothing in her manner now indicated that she had any memory of it, and between the flame blue of her dress, the yellow and amber of Rooney's, he felt like a shadow in his rumpled suit the color of fog. What was this house, who were these women? The chirping of crickets came in waves through the open windows, the sherry was sweet and warm on his tongue, and the green ferns of the clearing that morning rustled in his mind as he smiled pointlessly while they chattered on in a language that he felt he had not sufficiently mastered to join in himself. Irma was

weeping in her bedroom, the children hushed in their
bibs at her door. He had signed his grandfather's
name in the hotel register. "I need fresh air. I think
I'm intoxicated," and they seemed barely to acknowledge his departure then to stand for a while alone
on the front steps watching the last bands of salmon
sky dwindle on the horizon.

When he came in again through the back door
and found Lillian Flagg peering into the oven to see
if the chicken pies were done, he made a gesture to
Rooney of pushing her in and slamming the door
shut behind her. "Before she gets us," he whispered
as she carried their plates into the dining room. "The
house is made of gingerbread, you know. I just tasted
a piece of the porch. She's fattening us up." But
Rooney's smile was vague, unlistening, and it was
only once they were seated at table and Lillian Flagg
asked him to bless their food that he felt himself coming back into some kind of focus. "For all thy mercies
known and unknown, remembered and forgotten,"
he said, "we give thee thanks this night."

Lillian Flagg had asked why on earth he thought
he had been ordained: kneeling on the sanctuary steps
half smothered by the black robes of the ministers
with the trembling weight of all their hands hot on
his scalp—"Bestow upon him the grace of thy holy
spirit, confirming in Heaven what we do in thy
church on earth . . . let the same mind be in him
which was also in Christ Jesus." The moderator had
been a Negro with the face of a pharaoh, epicene,

bird-boned, and old Roy had sat in the second pew with a handkerchief pressed against his mouth. Now the plate burned the knuckles of his clenched hands, but he did not draw them away, glancing at Rooney with her head bowed self-consciously low in the candle light, Lillian Flagg sitting up stiffly with her eyes closed. "Blessed are they that hunger and thirst after righteousness, for they shall be filled." They ate almost entirely in silence, and soon after they finished, Lillian Flagg said goodnight and went upstairs.

When they had washed the dishes, they returned to the living room where Rooney sat down on the windowseat with her legs curled under her. "Go to bed, will you, Nick? You look like death, and I don't have two words left to rub together." For a moment he had almost obeyed her, longing above all things to obey her as he stood there with his hand on the newel post, one foot on the stairs, so tired all of a sudden that the lamplight seemed to dim and brighten with his pulse. Then he slowly walked the great distance to where she sat and stood beside her, looking down at her profile bright against the dark panes as she gazed away from him at nothing. With his palms flat against her temples, he tipped her face to him, and she raised her own hands and pressed them against his so that each seemed to be preventing the other's escape while robed in shadow he heard himself pronounce like a stranger, "The almighty and merciful God pardon and deliver you, forgive you every face you cannot look upon with joy," and what he saw was

Raggedy Ann with a mouth stitched shut in a ragged smile and the shoebutton eyes shining bright for maybe no more than a child to maul and mother her to life.

EIGHT

———◆———

IT WAS because the young Hauptscharführer, Heinz Taffel, took it into his head that she looked like a chicken that Irma Reinwasser had survived her imprisonment. He had been standing in a tar-paper shack warming his hands at the coal stove when he saw her stumbling through the snow with a rope over her shoulders knotted to a bundle of railroad ties that she was dragging toward the new section of track being built on the outskirts of the camp, and he had laughed out loud at the sight. Her head wobbled back and forth as she moved, picking her feet up high to avoid the drifts, and with her skin turned yellow and the great beak of her nose bobbing up and down, she looked not unlike a hen searching the icy ground for seed. Because there was no one else to share the spectacle with, Heinz Taffel had thrust his handsome young head through the shack door and honked his mirth out toward Irma herself, his breath rising in swirls of mist through the cold, north

German air. She stopped to look at him, at the same time trying to uncurl her frozen fingers and blow on them as though his amusement gave her leave to rest for a moment; and when he shouted at her, *"Du bist wie ein Huhn!"* so that she might share the joke, she did something in a moment of agonized madness that undoubtedly saved her life in the long months to come. So emaciated that she could encircle the upper part of her arms with her thumb and forefinger, she stood there in the snow and suddenly started to flap her elbows up and down and cackle—a raucous, falsetto clucking like a peal of broken bells—and before she could tell what he had in store for her, Heinz Taffel had rushed out and, throwing his arms about her in uproarious embrace, half carried, half dragged her, still clucking, back to the shack. *"Mein Huhn! Mein Huhn!"* She had laid an egg, he told her, and must hatch it by the warmth of the fire.

Dark-haired and dark-eyed with two little patches of red high on his cheeks like a doll, Heinz Taffel had the smell of life about him in a world of death, and even among the prisoners it won him a measure of wary popularity. He would always let them see him coming: he would leap and wave his arms, roaring like a young bull at their ragged clumsiness, kicking and thumping the laggards, but even his brutality was endurable not because it was any less brutal than the others' but because, though swift and terrible, it had a kind of boy's passion to it and was quickly spent. Among the officers as well as the other guards he en-

joyed what seemed almost a madman's license—on
one of the rare occasions when the commandant himself inspected some of the prisoners' huts, and Taffel,
more than half drunk, had wept like a child when he
showed him the bunk of a man who the day before
had been flogged to death for attempting to escape,
nothing had been done about it—and there were several rumors advanced to explain it. Some held that no
one dared thwart him because he was a bastard of
Rudolf Hess, whom he dimly resembled; others, that
the commandant, who was said to have a taste for
boys, had taken a fancy to him; but whatever the
truth of the matter, his exuberance and wild inanities
were tolerated to an extraordinary degree, and no one
made a move to check him when he seized upon
Irma Reinwasser and made her a kind of mascot.

He managed to have her taken out of the labor
battalion altogether and assigned to orderly duties in
the non-commissioned officers' quarters, where as the
hen of Taffel, finally Taffelshuhn, she came to experience all the hazards as well as the privileges of being
their creature. They coddled her with cigarettes and
chocolate when things went well, knocked and slapped
her around when things went badly, mocked her
skeletal ugliness by feigning, even to the point of
sometimes acting out, a barnyard lust for her, and
they never let her forget that original act of genius
when she had cackled for Taffel in the snow. She
crowed for them like a cock at reveille, flapping her
hands with their great knobs of wrist and knuckle,

and on all fours scratched across the barracks floor for the scraps that they occasionally brought her back from their mess. In their latrine, where a major part of her duties took place, they would menace and taunt her with their nakedness, making her dry them after their showers, massage them, and for a period it became the fad to make her lay eggs there, forcing her to relieve herself in front of groups of them in their S.S. uniforms, clucking and grunting with her great bony face somehow detached from the rest of her as it jounced up and down at odd angles like the plaster heads carried on poles in fasching parades. But as the camp went, it was little enough to pay for life and warmth, and Heinz Taffel remained her champion, defending her from the more brutal extravagances of his brothers-in-arms and the envy of the other prisoners.

But she learned that she could not depend upon him entirely. Sometimes when he had been drinking or when for some other reason his eyes glittered with crazy zest, he would bedevil her with the rest of them, leading them into still greater ingenuities, and nothing was as full of terror for her as this, when the face of the savior became the simpering face of a clown. But afterwards he was always penitent. Once when they found themselves alone by the coal bin where Taffelshuhn sat all streaked with black like a gnome but with some strange, gnarled gentleness in the glance that she raised to him, he had buried his head in her lap, vilifying himself to her unmercifully, and although she did not quite dare to speak, not knowing with which of his faces he might look up at her if she acknowledged his guilt by forgiving it, she had risked laying her stiff fingers on the back of his neck and held him there like a child until at the sound of approaching footsteps he had leapt up with his eyes bloodshot and helpless and cursed her superbly.

None of this was known, of course, to Will Poteat when he arrived at the house on Congress Street the evening of Nicolet's telephone call from Muscadine, but it was more as Taffelshuhn than as Reinwasser that she opened the door for him, her features heavy with shadow from the overhead light. It was Nicolet's call that had done it—her defender and tormentor-clown who had abandoned her only to announce his return to her, Til Eulenspiegel, calling her his own true love, and suddenly it was Taffel whom she heard, their gay voices, gay, dark faces, merging so that she could hardly hold the telephone but handed it to Lizzie and hobbled up the stairs to her room like a bird with broken wings to stand there by the window as still as death until the children had come up with ice cream on their faces and stared her into action.

"You don't know me," Poteat said. "I'm a friend of Nick's."

In her dreams the barbed wire sometimes flowered like a hedge of roses that stretched with wonderful straightness as far as the eye could see, but she could never follow it accurately because something always loomed to frighten her off her course; yet now, trailing the fingers of one hand along the wall to mark the clean line of her passage, she led him straight as geometry to the end of the hall where she paused to let him precede her in making the right angle into Nicolet's study, their footsteps clattering through the empty house, the children asleep in their beds.

"People tell their secrets here, don't they?" Poteat seated himself at the roll-top desk. "They speak of the odor of sanctity, but in a long life of sniffing I have never detected it once. This room, on the other hand—it smells of secrecy."

Of course, it was supposed to begin this way, Irma knew. The interrogator made some bland remarks that left a stain on his mouth like milk—*Haben Sie keine Furcht, kleine Taffelshuhn. Wir wollen nur dass man uns die Wahrheit sagt.*—perhaps he offered you a cigarette, lit one himself, and together you watched the smoke curl and tremble. The swivel chair creaked as Poteat tilted back in it with Nicolet's woodblock of the prodigal son above his head—the prodigal bent and exhausted with his face pressed against the old man's shoulders. Poteat said nothing; there was a trace of Goering, she thought, in the fixed, encouraging smile—*unser Hermann* with his eyes slightly protuberant as she waited for him to smash his fist down on the desk-top and with flakes of saliva at the corners of his mouth to begin whatever he had come for.

"There's a staleness about it," he said, "that gives it away—like an old ice-chest or a closet. They come in here to babble out their sins, and old Nick sits where I'm sitting, I suppose, rinsing them off with the blood of the lamb. We all have our sins, of course. I don't quarrel with that. I'm not really a quarreller at all, Fraulein. I'm a sniffer."

She had known a cross-eyed little undertaker from Mainz who had been dragged back from such an interview with all the fingernails of one hand missing and his face ever after a perpetual mask of astonishment because all that they had talked to him about, as far as he could remember, was the weather— doors had kept slamming, he said, and someone had held him by the ears. She had heard that at Sachsenhausen when a woman's labor began, they tied her thighs together. Torture was a beast's game, and there were beasts everywhere; no wonder that they had found her out here, deserted by Nicolet. She half expected him to burst out of the closet now where he had been hiding, posturing and gawking as he called her his own true love, Heinz Taffel, handsome and drunk with leather hands. But Irma had stared down darkness before, addressing herself fiercely at her dresser mirror where the plumed kewpie from the Palisades dangled, a pair of doll-size Indian moccasins, and a rabbit's foot of red, white and blue. Sometimes just the incantation *Amerika, Amerika*, was enough to save her although now she leaned forward and massaged her feet, enormous in their sheepskin slippers and gym socks, using that familiar pain to chin herself up out of shadow.

"What is the matter? Your feet hurt?" he asked.

"They hurt enough," and the sound of her voice speaking English was a platform for her to pull herself up to like an acrobat. "*Wass*——" She frowned at her error. "What's hurting you?"

"I'm not in pain," Poteat said. "I won't pretend I haven't sinned myself, such sins as come an old dog's way. I won't pretend there isn't some residual discomfort, a little throbbing of regret whenever the wind blows off the sea—not that I regret committing them but that there have been so few occasions to commit them again. But I haven't come in my own behalf. I've come in Nick's."

"Right now," Irma said, "he's not here."

"That's true, of course." He brought his fist down on the desk-top but soft as a dead leaf, rustling it back and forth over the blotter as he spoke. "He wasn't here today, and he wasn't here yesterday. It's a strange business, Miss Reinwasser, but I have a theory about it. I'll bet he's been taken up, like Elijah." Poteat tipped back in the chair and looked up at the ceiling. "I can see it clear as day. The sky's thick with angels and pink clouds, and plunk in the middle is the jolly saint soaring heavenward like a rocket. He's got his eyes rolled up in prayer and that black nightshirt he preaches in billowed out all around him by the winds of paradise, and his little black toes pointed down . . ."

Irma sat on the edge of her chair, staring at him in the effort to remember who he was, but the time for asking him had passed. It was his room now, and she was the one to answer questions; someone would come up from behind her soon and grab her by the ears.

"But unfortunately, there are always the people who live on dung," Poteat said. "They try to tell me that Elijah's flaming chariot is really hydromatic and flaming red. That it's a station wagon he made his getaway in, and maybe not all by his lonesome either. By God, you know, this world's an ugly place."

"Every week they put your picture in . . ." Sometimes in dreams when the beasts were almost upon you, the best you could do was turn on them and call them beasts, howl it out at them like a beast yourself. If sometimes it only crazed them further as they panted and slobbered toward you down the barricade of roses, sometimes it made them vanish. "You're the newspaper man, *nicht?*"

"I want to see the news put straight," Poteat said. "There are rumors all over town about where your man's gone, and why he went, and who went with him maybe. I'll tell you one thing for sure. The truth can't smell any higher than the rumors do."

"My man?" She leaned back in the straight chair, the mended sweater hanging loose from her shoulders and her great slippered feet hardly touching the floor. "My man . . ." By right not of possession but of protection he was hers perhaps: as a foot is the shoe's

that it wears, as in some curious way Heinz Taffel
had been hers whom she had protected from finally
brutalizing her by refusing ever quite to be brutalized,
not even at the last with her body fouled with sweat
and the cackling pain. Now Nicolet—with the shadow
of a smile, she prepared to protect him too against this
figure who sat at the desk speaking of dung and an
ugly world. "He is his own man, God's man. You don't
hurt such a man with crazy rumors."

"Some of them say there's a lady involved."

"Here is a lady. *Komm.*" She held out both hands,
and Lizzie, who had appeared in her nightdress at
the door behind Poteat, came padding across the floor
barefoot to where Irma sat. "Sleepy lady," Irma said,
taking the small face between her hands and tipping
it up to her, then letting it sink to her lap where she
covered it with her hands. "The lady you mean is Mrs.
Rooney Vail, I'm not so dumb." She spoke in a voice
emboldened by the presence of the child. "If you want
to know more, I will tell you also the rest. I talked to
him tonight, and she is with him now, this lady Mrs.
Rooney Vail."

Lizzie murmured beneath her hands. "I want a
glass of water."

"Rooney Vail," he repeated. "Rooney, Rooney—
there's witchcraft in a name like that. It could turn a
man to stone. But this beautiful story you've told me,
Fraulein." His smile deepened. "How am I going to
thank you for it."

"It's nothing like how you think, Mister." Irma

picked Lizzie up and set her on her lap. Wrinkles from the bedclothes were imprinted on the sleep-flushed face, and putting her thumb in her mouth, she buried her face against Irma's chest.

"Don't you want to put her back where she belongs?" Poteat leaned forward and drew his finger lightly across the sole of Lizzie's foot. She drew it back.

The weight of the child felt heavy against her, the slightly sour smell of a child with the wet thumb slipping from her mouth as she fell asleep. Irma shook her head. "She's all right. She's sleeping." Like Goering, he had dimples, would look almost handsome in a uniform with his hair brushed back, but the room was no longer his. She could see that the irrelevance there of Lizzie had set his face faltering for an expression that would accommodate both what he had come for and a sleeping child. Once before she had been saved by irrelevance: fat old Maxl wandering in with his snout to the floor just as Taffel had bent down to her again.

"The young buck vicar and the gentle-eyed doe have taken to the woods, and their white rumps are seen flashing through the brush. I'm not a villain, Miss Rainwater. A villain rejoices when the guilty secret is revealed. I mourn. The prize has turned to ashes in my hands."

"Now you must listen to me," Irma Reinwasser said, "newspaper man, whoever you are." She spoke without raising her voice but her face snapped like a flag. "All this dung you call it, for weeks I've been getting it everywhere I go, taxi drivers, waitresses, even the milk man. Always the same question—what is going on? And all the time in the newspaper you keep the fire hot. Why do you do this? Nothing is going on, that's the answer. Nothing. They don't leave here together like crooks. He leaves by himself in the morning early, writing a note for me and kissing the children goodbye. That sounds like Don Juan? He left this house like a pastor because she wanted him, I don't know what kind of trouble, and he went away to help her and bring her back—tomorrow they come—because he called me up and told me this. He is a good man," she said, "God's man—none of this dirtiness on him. I know it. I live in this house and see him come back tired and sick from his work. He doesn't eat good, he's so skinny. This is the news for your newspaper, write it. In Myron there is a good man doing his work."

Poteat swung around in his chair so that he was no longer looking at her but down at his own hands that lay palms down on the blotter. "Do you believe all that?" he asked.

"I should be saying it if I didn't believe it? Who is he I should make up lies for him?"

Poteat shrugged. "You say a good man. Maybe so. If he really is, I admit it could explain pretty near the whole damn thing." He tapped his fingers lightly together in front of his face, staring at her over them again. "I'll tell you something about goodness, Fraulein Reinwasser. It brings out the worst in us all. Every time the world sees too much goodness, it secretly lets loose in its pants."

"What are you saying?" She grimaced, her small eyes wary.

"You see a good man, and deep in your large intestine you yearn to cut him down to size, your own size. You and I know the world, Fraulein. If he is really what you say he is, your little saint-man, why else do you think the red-head picked him out except to muck that goodness up a little? If I may make so bold," he said, lowering his hands and resting them on the arms of the chair, "why else do you think you were so quick just now to tell me all about it? I didn't even have to twist your arm."

"You would twist my arm?" She paused. "I told you he went to her because she is one of his people, to help her out someway. I told you the truth to keep him safe from the filth people think." Her words came slow as if she was reading them, her lips touching the child's hair.

"Just the way I came here tonight so I could vindicate him in the public press?"

"You told me you were his friend."

"When all this gets spread around and ploughed under, I may be the only friend he has." Poteat got up from his chair and touched Lizzie's cheek with the back of his hand. "You better put her back to bed."

"You really think I want to hurt him?" She did not rise, and Poteat stood there for a few moments, looking down at her.

"Why not?" he said. "It's the kind of pleasure that's very hard to resist." Then he left her sitting there to walk alone down the dark hall and let himself out into the moonlight.

They had decided that she did not have the proper kind of feet for a chicken. They could none of them remember how many toes a chicken had except that they were fewer than Taffelshuhn's, and while a chicken's toes were long and skinny, Taffelshuhn's were cramped together and short. A group of guards had discovered this in the barracks where they had been lounging on their bunks after the evening mess idly watching her with her feet bare and her trousers rolled up to the swollen knobs of her knees as she scrubbed down the floor with a pail of soapy water and a long-handled brush. It was shortly after the surrender in North Africa of the last German units there, and there had been long, grim conversations all that week and considerable drinking so that once the new joke about Taffelshuhn began, it gathered momentum quickly. To crown it, they searched for Taffel in order to confront him publicly with the deficiency of his hen, and they found him at last in a storeroom behind the barracks where he was on his hands and knees, quite drunk, trying to pry open a wooden crate which he thought contained champagne for the officers' mess. They had brought Irma Reinwasser with them, and while two of them held her under the arms, another picked up her feet to show

them to Taffel so that she was suspended there like a
doll making no move to break way or to protest but
only keeping her eyes fixed on Taffel to see what he
meant to do. In his gloved hand he was holding the
pliers with which he had been trying to pull nails out
of the crate when the group had entered, and with
these he had inspected the offending feet, gripping the
toes just firmly enough to be able to move them back
and forth gently, like a doctor. He acknowledged that
they were no ordinary chicken feet, but then he swore
that she was no ordinary chicken, his Taffelshuhn,
and with the patches of red on his cheeks fresh as a
girl's, his lips moist and smiling, he laughed his
honking laugh as if to bring the scene to an end, and
one or two of the men had already turned to leave
when suddenly, with a quick clenching of his leather
fist, he had crushed the pliers shut upon her. By lamplight then with a spring rain falling on the tar-paper
roof and the storeroom smelling of the green wood of
the crates and Taffel's laden breath, the operation
somehow to give her the feet of a chicken had begun
as the men pressed close to watch Taffel with the
sweat dropping off the end of his nose and the whimpering shape that he bent to, astride her knees, until
from nowhere the Commandant's old dachshund Maxl
appeared among them looking up at Taffel's dazed
and grunting face and wagging his rat's tail slowly
from side to side.

Taffel stopped as soon as he saw him, an obese old
dog with the lining of his eyes showing red and his

privates just clearing the floor as he stood there swaying back and forth feebly with the movement of his
tail; and stumbling forward on his knees, Taffel gathered him up in his arms, pressed his glistening cheek
against him, and then was sick violently and for a
long time with old Maxl struggling to get free. His
fellow guards had disappeared when he recovered.
Only Irma was left, dead he thought at first with
her arms and legs sprawled awkwardly as if she had
fallen from a great height, but he found her eyes
alive and bent his face to them: *Verzeihung, Taffelshuhn. Verzeihung, Verzeihung*—the same word over
and over again, at first a supplication but gradually a
kind of lullaby—forgive, forgive—as though he was
coaxing a child to sleep. With one hand he brushed the
drowned hair back from her forehead, then picked her
up in his arms like a child and carried her out into the
rain with her ruined feet flopping at his side.

Irma Reinwasser rose now from her chair with
Lizzie and carried her back upstairs to bed without
waking her. The room was drenched with moonlight,
and a breeze stirred the curtains. She pulled the sheet
up over Cornelia and watched her there for a while,
unwilling to leave the only room in the house where
there was life. By the window stood a carrousel
horse that Franny had found and painted snow-white
with a scarlet mane and tail, its bridle studded with
bits of colored glass that glinted in the moonlight.
Irma Reinwasser mounted it and looked down
through the window at the shadows of the catalpa

tree on the sidewalk across the street.

She wanted to hurt him, the newspaper man had said; but to hurt which one, Heinz Taffel or Nicolet? She tried to peel the two faces apart, but they remained one: savior betrayer, gentle torturer—did God himself have such a face?—with bright, deep eyes that studied her now through the dark of the children's room. She raised one hand to her cheek. Nicolet, what had he done after all that she should hurt him— had just left her to watch over his children while he stole off at dawn to another woman's rescue, and why not, with herself only the remains of a chicken woman and not now in need of rescue, not that he knew; had just for a moment mocked her with the gay, dark words that filled her still with what she could see only as their emptiness: *my own true love*. The newspaper man was wrong. She had no wish to hurt Nicolet, her man, not even, through him, somehow to hurt Heinz Taffel, hurt back God, the world, for hurting her. *Verzeihung, Verzeihung, Taffelshuhn*. There was hurt enough.

She gripped the reins tight at a murmur from Cornelia, who rolled over on her side with one hand like a starfish on her pillow; what could she be dreaming? Always they dreamed about angels, the father said; Lizzie said little and black like flies, and that was always the joke of it until now with Poteat's words in her head they became the swarming mat of flies on the dung-heap world. Her hand still at her cheek, forgotten, she looked up at the moon with the light of it bathing her great face. There, perhaps, there was cleanness, cold purity of line. Here all was shapeless, random. She had told the truth about Rooney Vail to save him, and it had only given his enemy the means to destroy him as perhaps she had wished all along. *Wie man's macht ist's falsch, falsch.* And fierce as a gypsy with a sword between her teeth, she spurred her charger on into darkness.

NINE

I T WAS still early morning, but the sun was hot, no movement of air, and they had been standing in the driveway saying goodbye when Rooney had suddenly leaned against the car and let escape the laughter that all through breakfast she had guarded. "I'm sorry, but just look!" and their frail attempts to laugh with her had made it only worse until she could feel the tears warm in her eyes: Nicolet in his shirtsleeves and baggy pants with a day's growth of beard because there was no razor in the house, Lillian Flagg with a blue kimono over her nightdress and lipstick on her teeth——"A madam, the village idiot . . ." She let her overnight case drop to the ground with part of a pink slip protruding. "Orphan Annie." Then Lillian Flagg had taken each of them by the hand so that they stood there in a row, and tilting her face upward with her eyes tight closed, she had breathed deeply several times like a swimmer about to dive: "Lord, Lord, surround them with your love like a cloud so that no harm can come. . . . to them or from them." She had raised their hands in hers to shoulder height so that the nightdress was hiked to bare her white shins. "With healing in your wings, descend upon them. We are freaks, but we are your freaks. Fill them with life, yea and to overflowing. Even now, Lord, pour it out upon them. Oh yes, thank you, Jesus, even now. It will be so. It will be *so*." The great plumes of cloud slowly arched and scattered, and she held their hands so tightly that her arms trembled, then brought them down again and released them. "Thank you, Jesus." She blinked her eyes open. "From here on out, you do your own praying."

Was it true, was there anywhere such power? Almost as soon as the house was out of sight, Rooney had turned to him with this only to find him so intent on what in the next instant he began to say to her that he had apparently not even heard her question. He was not going back with her to Myron, he had told her. His father lived only a few hours farther north, and he had decided to go on up there and return to Myron the next day. Would she explain this to Irma and the children as soon as she got back? Would she call the church? Did she have money enough to lend him what he would need for the journey?—this last as she drew up to the curb in Muscadine to let him out, handing him through the window what she had in her wallet which he took and kissed before thrusting it into his pocket.

Then he had hesitated for a moment, bending

down to look in at her, and she felt that she saw in his face not only all that had happened between them in Muscadine but all that had not happened between them, and she felt that he saw it too and was looking at it now rather than at her, was saying goodbye not to this time that was, but to whatever lay just the other side of time that now would not be. The next moment he had gone—in the mirror she saw his narrow, dark figure retreating quickly down the street—but almost at once it had seemed to her less that he had gone than that he had never really come, at least not the Nicolet whom she had dreamed that she was summoning with her postcard: part priest, part lover, with whom in a single act she could find both escape and forgiveness for escaping. Before she lost sight of him altogether, she had come close to running after him, and with part of herself she did this as she drove away, overtook him there on the blinding sidewalk and went on with him to wherever he was going and beyond so that in the end it was a vision of them both that she had left in Muscadine.

She had driven too fast with all the windows wide open and her hair flying and had felt a recklessness too in being for the first time in her life entirely without money because she had given all that she had to Nicko and had none left for lunch, nothing, not even for gasoline with the gauge running low. The faster she drove, she believed, the better her chance of reaching Myron before it ran out altogether; the faster she drove, she came half to believe, the better

her chance of reaching Myron before she herself ran
out altogether. Part of her had gone chasing after
Nicko—where would they be by now, she wondered,
what would he be saying as he turned to her with his
turquoise eyes, unshaven jaws of a tramp, and the
thin, priest's hands?—part of her had been diminished
by being named, the memory of the window's crimson burning and the drowning face that she had
pulled down to hers, by Nicko's saying with a stranger's voice, *Forgive you every face you cannot look
upon with joy.*

The air roared through the window, billowing her
skirt, as the red car raced, and she tilted her head for
the wind to whip the hair from her eyes. She felt
light-headed, giddy and bled, and everything seemed
to depend upon her getting back to Clem while what
there was left of her lasted. It was Clem's face that
she raced to as the red needle trembled toward the
bottom of the gauge.

He was not there. She had stopped first at the
Something Shop, rapping at the glass of the locked
door and peering into the dark interior before she noticed the Help Wanted placard, which became suddenly her heraldry as well as his: searching for his
life in order to become herself a life. She ran back to
her car with her heart drumming out the fear that she
had come too late, that Clem had waited there for her
with his need emblazoned on the door for all the ages
of her absence until finally he had moved on in de-
spair and they were destined now to spend their lives

searching for each other, missing each other by seconds at each accustomed place. It made reality of all the dreams that she had ever had of separation—standing on the deck of a ship as it pulled away from the shore where all the faces were gathered to wave her goodbye, goodbye, through the widening dusk—and it was with dread that she drove on to their house, certain now that she would not find him there either.

Letters like dead leaves lay on the carpet just inside the front door, and a raincoat hung from the banister with its empty sleeves touching the bottom stair. She ran from room to room, calling his name in a voice that reassured her where the house itself failed. His pajamas lay in a heap by their unmade bed, beside them the crumpled ball of a handkerchief. The floor was stained milky white where rain had blown in through the open window, and she paused there to stare out at the pasture where the old Morgan was rubbing her hindquarters against a tree. The air that rose to her was warm and sweet with grass, and she watched a starling light on the sky-blue salt lick. Beyond the pasture, a path sloped sharply to where they had dammed the stream for a place to swim; and not suddenly but as though for some time her eyes had been watching what only now her mind began to grasp, she saw Clem standing toward the top of the path with his hand raised to shade his eyes as he looked up at the window that she haunted. The water still glistened on him from his swim, a towel about his waist, and unable for the moment to call to him, she waved from her window. At first uncertainly then quick and high, he raised his arm.

"My old Clemmy, Clem . . ." nothing more, only Clem rushing to her half naked up the flight of stairs where she stood with her face between her hands, but she had seen him as a warrior, a young archangel drenched in light as he had saluted her from below, and she clung now to a hero's chill flesh, burying her face between the great wings, the wet, soft feathers of his chest.

"Where the hell have you been?" He held her off at arm's length, his voice fierce but hushed with the fear that the fault had somehow been his. "Everything's been haywire here."

"The rain came in all over the floor." The same rain, she thought, that she had watched through Lillian Flagg's bay window when she had felt a rustling of life, felt now the trembling of his hand on her shoulder so that she bent forward and touched it with her cheek. "Who cares about the rain . . . Clem, I'm so sorry. My old Clem . . ."

"I thought maybe I'd never see you again. I I couldn't believe it except . . . I believed it. I thought you'd gone for good, and I thought Nick was mixed up with it. They said he'd taken off too." He half whispered, his forehead wrinkled as though trying to make sense of his own words. "Was he . . . Nick?"

"He only came to bring me back, but I was always

coming back. All the time I was—"

"I never thought you would," he said.

"Everything was haywire there too. This queer little place called Muscadine." The name sounded to her as if she had just invented it. "Up there in the woods. There's a woman who prays for people. They say she's worked miracles. God knows what Nick thought, lipstick on her teeth. She teaches you how to pray."

"How to pray?"

"It's crazy, isn't it?"

"I don't know. The world's crazy." He still held her there with his wet hands. "That's why you went —just to learn how to pray?"

She nodded.

"What did you pray for?" he said.

Drops of water ran down his neck onto his bare shoulder where she touched them. "A baby."

"Oh Christ, Rooney . . ."

"Don't cry, I couldn't stand it!"

"I'm just freezing to death." He was shivering. "I'm sopping wet, that's all." He took the towel from around his waist and buried his face in it, rubbing his head as hard as he could, and there was some kind of precarious victory in his smile when he looked up at her again, his face flushed from the rubbing, his short hair standing upright. "I better not hang around here bare-ass."

In Muscadine there had been only faces—Nicolet's, Lillian Flagg's, searched, searching, and all the faces that she had remembered in Muscadine, her own; she had forgotten bodies, calf and thigh, hips squared to support the earth if need arose, and she saw his nakedness as if for the first time. Then with a yelp of mock horror he clapped the towel around himself again to hide the stirring, secret life—"I'm a damned satyr, a goat!"—and with a boy's hoot stalked off toward their bedroom. Suddenly he turned in the doorway, grim-eyed, wings spread. She fled to him, terrified.

The noon sun glanced white from the sheets, and she laughed into his throat as the sunlight pelted her like rain, the dandelion eyes and ragged, glistening leaf of mouth, the chill weight pitched over her, warm beneath the chill. The wantonness of it at noon with all the summer world at work and in the hot street faces meeting, merging without joy like raindrops while with the furious young angel she mounted higher, deeper, until with a shudder the blue air burst and they fell, an amen of exhausted wings. "I prayed for life. Are you life?"

"The answer to a maiden's prayer . . . goat-foot."

"You're killing me . . ." and they continued to fall, now side by side on their backs, until they reached earth and earth fell.

"She did but see him passing by," his lips barely moved, face flattened by sunlight on its side close to her.

She touched. "Oh God, Clem . . . stupid, lovely stupid, stupid . . ."

"Lovely." His eye was dead fire. "Yet she will love him till he die."

"Always now. Fold your wings." A dog barked, and her hand went stiff.

"Come up and join us. The Vails at home." They listened together to the silence.

She said, "Peace."

"Spell it."

"Both ways." She rose on one elbow and looked down at him. "I've had it with somebody else—a long time ago." Her mouth trembled at the ease.

"I knew."

"How did you?"

"God knows. Was it Nick?"

She shook her head. "Have you too, ever?"

"Only with myself."

"You mean that awful time for the hospital."

"No." He took her wrist between his fingers. "More since."

Tears came. "Why?"

"Maybe for spite." He turned his head on the pillow so that he looked up at her, slow and dreaming. "Maybe loneliness."

"Oh, I know, I know," and she leaned forward, her hair hiding them both.

Lizzie wept. With her mouth wide open and her eyes streaming, she sobbed until her face was covered with pink blotches as Rooney knelt in the grass to comfort her. Clem and Irma stood by the lilac bush watching, Clem holding two balloons attached to sticks and Irma in a cap with a transparent visor that tinted the upper part of her face green.

"You see, that's because she misses him very, very much." Cornelia shook her head slowly from side to side, her hair skinned back into two little tufts fastened with elastic bands. "He told us he was coming home today."

They had come across the lawn like some strange deputation, Clem with the balloons, Rooney just behind him in yellow slacks with her arms stretched out toward the children as though the message from Nicolet was an offering that she carried. If at first it had seemed to her easy enough to tell them that their father would not be back for another day, at the sight of their two heads springing up from the sandbox as the red car pulled up at the curb in front of their house, she had understood quickly that it would not be so. Totally unmoving, they had watched her advance with Clem across the grass, Irma looking up with them from where she sat with her mending on the back porch, and it had seemed to Rooney as if the summer itself held its breath until finally she reached them and set them in motion with her words. Irma came down the porch steps, Cornelia climbed out of the sandbox to shake her head at her sister's tears, and Clem stood by the lilac bush with the balloons—"Hey, you kids, these are for you. He'll only be gone one more day."—while Rooney pressed her cheek to Lizzie's hot, hopeless face.

"He just thought he'd go see your grandpa, poor old guy all alone up there." Only one more day, she thought, except that for a child each day was the only day.

"Only one more day, Lizzie," Cornelia said, but it was Irma at last who quieted her. She lifted her out of the box by the hands and swung her around in a circle as she half chanted, like part of a children's game, *"Nun kommt er nimmer und nimmermehr."*

"No, *morgen*," Clem said. "He's coming *morgen*."

"Ja, ja?" Setting Lizzie down on the ground again, Irma gave her a pat on the back that sent her running off with Cornelia to the other side of the lawn where Clem followed them with the balloons. They took them from him and waved them in the air as he pushed them in their swings.

"You think he is ever coming back?" Irma asked.

Watching Clem with the children across the wide stretch of green grass, Rooney had forgotten Irma's presence but turned to her at this, the short figure at her side with her gray hair frizzed out under the baseball cap. She had spoken in a new voice, lower pitched, almost a whisper, like an old actress speaking finally as herself behind the scenes. Rooney's impulse was to take her by the hand and run with her back to the children, to talk to her only there in the sunlight with Clem beside them, but in her frayed sneakers Irma stood immovable as stone.

"He was all set to come back with me this morning, but then he thought he'd see his father and come back alone tomorrow."

"It's going to look better that way, *nicht?*"

"I'm sure he never thought of that."

"Then maybe you thought of it. You take him away and you tell him when to come home. Now maybe someday you'll decide to take him away for good, how should I know?"

One red, one blue, the balloons bobbed in the sun as the children swung back and forth with Clem to push them, and suddenly they seemed so far away that if she cried out to them, they could never hear her. Like the bad fairy at the christening, Irma Reinwasser held her there, and the christening, Rooney thought, was her own—a life anointed and named: Lillian Flagg with her arms raised to the sky, Clem now. She looked down into the dwarf face.

"You already got a nice man only you can't get a baby with him. So you try another." The little eyes tried to hold steady. High in the air, the children screamed.

"I don't even know who you are . . ." Rooney found herself whispering; it was like a shipwreck in sight of land.

"*Eine Jüdin . . . niemand.* Nobody," she said. "The mud on his boots."

"Oh God, no!"

Irma teetered for a moment—"*Pfui, pfui . . .*"— brushing her face clumsily with her hand as though she were dizzy, knocking her cap askew. "I think I'm sick."

Rooney led her to the porch with her hands on her bony shoulders as she wobbled along, slew-footed, the cap falling off her head. Rooney lifted it away and helped her sit down on the steps.

"Just get this straight—he couldn't possibly get along without you. You just came in and took right over. The kids adore you."

"Don't listen to anything I said. I don't even believe it myself. I must be crazy." She leaned back against the railing, pale and out of breath.

"Never mind, never mind. People say things— God knows what's true."

"Here everybody's treated me so good always. Blue-beard said such kind things yesterday on the phone . . ."

"He's a kind man."

"Rooney, *help!*" Brandishing their balloons, they were chasing him toward the fence, and he leapt like a dancer as he called out, then disappeared with them around the front of the house.

"Last night a man came asking questions," Irma Reinwasser said, "and I told him the two of you were away together."

"What man?"

"From the newspaper."

Surround them with your love like a cloud, she remembered, and as if through a cloud she saw him now, or himself a cloud, drifting out of shape.

"What did he say?" Rooney asked.

"He's going to make trouble."

"Don't worry. I know him. I'll go and talk to him."

"I'm so sorry," Irma said. Rooney had crouched down on the step below her, and Irma leaned forward now as she spoke so that their faces were only inches apart. "Sorry . . . sorry . . ." The words came slow and quiet as she wagged her big head, the breath sour, the skin the color and coarseness of sand, and could it be that Irma Reinwasser loved him, Rooney wondered, loved Nicko—could loving be what bound them all, bound every life, stranger to stranger, victor to victim. For a moment she almost said this, but then she did not as though for fear that to speak this deepest secret would be to bring heaven in all its terror crashing down upon them unawares.

"Oh don't be sorry! For God's sake." Tossing the baseball cap into her lap, she jumped up from the step and ran off to find the children and Clem.

TEN

———◆———

E CALLED IT the Comet Fire Kindler, and I think of it as a mute but eloquent symbol of his life. You took this cone of stout brown paper—I have always treasured this one—" leaning forward in his rocker, Roy Nicolet held it out for his son to see, "and you filled it first with little bits of soft coal, then with larger pieces, and you covered it all with coal tar. To use it was very simple. You merely placed it in your stove in front of the draft, banked it with your ordinary coal, and lit it. It made a quick, hot fire which ignited the coal very well, but in a large fire box . . ." he slowly shook his head, "it was not sufficient."

Through his sheer white sport shirt, the wide collar unbuttoned and laid out flat, the outline of his undershirt was visible, the faint pink of shoulders and upper chest. His thick hair was the white of cotton, and he smelled of talcum powder, his face itself a powdery white and curiously flat as though the features had been partly rubbed away by too much handling. The skin beneath his eyes was tinged with brown, scorched. "My father was a quick, hot fire," he said. "He ignited little and burned out young."

Nicolet took the Comet Fire Kindler from him and placed it beside him on the bed where he sat. "Well, everybody's fine at home. Pie Face and Lizard Boy are burning bright."

"Lizard Boy?" His whole face seemed to slip forward slightly toward the pucker of his mouth.

"Lizzie," Nicolet said. "It's been Indians for over a year now. Franny was Needle Pin. Then for me they dreamed up Bluebeard."

"I can see why. We'll go downstairs bye and bye, and I'll give you a shave. The velvet touch I've never lost." He drew his finger flat down the length of his cheek. "Your poor Frances. A year ago spring I stood with you beside her open grave and thought, 'The good die young, and those whose—'" At a clatter from outside, he stopped and squinted down from his bedroom window into the dusk. "Tinny damned bike always toppling over where he insists on leaning it." He reached up and gave the window-shade a little tug and let it snap to the top. "'And those whose hearts are dry as summer dust burn to the socket.' Is there anyone else yet, son?"

Nicolet shook his head.

"I am sorry to hear it. You need a wife, Theo. You have let yourself go. I was ashamed just now to have Miss Zimmer see you." Miss Zimmer, one of the boarders, had let him in, calling up the stairs to Roy and then standing there in the dark hallway to watch the old man come slowly downstairs with both of his arms spread wide and embrace his son, kissing him on the cheek. "How long has it been since you shaved."

"There was no razor where I stayed last night."

"And no luggage. I would not be smart to take in a guest here, Theo, who had no luggage."

"I just decided to come at the last minute—a filial impulse."

"You could at least have slipped a razor into a briefcase—a toothbrush, a comb, perhaps a clean shirt . . ."

"Mail me the list." Nicolet stood up abruptly as he spoke and extended his hand to his father. "I don't want to cause you any further embarrassment." He knew in advance what Roy would do—the little catch of breath, eyes suddenly veiled as he tipped up his flat, white face, startled, like a man afraid of being struck from above, and Nicolet struck out with what words he could find, revolted by himself. "A toothbrush, a comb. An eyebrow pencil."

Roy reached out and seized Nicolet's hand in both of his. "Stay, Theo. I haven't been well. I've had this cold for months because I don't have the strength to throw it off."

On a small tin tray hooked over the windowsill at his side stood a half empty bottle of brown cough syrup, the sugary spoon, and a ruby glass tumbler with the name Roy painted on it in an elaborate, old-fashioned script. "You wouldn't leave right off—" but it was rather the tumbler that held Nicolet there, Roy's own ruby glass tumbler with his name on it, something a little special for Roy to remember somebody by or someplace and given to Roy because he was somebody himself, cherished somewhere, not nobody, at the mercy, Nicolet thought, of his only son, that up-and-coming young man of could you possibly at this point, he wondered, say God.

"You old cry baby." Nicolet said it because he had to go just that much farther before he could decently come back. Whoever had given the tumbler could never have dreamed of such a scene—what killed him was that maybe Roy had given it to himself—or else had given it just because of such dreams: whatever happened, he would always have something with his name on it. "I'll let you give me that shave if you're still game."

So they found themselves downstairs in the small back parlor with the old barber chair bolted to the middle of the floor, its footrest a spider's web of cast iron and upholstered in slippery imitation leather. There was a large mirror hung over the sealed-up fire-place, and on the mantel bottles of hair tonic, witch hazel, two stone marmalade crocks full of combs. The light was poor, and Roy switched on a fluorescent circle directly above the chair that hummed faintly and turned their lips blue.

Warm as the evening was, Roy put on his green

and black checked lumberjack shirt before seating
him in the chair with a sheet draped around him, then
raised the chair and tilted it back, placing a folded
towel just beneath his son's chin.

Nicolet closed his eyes to the sound of the floor-
boards' creaking as Roy moved to the sink and back,
the tocking of the brush in the mug; felt a hand on
his forehead as the tepid lather touched him, soap
smell, the soft brush working over his jaws and knob
of chin. When he opened his eyes, he found himself
staring up at his father's face, above it the ring of
harsh light that cracked and dazzled while delicately,
his little finger crooked, he held the razor poised
above him with its long blade glistening; and if nothing else, Nicolet thought, he would offer him his
throat to cut because a man could not die more justly
than at the hands of his father, at least of this father
whom he had journeyed to see for the purpose in part
of proving that he had no father, but only a shadow,
a ghost, who must somehow be exorcised before he
could continue on his way unhaunted. He neither
flinched nor cried out as the old man took him by the
lobe of one ear and came at him with the sharp
steel, drawing it rasping and gentle down an inch of
cheek from the sideburn. "They call you Bluebeard?
Well . . ." He wiped the razor on the towel, gazing
at the face as though the face was all that there was.
"When I'm through, they'll be calling you Prince
Charming."

"Tell me more about Léon." It was partly the con-

versation that you made with an old barber—tell me
about the weather, the ball game—partly a plea for
some clue to the mystery of this journey that he had
taken to find Rooney only to find that Rooney was no
more than a stage on the way.

"You've got him on the brain, do you? I have sometimes thought that we see our fathers for the first
time only when we begin to need them. Surprising,"
he said, the razor hovering like a bird, "that after all
these years you should need a man who died half a
century before you were born. Perhaps it is his only
immortality, but he would probably have settled for
less."

"I registered at a hotel once as René Laliberté.
What do you make of that?"

"Well, it is a good name to travel by. He made it
up when he left his native hearth to fight over here for
the black man's liberty. *La liberté*, you see. He was a
romantic, my poor young dad, and an idealist, but it
was one bad joke after another for him all the way
through. He was born with a caul which the midwife
who attended his mother said showed that his life
would be remarkable, but though he was a man of
more than common ability, his life was not remarkable."

"The rifle pits at Petersburg," Nicolet said. As Roy
had leaned over him, his face seemed empty of all
but the task of barbering, and Nicolet spoke the
elegiac formula to bring something to life in it. With
the old ladies who were his daughters, his flock,

most of what he said on his pastoral visits, chattering, teasing, was to keep them from remembering, keep them from weeping; but his father now he wanted to weep and remember, his barber now he wanted to hurt into becoming a father to weep with, weep at, more than a ghost. Roy gave a deep cough, pressing the back of his hand to his mouth and turning his head aside, flushed, but the withered flesh beneath his eyes was dust dry still as he turned again to his work.

"A Southern sharpshooter got him in the right arm just beneath the shoulder, and they should have amputated immediately, but instead they performed an operation called excision to remove the shattered bone, only they did not do it well because years later an abscess formed, and he died of blood poisoning on a pension of eighteen dollars a month from his adopted land. They sent from the place where he died for his broadcloth suit, and as a small boy I placed the studs in his shirt. But the worst of it was the field hospital where they left him because he was too near death for them to move him off behind the lines. I remember him telling it," he said, pausing there round-shouldered with a trickle of perspiration staining his Byronic collar. "He never lost his French accent though he lost everything else. How for three days he lay there with his wound undressed in that southern June while the rats came out and waited by his bedside. It makes you wonder a little about *le bon Dieu*. He said it would have seemed like Heaven if only he had been able to raise himself up just enough to let the cool air under his back."

Finishing the shave, Roy sprinkled some lotion into the palm of his hand and rubbed it into Nicolet's face, the sharp, sweet chill of it stinging his flesh. Pulling the lever, he snapped the chair back into an upright position so that in the mirror Nicolet could see them both—Roy standing beside him with the razor in his hand, his own head jutting dark and unfamiliar out of the white sheet. "There now, you're a new man."

"That would be nice." His father's hands had lulled him, and he felt too drowsy to get up out of the chair as though, for as long as he sat there, he was safe from the necessity of pursuing any newness greater than what the shave had produced, safe in the arms of an old nurse from all his pursuers, from himself, from Harold. He ran his hand over his smooth chin and wondered if Léon had felt any such languor as he lay with his rats beneath the hot canvas, safe from all his dreams but death; and Roy could be death, he thought, eyes scorched into the crumpled white napkin of his face, his hands now on his son's shoulders, kneading them softly as he gave the chair a little turn to show him a better view of himself in the mirror. Come live with me and be my love, be my son—the dry-eyed old cry baby, shuffling and majestic old ghost who had spent years composing deathbed summonses to convince himself that he was alive enough to die. "Just hold your horses a few minutes more, Theo, and I'll trim up that hair a little." Out of the breast pocket of his lumberjack shirt he drew the scissors snapping and flickering with a life of their own.

"You're not telling me the worst of it, are you?" Nicolet said. "I mean the scandal that came later, whatever it was—the heart break, heart ache . . ." With his father's own language, he thought, perhaps he could stir him to something. "A noble young stag . . . hunted down to his death."

Roy bent almost double with coughing, staggered across the room, his hand on his chest. "A little midget of a man called Durfee," he half gasped from the sink where he stood, making harsh, gargling sounds—"Durfee"—then cleared his throat violently and spat before he returned to the chair, dabbing at his eyes and mouth with a towel. "I don't have the reserve you need to throw it off. At my age you don't."

Nicolet nodded as the scissors began their chattering again at his ear.

"A man diminutive in stature as well as in honesty," Roy said. "Chief of the Bureau of Engraving and Printing where Léon worked as his assistant during the second administration of General Grant. They were great friends at first—my father boarded with him and his family in Washington and looked up to him greatly, always eager to believe the best of any man. This was before my birth, of course, but I have seen his picture—a dapper little gentleman with a handlebar moustache and a high and scholarly forehead—and to give him credit, after a fashion he ran things well enough, it seems. The Bureau was a small empire that occupied an entire wing of the old Treasury Building. There were bookkeepers and engravers, plate printers and machinists, superintendents, clerks, artists. And there were dozens upon dozens of women and girls who did mainly the counting and trimming and calendering of endless sheets of paper from the blank sheets themselves to the completed bank notes and stamps and bond issues of every sort. Over all of these people Mr. Durfee presided, and they were all completely dependent on Mr. Durfee's good will because Mr. Durfee's power was absolute. He could hire and discharge as he saw fit. He was responsible to no one. This was a great many years ago, Theo, but to me it is very real because the last months of his life he spoke of it constantly, and his memories of it were most of my inheritance. There," Roy said, tipping Nicolet's head slightly to one side. "Now a little off the top.

"The pay was not as good as in the other departments because few of the positions required much education and the hours were more strictly kept, but even so the demand for jobs there was considerable, especially among women. Congressmen who wanted to stand well with their constituents or to help some needy widow or orphan or who from some less worthy motive wanted to provide for some female friend would come to Mr. Durfee and ask a place for them. And if the Congressman was insistent, especially if he was a senator who was going to be in Washington for some years, the place was generally found and the girl would be crowded in even if it meant that some other girl had to lose her place so the payroll wouldn't look too large. There were some girls who were never seen about the Bureau at all except to pick up their wages, and it was said of them that they did their work at home. But the question was what kind of work was it that they did at home and who did they do it for. You get the point, Theo," he said, pausing behind Nicolet and addressing the mirror. "If it was not so tragic, it would be a proper subject for farce. René Laliberté—although by that time he had long since taken back his proper name—this ardent young Frenchman with all his glorious ideals and dreams found out after a few years that he was working in a bordello!"

Behind him, Nicolet could feel the widows and orphans crowding into the makeshift barber shop with their long dresses rustling as they jostled each other to make room for the little Victorian dwarf himself in his flowered waistcoat. "Break, noble heart . . ." Roy said, his voice unsteady as he raised his comb in the air. He had needed only an audience, Nicolet thought, staring down at the sheet that shrouded him, his face burning, and now he had created one for himself.

"In summertime the heat of the place was infernal, and Léon always held that the heat was partly responsible for what went on—all those women with their blouses unbuttoned and their sleeves rolled up, the odor of their bodies. Mr. Durfee strutting around among them like a bantam cock. But not all Léon's dear charity could lay the rest of it at the weather's door—the bribes shamelessly accepted from plate printing companies who wanted Mr. Durfee's good word in getting contracts. Profiteering, rake-offs of every kind . . . It's hard to see how he could have remained ignorant of it all as long as he did. Then he wrote a pamphlet, Theo." He had placed a hand on Nicolet's forehead to tilt his head up and paused there, holding it so firmly against his chest that Nicolet was forced to meet his father's stare in the mirror. "He exposed everything, naming names and giving facts. He had it printed up at his own expense and mailed copies to all the important men in Washington at the time. All he thought he had to do was tell the truth, you see, and the world would rise up in indignation and stamp out the evil. Imagine such innocence. The New York regiment he had fought with in the war—mostly foreigners and roughs—they called themselves *les enfants perdus*, and he was the real *perdu*, my dad. They crucified him, Theo. It wasn't enough to force his resignation from the Bureau of Engraving and Printing. That little whoremaster hounded him through the city until there wasn't an office that would have him. He was—"

Behind them the door opened, and Miss Zimmer entered the room—"Ruined, ruined," Roy said—a bony woman with blue hair, squinting through the smoke of the cigarette that trembled between her lips as she spoke. "Sorry to bother you with a customer, Roy," she said, "but somebody's got to do something about you-know-what."

"It's not a customer, Miss Zimmer, it's my son. You let him in yourself. The Reverend Nicolet." She shook the hand that Nicolet extended from beneath the sheet but otherwise scarcely acknowledged him, giving all of her attention to Roy, who in turn seemed determined not to acknowledge her as he redoubled his speed with the scissors, every muscle in his face drawn tight. With one eye half closed against the thread of smoke, she watched him keenly, as sensitive as a connoisseur to every refinement of his displeasure and not unappreciative of it or of her own ability to evoke it. "It's been plugged up since lunch, and the whole upstairs smells like a sewer."

"I'm not a plumber, Miss Zummer—Zimmer," he corrected himself, still not looking at her but taking a fistful of his son's hair and shearing off the top. "I've put in a call to the proper authorities, and they will come when they will come." He swung around so that he stood between her and his son.

"Roy, don't turn your back when I'm talking to you. Roy . . . Roy . . ." She put all of him into his name which she repeated insistently but without raising her voice, more of him, Nicolet thought, than he himself knew as his son—much of what the ruby tumbler knew of who he had been and most of who-ever he had become since. "Roy, I'm speaking to you. Roy . . ." a monotonous, admonitory chant with the old man's face contracting at each repetition of his name until his features seemed a tight knot at the center.

"Isn't there something I can —" Nicolet began, when his father suddenly turned and let the scissors drop to the floor.

"Yes, Miss Zimmer!" He spoke with exaggerated politeness. "Wouldn't you like the Reverend Nicolet to accompany you now to your toilet and see what he can do with it? I'm sure it would make his whole trip here seem worthwhile. Oh God . . ." He reached backward to support himself on the arm of the chair.

"Roy, you'll end up burying us all." Miss Zimmer spoke calmly, dropping her cigarette to the linoleum and stepping on it with a kind of slow finality as though in some fashion she had accomplished her purpose. "As for the Reverend . . ." for the first time since entering, she took her eyes from Roy and looked at Nicolet. "It's too bad he's not enough of a son to make the trip more than once a year."

As she left, Roy slumped down in a chair by the fireplace, leaning forward with his face hidden in his hands, and Nicolet, the sheet still pinned about him, came over and crouched at his side. "Are you all right?" As he put his hand on his father's shoulder, it felt to him like someone else's shoulder, someone else's hand.

"That damned thing," Roy Nicolet murmured with his face still hidden. "It's always getting plugged. I don't know what she does with it."

"Probably no more than she has to."

"You'd be surprised." There was a muffled choke that Nicolet took for a sob until the old man uncovered his face and turned to him. Nicolet could not remember the last time he had seen his father smile, a great sprawl of crooked teeth and shadows that seemed to expand until it embraced not only Miss Zimmer but Léon too, as though he recognized at last that even at Léon you could only laugh as now he did, a slow, helpless shaking of the shoulders, his eyes watering, as he spoke from behind his hand. "She'll do anything to get a rise out of me."

With his sheet hanging like a cowl, Nicolet rose and returned to the chair where he threw back his head to free one clear laugh of his own: Léon dreaming his noble dreams among the federal whores, old Roy playing tragedy in a house that smelled like a sewer, and himself, the adventures of Bluebeard . . . He could see Lillian Flagg with her white shins bare as she prayed for him in the driveway, the bored boy listening to his blasphemies as they drove through the rain, the one tear that had glistened like a pearl on Rooney's nostril when she had confessed to the act of her loneliness while he, her confessor, aching, had touched with his knuckle only the tear. The world was a bordello—the old man must know this, he thought, watching him get up from his chair, still wet-eyed, and bend down for the scissors where he had let them fall, his face dark as the blood ran to his head. Confession and tears, the preacher had said, hunched like a monkey in the high college pulpit and plucking the air. And yet at the heart of it, the great laughter—not, by some miracle, bitter, broken, but splashing like a fountain and spilling over the sides. Joy, Nicolet, joy, Lillian Flagg had said. Joy, little man, he thought, love-sick, God-sick little man, homesick, and he had taken the girl's face in his hands to forgive it, Roy's face appearing now above his own, a totem pole.

"After that he imported music boxes," Roy said, the scissors flashing once again. "He left Washington and moved to Chicago, married a gentle soul there who died having me—a life for a life. The good Lord seems to want there to always be Nicolets, but it's catch-as-catch-can for us once we appear. Our women die young, Theo. Your mother too. The music boxes didn't sell. Then the fire kindlers. But he had a merry heart. I can still remember songs he taught me. *Mademoiselle . . . voulez-vous danser?*" He paused, his mouth slightly open as he searched the dim room. "*Non, Monsieur, j'ai mal au pied.*

"All these things, Theo—memories, scraps of foolish songs. *La Fille de Madame Angot*, he loved, and Brignole singing the *Miserere*. I've carried them down the years the way a snail carries his shell on his back, and maybe that's why I've traveled so slowly and covered so little ground. I've carried his dying especially. When a man's time comes, he should go with dignity, and in some ways my father did that except that like the rest of his life, it was not unmixed with elements that were not dignified.

"The bone of his right arm was gone at the shoulder joint, you see, and he could not lift the arm or stretch it out. When the elbow was supported, he could use his hand, but it had to be supported at just the right height—not too high, not too low—or he got very tired. When he walked, he usually carried his hand in his trouser pocket, and when he was in a crowd or riding the street car, people often hurt him without knowing it. So finally it got to the point where he went to the examining surgeon at the pension board and begged to have the arm taken off altogether, but the medicos always discouraged him and said it was better than no arm at all. And they also gave him some pills that had morphine in them although I believe that he did not know this at the time; and for several years he took them every night, and they helped him. But then the day came when they did not seem to help him so much, and one afternoon he came home from work—by then he had a position as bookkeeper in a hardware concern, selling his fire kindlers on the side—and went to bed. To a ten-year-old boy, it is a very frightening thing to see a grown man in bed in the middle of the day. You think the world is coming to an end. The next morning he could not get his shirt on, and the pain was so severe he could not stay in bed any longer but walked the floor for hours holding his poor arm in his hand and not able to keep back the groans until finally the woman who cooked for us persuaded him to let us go for a doctor. It was all swollen and inflamed, and you could see

that something terrible was happening. I remember
the cook telling me that if I wore a dime in my shoe—
something silver—maybe he would not die, and for
the few days more that he lived, Theo, I wore a dime
in my shoe, but it did no good. The doctor had us
put flaxseed poultices on the arm—I would help wring
out the cloths in hot water—and this went on for days
while he kept on taking larger and larger doses of his
pills to ease the pain. Then one morning, we found
that a small pimple had formed on the line of the old
scar, and it kept on growing until suppertime when it
broke and began to discharge. He told us that now
he knew an abscess had formed on the bone, and we
must take him to the hospital."

As Roy spoke, Nicolet kept trying to see him as the
child he had been, Léon's boy with a dime in his
shoe, and to see him through Léon's eyes, his child
grown old, his face a landscape where someplace a
child was buried. He remembered Lizzie sitting in
the wet sand naming waves—Franny curling in flat
and gentle, the slap and sizzle of Irma—when suddenly she started to run in panic through the boiling
foam and he caught her up, chill and shaking, in his
arms, and thought that this must be what it was
like to be Harold, tried now to look at the old, blue-
lipped child through Harold's eyes.

"They took off the arm," Roy said. "An aunt of
my mother's brought me to see him every day after
school, and I would stay with him hours at a time.
He could not stand to be alone. He said the rats would

come into his room when I was gone. And sometimes Mr. Durfee would come. Mr. Durfee would climb in through the window and sit on the foot of his bed all night, smoking a cigar and chatting away like old times. Father told me how he said he was sorry for all he had done and asked to be forgiven, and Father forgave him. There was nobody there, of course. But the worst of it, Theo, I did not know till later." Replacing the scissors and comb in his pocket, he unpinned the sheet and shook it clean.

"At night there in the hospital, he would scream and scream until no one on the floor could sleep. And it was not because of the pain, they said, or the rats or Mr. Durfee. Although I could never believe that he knew what those pills contained, over the years he had become so dependent on them that when the doctors tried to take him off them, he went out of his mind. He had become an addict, Theo. It was morphine he screamed for, and a few days later when he finally died, he died whimpering like an animal—his arm gone, his wife gone, finally even his dignity . . ." There were several thumps on the ceiling as he paused, but Roy gave no sign of hearing them as he stood there, with the sheet in his hands, his mouth puckered and his cheeks going in and out as though he was about to whistle. "Rest . . . rest . . ." he said, pushing the lever so that the chair sank unsteadily to the floor. "Rest, perturbéd spirit."

It had sounded as though someone was moving a piece of furniture across the room above them, but now the noise became insistent, a steady, loud rapping. "That's Zimmer," Roy said finally, and as he looked up at the ceiling, the smile slowly began to return— "She won't stop till I go up there and tinker with the damned thing"—then froze as Nicolet, half rising from the barber chair, seized him by both arms and suddenly pressed his cheek flat against the old man's chest like a doctor listening to the beat of a heart.

ELEVEN

H E LAY behind the barn with his jacket
folded under his head. The rim of the sun
had just appeared above his father's house,
and long diagonals of light came slanting down at him
from the peak of the roof. "The birthday of the church
took place in the midst of terrible fire," he began, his
thin lips barely moving. "I've got this sermon to do
. . ." *Don't ham it up, Nick. That's cheating.*
"Franny." He could invoke all of his saints now, he
thought, stretching his bare arms out into the damp
grass. *Voulez-vous danser?* "Yes, *dansez, dansez,*
Léon." The drawn sky swarmed, cloudless, beyond
the apple branches.

A little notebook lay open on his chest. "Pentecost,"
he had written. "The fourth Sunday after—better late
than never." Then, in parentheses, " 'Have you ever
received the gift of the Spirit, Mr. Nicolet?' Saint Lillian the Less. *Non, Madame, j'ai mal au pied.*" Beside the notebook lay a pocket-sized New Testament in

French, bound in rusty black cloth with part of the spine torn away and inscribed, "René Laliberté, Front of Petersburg, August 28, 1864." He had found it on the pillow by his head when he woke up, and reading it in French was like reading it for the first time. He had looked at the last chapter of Luke as he dressed— the eleven hiding out somewhere in Jerusalem after the crucifixion: *"et Jésus lui-même se présenta au milieu d'eux . . . et il leur dit, 'Avez-vous ici quelque chose à manger?'"* The fraternity brother with pimples on his chin knew the answer to that, he had thought. And the boy had been right. That was what the world gave him to eat all right, the disciples no less although on this occasion they had come through with a piece of fish. It was like them to be eating when he appeared—scared stiff but with their mouths stuffed full. One of them probably slid a piece of it across the table without daring to raise his eyes. Then, *"Demeurez dans la ville de Jerusalem jusqu'à ce que vous soyez revêtus de vertu d'en haut."* Stay in the city until you are clothed with power from on high, the promise of Pentecost, and he thought of Harmon Falls where he had stopped on his way to Muscadine, the faces bursting into flame, the sermon.

As the sun cleared the roof, the light became almost intolerably clear. Every detail of texture and color seemed too visible, dazzled him; it was like looking at pebbles through the flashing water of a stream —the flakes of rust on the wheel of the ruined cider press, the beaded brilliance of orange rinds that lay tumbled down the slope of the compost heap. "You tell me, old Lillian, bare-shanks, how do I preach the power from on high?"

Just look around you, Nicolet. Her eyes swelled the chipmunk smile.

"I see a tiny red bug crawling up a tree trunk. I see where my tragic old dad dumps the slops."

Call on his name now.

"The bug's?"

The Lord's.

"Oh Lord . . ." he began, stopped then. "My prayers move creepy-crawly like the bug. Help me."

His real name.

"Jesus?" He whispered it. "Makes me think of corn belt parsons with china teeth and ghastly old Jesus hymns. Beulah Land. Melodeons."

It's his name. Call upon it.

"Later." There were other saints. He leaned over on one elbow and took the pencil in his hand. "Power," he wrote, "from on high," with a little feathered arrow pointing up. The professor of homiletics had told them always to put into one sentence the central point and never to preach for less than twenty minutes— "Sermonettes make Christianettes," he had said. "It comes down," Nicolet added. Did it? He crossed out what he had written and in block letters wrote, "IS IT TRUE?" Was that, secretly, what they came to find out Sunday after Sunday, just that, yes or no? He thought of them settling down to silence, old jaws clamped in a look of imbecile concentration, as he took his place at the lectern and unfastened the paper clip from his notes, glancing down at where they sat —the queer old lady hats set square like little mansard roofs, hearing-aids in the front pews, here and there a palm leaf fan flickering and the muted complaint of a cough. Rooney would sit in the back with her hair tucked into a bun getting ready to add up the hymn numbers but not yet. For those few moments before he began to speak, he could believe that they had come for something, were dreaming that maybe this time he would tell them: IS IT TRUE? "It's the awful question you avoid like death," Rooney had once said in a fury. Like life, some saint said to him now. They waited. You waited. Sometimes you felt as though you had swallowed an anchor, waiting there. *May the words of my mouth and the meditations of our hearts be acceptable in Thy sight. . . .*

Then "This morning," he could say, "may the words of my mouth be just this—Yes. It's true, all of it. Yes. He lives. He has power. Can you believe it? Yes. It comes down." Hearing-aids would be turned up or off, hat pins trembling jet. "Oh the world's a great bordello all right, saith the prophet—down to the last square inch. What's a minister like me even but God's pimp, maybe half in love with the flesh he's peddling but only half? What's any one of you?" What was Rooney, chaste as a nun in black linen, dreaming of a stranger—Léon screaming in the night? "Beloved, don't believe I preach the best without knowing the worst, that's all I mean. I know it, beloved—a flop of a son, comedian of a priest. But the worst isn't the last thing about the world. It's the next to the last thing. The last thing is the best. It's the power from on high that comes down into the world, that wells up from the rock-bottom worst of the world like a hidden spring. Can you believe it? The last, best thing is the laughing deep in the hearts of the saints, sometimes our hearts even. Yes. You are terribly loved and forgiven. Yes. You are healed. All is well." They would file past, shaking his hand. "It was so lovely, so spiritual . . . A fine message . . . You really put it to us that time, Nick . . ." The cars pulled out slowly onto Congress Street and rolled on toward Sunday lunch, the papers. He flopped his head over on the folded jacket, gazing out into the trees.

"Why was 'beauty' on your list?"

I can't remember. But don't ham it up, Nick. Never say more than you really feel.

"I feel slightly dizzy. . . ." The smile was half agony.

He closed his eyes in the warm sunlight. Soon it would all begin—breakfast with Roy, then the bus back to Myron, the children and Irma, the sermon to write—but for as long as he lay there, none of it could touch him. There would be time for all of it, but for the moment he held it all off, time off, and the earth beneath him seemed to tilt this way and that like a great disc. There was the smell of oranges, his arms heavy as stone on the grass. He could hear the buzz of yellow jackets drifting over the compost. Death

must come like this. The Reverend Nicolet found behind his father's boarding house, no sign of struggle,
only a picture postcard—someone was thinking of him
in Muscadine. Only it was not death that was coming, whatever else. His heart pounded, and he did not
dare open his eyes not from fear of what he might see
but of what he might not see, so sure now, crazily, that
if ever it was going to happen, whatever it was that
happened—*joy, Nicolet, joy*—it must happen now in
this unlikely place as always in unlikely places: the
road to Damascus, Emmaus, Muscadine, stuffy room-
ful of frightened Jews smelling of fish. Now, he
thought, now, no longer daring not to dare, but opening his eyes to, suddenly, the most superbly humdrum stand of neglected trees with somebody's shoe in
the high grass and a broken ladder leaning, the dappled rot of last year's leaves.

"Please," he whispered. Still flat on his back, he
stretched out his fists as far as they would reach—
"Please . . ." —then opened them, palms up, and
held them there as he watched for something, for the
air to cleave, fold back like a tent flap, to let a splendor through. You prayed to the Christ in the people
you knew, the living and the dead: what should you
do, who should you be? And sometimes they told you.
But to pray now this other prayer, not knowing what
you were asking, only "Please, please . . ." Somewhere a screen door slammed, and all the leaves were
still except for one that fluttered like a bird's wing.

"Please come," he said, then "Jesus," swallowing,

half blind with the sun in his eyes as he raised his
head to look. The air would part like a curtain, and
the splendor would not break or bend anything but
only fill the empty places between the trees, the trees
and the house, between his hands which he brought
together now. "Fear not," he thought. He was not
afraid. Nothing was happening except that everything
that he could see—the shabby barn, weeds, orchard
—had too much the look of nothing happening, a
tense, self-conscious innocence—that one startled leaf.
He listened for "Feed my sheep . . . feed my lambs
. . ." —the old lambs, faces where children lay
buried, Roy with the dime in his shoe; his children's faces, Rooney's, where the old women they
would be lay buried: Cornelia, bony and pigeon-
breasted at eighty, boring some young divine with
memories of "My father . . ." her eyes blurred behind the heavy lenses. "I believe that once by Grandpa's barn he said he saw. . . ."

Two apple branches struck against each other with
the limber clack of wood on wood. That was all—a
tick-tock rattle of branches—but then a fierce lurch of
excitement at what was only daybreak, only the smell
of summer coming, only starting back again for
home, but oh Jesus, he thought, with a great lump in
his throat and a crazy grin, it was an agony of gladness and beauty falling wild and soft like rain. Just
clack-clack, but praise him, he thought. Praise him.
Maybe all his journeying, he thought, had been only
to bring him here to hear two branches hit each other

twice like that, to see nothing cross the threshold but to see the threshold, to hear the dry clack-clack of the world's tongue at the approach of the approach perhaps of splendor.

He sat up, clasping his knees in his arms. Someone was calling "Nick oh Nick . . . oh Nick," and as he watched, wooden-throated, a neat, dark figure appeared around the corner of his father's house. "Denbigh!" It came out an unfamiliar croak and he tried again. "As I live and breathe."

Denbigh did not see him at first but raised his hand to shield his eyes and looked in the wrong direction until Nicolet reached for an orange rind and tossed it toward him. Then he came trotting through the high weeds. "Nick, old man! Your dad said he saw you out here through the window, and there you are."

There was the handsome little flash of a smile as he shook his hand, the steel-rimmed glasses glinting in the sun. His crisp, black suit and the immaculate white of his clerical collar warred with the dilapidated place, but the advantage was all Denbigh's—the place had already grown dim and irrelevant.

"There's nothing wrong with the kids, is there?" Nicolet felt suddenly sick; it always came when you were looking the other way.

"Oh Hell no!" The jaunty little oath was Denbigh's penance somehow for the collar, Nicolet thought, because Nicolet himself had none, standing there in his shirtsleeves, a renegade. Denbigh reached out and plucked off a damp leaf that hung from Nicolet's shoulder. "They're in great shape. I talked to Irma on the phone last night."

"Then pull up a chair. Tell me what's on your mind."

"Don't mind if I do." He spread his handkerchief on the ground, and as he sat, the ground became a chair, the trees a manse; Denbigh would not have heard clack-clack, Nicolet thought, but the Apostles' Creed. "Irma told me where you were. I thought I'd hop over and catch you up on the news."

"Well, you're a breath of sanity, a ring of truth," Nicolet said. Poor Denbigh—for all the brave little smile, you could see that it was some kind of ordeal for him, his forehead shiny with perspiration. "But she should have saved you the trip. She knows I'm coming home today."

"Frankly, she doesn't really think you're ever coming home, Nick. I'm afraid she's in pretty much of a state."

"Didn't Rooney give her the message?"

Denbigh paused for a moment at Rooney's name, his eyes suddenly going dull, and for the first time Nicolet realized that he must have gotten up in the middle of the night to be here now.

"It's nothing you can't handle, I know. But you've been gone three days now, old man, and your own church doesn't know where you are, so there have been all kinds of rumors, that's all."

"Such as?"

"Well, it's what you might expect. The word got

around that Rooney Vail was gone too, and now that she's back, they say she's just come back to pack up her stuff and leave for keeps. You're supposed to be waiting for her somewhere."

Nicolet nodded. He had prayed "Please come," and it was little Ralph Denbigh who came. "It's a strange world." He smiled.

"And there's also this." From his wallet Denbigh drew a newspaper clipping and held it out to him. "Poteat's latest. It came out yesterday."

"What's in it?"

"You better read it, Nick. This is pure poison." Denbigh watched him tuck it, unread, into his shirt pocket. "Poor old Irma thinks she's responsible. She says she's the one who let it slip you and Rooney were together, and now she's dying a thousand deaths."

"We were together, you know."

"I know. Irma says you came to help her out with something." Denbigh took off his glasses to wipe the perspiration from his eyes, and without them, squinting near-sightedly, he looked suddenly forlorn. "That's all there was to it—right, Nick?"

"Poor old Denbigh, how many deaths have you been dying? Yes," he said. "That's right as rain."

"Of course it is," Denbigh said. "So now the thing to do is get you back pronto and slay the beast. That's why I came."

"Just one thing first." A rung of the broken ladder lay near Nicolet's hand, and he picked it up. "I want you to listen to something. Just sit right where you are." Nicolet had risen to his feet and walked over to one of the trees as he spoke. "And listen."

Denbigh hooked his glasses back over his ears and craned around to see what Nicolet was doing. Nicolet took the ladder rung and gave one of the branches two sharp raps.

"What's that supposed to be?" Denbigh asked. He looked to Nicolet the way he had when he was conducting Franny's funeral—as though it had suddenly come to him that she was not really dead at all and that he was committing the blunder of his career; as though now his friend had lost his mind and he should be running for help, not sitting there in the weeds listening to him strike a tree. Nicolet struck it again, two blows spaced somewhat farther apart, and looked into Denbigh's eyes with a kind of half amused intensity.

"Could you dance to that?" he asked.

"Dance?" Denbigh raised one hand, the fingers spread apart, and touched his brow with it, staring at Nicolet through the fingers—a small, intelligent animal peering out of his cage of flesh.

"If the life of faith was a dance, Denbigh, and this was the only music—all you could hear anyway—" with a few more double raps he began to suggest a kind of erratic rhythm "—do you think a man could dance it, Denbigh?"

"It sounds like calypso or something. I suppose you could dance to it," Denbigh said. "I'm not sure what you're talking about."

"I'm not sure what I'm talking about either." He tossed the rung toward the barn which it struck and fell. "But whatever this is we move around through . . ." He raked his hand slowly back and forth through the air. "Reality . . . the air we breathe . . . this emptiness . . . If you could get hold of it by the corner somewhere, just slip your fingernail underneath and peel it back enough to find what's there behind it, I think you'd be—"

Roy had appeared on the back porch and cupping his mouth with one hand, called to them through the still morning haze. "Breakfast," he called. "Breakfast." His shoulders hunched, he leaned forward on the railing.

"I think the dance that must go on back there," Nicolet began, "way down deep at the heart of space, where being comes from . . . There's dancing there, Denbigh. My kids have dreamed it. Emptiness is dancing there. The angels are dancing. And their feet scatter new worlds like dust." He raised one arm to show his father that he had heard him, but he did not turn. Some magic in his voice had lulled Denbigh, the frown had gone. He sat there listening as though he could hear the angels himself, the lenses of his glasses afire with the splendor of their wings. "If we saw any more of that dance than we do, it would kill us sure," Nicolet said. "The glory of it. Clack-clack is all a man can bear."

" 'With two wings they covered their eyes,' " Denbigh said, " 'and with two they covered their feet.'

And with two they danced."

"Hoo . . . hoo. . . ." Roy was calling them through his cupped hands.

"It's holy ground," Nicolet said, tamping down the loose earth with one foot. "The whole bloody earth is holy ground."

"Let's eat." Denbigh rose to his feet finally, brushing off his trousers with his handkerchief.

"Let's dance," Nicolet said.

Denbigh tapped the pocket where Nicolet had placed the clipping. "After you've read that, friend," he said, "you may not feel like dancing."

TWELVE

———◆———

"THE infernal loveliness of a New England spring," Poteat wrote. "At sunset when the tide is out, the wet sand turns lavender and becomes a looking-glass. In bare feet a woman walks along the water's edge looking for her lost youth, a gull sits on a rock waiting for the Second Coming. Next week is Independence Day, and summer trembles on the lip of June."

His friend Metzger, who taught English at the Myron High School, amused himself by occasionally clipping Poteat's column out of the newspaper and mailing it back to him corrected in red pencil. He would underline 'infernal,' Poteat thought, and write in the margin "wordy," or "how come," or "horse manure"; but 'infernal' was at the heart of what he wanted to say, and 'infernal' it would remain. Loveliness was infernal because it only masked inferno, just as living flesh was deadly because it only masked the bones of death; the temptation was always to fall in love with what in the end would destroy you. Anyway, Metzger was an ass, he thought, Squirrel as his students called him; and once when Metzger had expressed puzzlement over the nickname, Poteat had explained that it was because he looked like a squirrel—as simple as that— and he did, the busy little grey bachelor face, all whiskers and teeth. You made friends with the ones who in the end would destroy you if only by boring you to death.

When he began to write the column that disturbed Denbigh, Poteat did not know how far or where his words would take him. He never knew. The *Repository* was his own paper—"Suppository," Metzger called it, of course. "What do you think people use it for, Willy?"—and answerable to no one, he followed wherever the words led. "Words are my undoing," he told Metzger one evening over a plate of fried clams at the Old Myron. "My undoing literally," he said. "My unraveling. Like a golf ball when you take the cover off—all those miles and miles of rubbery string. I've been reeling words out of my gut for years, I suppose to find out one day what there is at the middle of me." Metzger told him that at the middle there was a little kernel of warm, stale air.

"A flock of sanderlings," Poteat wrote, "tilts through the salt air, furling and unfurling like a scarf." Or like a handkerchief, he thought. If it had not been for the handkerchief, he might have lost his mind. And even as things stood, who could possibly count his loss? The column had to go to the typesetter in the

morning, but late as it was—he had just returned from
his meeting with Irma Reinwasser in Nicolet's study
—he put it aside in order to savor once more the full
richness of his longing, his regret, the thick, dark
honey of his anger. He switched off the lamp on his
desk and sat staring out at the Myron river. From the
tall chimney of the shoe factory, a feather of smoke
drifted down toward the black water.

Rooney had told him to go. She had sat there with
one of the green ponchos clutched about her shoulders,
and picking up the keys to the shop from the counter,
he had let himself out without looking back. The store
fronts were ruddy with the setting sun, and he had
walked slowly up McKinley Street carrying his secret like water so holy that it would mean death to
spill a single drop. He could remember glancing
ahead to where his house stood just beyond the bridge
and thinking that once he got there, he would be safe
with his secret but that if Metzger or any of the rest of
them should suddenly come at him out of one of the
shops, he would be in danger of blurting out the
whole thing: that he was no longer trapped with them
in the airless middle of middle age but that he had
been rescued by a pair of young arms and drawn back
into something again like youth, only youth as he had
never known it, youth as he had never wanted to know
it, not even when he was young.

From the time of his boyhood, he had yearned to be
quickly old. While his contemporaries dreamed of
their hearts' desire, he had dreamed of a time beyond

desire, of resting secure and dry at last on the other side of the treacherous river. Even in High School he had emulated the manners, the dress, the speech of middle age, and what he had studied was not what was taught but the teachers themselves. His classmates thrilled to the sight of what was daring, beautiful, wild, but he had thrilled to the sight of a man like old Killian, the Principal, who could sit superbly unthrilled through the wildest and most daring that beauty could do on the football field, the dance floor, anywhere. He had learned to be world-weary before he had learned anything very much about the world, and as he walked up McKinley Street, he felt that he had made a nearly fatal mistake with his life and that the strange young woman had saved him in the very nick of time. He dreaded the possibility of meeting Metzger because Metzger would laugh, of course, his squirrel face cracking and chittering—grow old along with me, the best can never be—and yet he yearned to meet him too, even paused for a few moments in front of Thelma's grill where Metzger sometimes came for an early supper with his briefcase of papers to correct, because there was also a crazy bravado in him that wanted to boast of the cool and conquering young mouth that he had conquered, to astound the old, grey squirrel who was his friend and to astound him right there on this street that he had known all his life which had not been a life at all, as he saw it now, but a longing for death.

But he met no one on his way, and when he got

back to his empty house, he went straight upstairs to his bedroom, opened his closet door where a full-length mirror hung, and stood there in the autumn dusk trying to see the person that Rooney Vail must have seen, trying to smile at himself the same smile that she had touched with her fingers—had she? For only an instant then, but at desperate length later, he doubted the whole thing. He could imagine Metzger's cackle—"My God, Willy! Don't you know about the male menopause, the last little fling before the sap stops flowing?"—and as much to Metzger as to Rooney he had parted his lips to speak, had held out one pleading hand toward his own reflection. It was not true; he was still a young man, probably no more than fifteen years older than Rooney Vail if that. He could almost have wept at how much it was not true, and just at that moment he thought that he saw who it was that Rooney had taken for a lover—this stout, pale, melancholy man, reaching out in shuddering disbelief for anybody's hand. She had rescued him. He was deeply moved by his own sad smile. Perhaps in some way he had rescued her. He shut the closet door slowly, no longer even hating Metzger, and when he went to bed—he did not undress but lay down on top of the covers fully clothed—the chill October air lulled him to sleep like October's weary but victorious prince.

When he woke up, he was sick with love. Dreams that he could not remember had flung open doors that Rooney herself had only unlocked. His life was no longer a familiar room but a corridor swept with bright wind that might lead anywhere. He lay on his bed as though he had been drugged, unable to get up and go to work, unable even to think very clearly about Rooney—when he would see her again, what Clem would do, what was to become of them—but aware only of the workings of the drug itself. He felt a soft, heavy pain all through him, but he felt too that beneath it, waiting, lay another pain so much greater that if he had to endure it undrugged, it would be the end of him. Once or twice as he lay there, he whispered her name to himself although he could not really remember now what she looked like or the sound of her voice; and when he did this, he felt stabs of the deeper pain so sharp that for the rest of that first day he did everything that he could to put her out of his mind altogether. The newness and rawness of his love made even the thought of his beloved unendurable.

Before a week had passed from the time of their meeting, he came to believe that he was going insane. Crack-up, going to pieces, break-down—all the accustomed metaphors became suddenly clinically accurate. He knew that whatever held him together as a self could not hold much longer. The mortar was drying out and crumbling, and one by one the stones would fall until finally there would be no more wall to mark the boundaries of who he was, and he would return to wilderness. He was certain that the scene with Rooney had never taken place.

It was the gaudy stuff of dreams—the lonely young wife offering her body to a stranger, Titania in love with an ass. The only evidence that he had of its reality was a lingering sense of being sick, the throb of pain up through pain at suddenly thinking of her again after a little time of forgetting her; at remembering—or so it seemed—a silvery jangle of bracelets as she had stirred beside him, the shadow of the lashes on her cheek when her eyes were closed. Was it possible that she had slept for a moment? But he knew that dreams alone could haunt and sicken you like this. He could remember still a dream that he had once had when in water spilled on a table top he had written with his finger a name that had made him weep, and how he had woken up weeping although he could no longer remember the name or why he had written it. And then, just as he was leaving the newspaper office at noon a few days later, he had seen her coming towards him across the street. Her hair was brushed back under a yellow band, and she was carrying a plant of yellow chrysanthemums. He had waited for her in the open doorway, his face lost somewhere between expressions, and she had passed close enough for him to have touched her if he dared, but she had neither looked at him nor avoided looking at him, had just walked past as though he was not there, and he had felt the top of his scalp go cold as death. The wall was crumbling fast.

The handkerchief saved him. He had discovered it not long afterwards wadded up in the breast pocket of the jacket that he had worn at the shop that day, and it was stained crimson with her lipstick. It proved nothing, of course, except his sanity, but by then he was only too glad to settle for that. He knew that at least it had really happened—for weeks he kept the handkerchief unlaundered in his top bureau drawer like a relic stained with the blood of a god —and so if she had not given him a new self, a youth that he had never known, at least she had restored to him the old self that he had thought never to find intact again. The discovery of the handkerchief marked the beginning of convalescence, and it was not long before he was strong enough to play the game that she played. On the few occasions when their paths happened to cross again, you would have thought that they were blindmen passing.

The gull, the woman, the infernal loneliness . . . He switched the light back on in his office: his littered desk with the double-decker tray marked In and Out. He thought of Irma Reinwasser sitting there in Nicolet's study where he had left her with the child asleep in her lap. It was the child's velvet cheek that he had brushed with the back of his hand, but he had meant it for Irma, some little touch of comfort to see her through the night because once she had told him what he had gone to hear, his heart had gone out to her. She looked so helplessly ugly with her great empty threat of a nose, a gristly old fowl guarding her pillaged nest.

"Not a religious man," Poteat wrote, "I nonetheless found myself thinking of religious things. I thought of the Apostle Paul, that sawed-off little founder of churches in an alien world. I looked at the lavender sands and thought of him shipwrecked on the Isle of Malta. I thought of the letters that he wrote back to the churches at Corinth and Galatia and Philippi, and then I thought of the letter that he might have written to the church at Myron . . . The Epistle to the Myronians, chapter one, verse one:

" 'To all in Myron who are called to be saints, grace be unto you and peace,' " Poteat wrote. " 'What is this I hear, brethren, of stirrings and uneasiness among you? Though absent in the flesh, yet am I present in the spirit to behold the face you turn to the world. It is a fair face to please both men and angels. This year's bake sale more than doubled the take of the last. The new Sunday School rooms with their eye-ease green blackboards bear witness to the good works that proceed from faith. Who does not rejoice that the Every Member Canvass flourishes like a green bay tree? I give thanks always for these things, yet, brethren, ought I not also to mourn?

" 'For it is reported that beneath the fairness of the face there is an evil smell among you even as there are evil smells among the pagans. One who is not the least of your number has vanished. And she who is another man's pearl of great price has vanished with him.' "

From the first, Myron had eaten out of Nicolet's hand, Poteat knew. They had eaten the Gospel out of

his hand—his own brand of it, warmed and sweetened
by no particular skill that he had as a preacher but
by some curious lightness of heart that seemed to be
in him, a way that he had in the pulpit of smiling
sometimes as though he knew beyond all doubt a hilarious secret which was that the glory that he was
proclaiming either really was, or really was not, true,
but that in either case it was a cause for lightheartedness: life was a joke too terrible or too wonderful
to take any other way. They ate up anything that he
chose to give them, jolly Saint Nick. Even the death of
his wife they had fallen upon hungrily not as a thing
to pity him for but as another tie that bound them—
a wound that he had suffered gallantly, almost gaily,
in their service. And when it became known that he
was seeing more and more of young Mrs. Vail, his
elderly congregation had thought none the worse of
him for that because he had become for them not only
a spiritual father but a debonair and devoted son,
and what might have seemed unbecoming in one
role only added to the enchantment of the other. Besides, it was unthinkable to them that what he held
out in his open palm to her was any less innocent and
bland than what he gave to nourish them.

Here, kitty, kitty, kitty, was what Poteat heard the
few times that he had gone out of curiosity to hear
Nicolet preach—had seen Nicolet's deep-set blue eyes
brimming with their strange mirth as he coaxed the
lean young tabby forward not to mention his old
daughters- and mothers-in-God, God himself he

coaxed, *veni spiritu sancto*—and although Poteat had
tried to hate her for going to him, he failed in the at-
tempt. It was like trying to hate his own youth, the
whole belated twenty-four hours of it. Instead it was
Nicolet that he turned his efforts to, not only for his
evident success with Rooney Vail but for his success
with the world and for the absurd ease of his success
because for Poteat nothing had ever been easy. He had
worked endlessly to become what he was, had raveled
himself out in words, and what he had become, as more
and more he grew to believe, was only the town eccentric and scandal-monger, the friend and confidant
of Metzger the squirrel.

An evil smell. " 'Oh foolish Myronians, who has
bewitched you?' " he wrote. " 'You have been called
to be in the world, not of it. But you reverence one who
stands knee-deep in the fragrant muck of the world.
Let no one be deceived. The little world of your church
has become an image of the world as it is. Beneath the
spotless napery of your sacred table lurk all the ancient beasts—darkness and deceitful lust. Falsehood.
Licentiousness. Brethren, believe me. I mourn for the
Gospel. The good news proclaimed in your midst is
that only the surface is good, only the face is fair.
But is such a gospel either good or new? Do not even
the pagans proclaim as much? Do not the pagans
also rejoice at the beauty of the surface of the world?
Are they not also moved to eloquence by the loveliness of sunlight on the outer skin of things?

" 'But the pagans are more honest than he among

you who has vanished because although with his lips
he proclaims that underneath the fair surface are the
everlasting arms, with his life and with his vanishing
he confesses unintentionally what only the pagans
have courage enough to declare openly: that the only
arms to save are the soft, young arms of mortality
which cannot long deliver either him or the world from
the everlasting stench and emptiness that lie beneath.

"'Peace and mercy be upon you. Greet all the
brethren with a holy kiss, and I adjure you that this
letter be read to all . . .'"

The light of his desk lamp hurt his eyes, and his
head ached. He took little tufts of hair and pulled
them until the scalp stung. Before he went home, he
left what he had written in the tray marked Out.

If Nicolet sometimes prayed to the best in the people whom he knew, on occasion Poteat too held such
exotic converse. Before the paper came out with his
epistle, he indulged himself in imagining a number
of confrontations resulting from it—most of them, of
course, confrontations with Nicolet. Nicolet denied everything and swore vengeance. Nicolet admitted everything and begged mercy. Nicolet never came to
him at all but was finally discovered with the column
half chewed up in his gaping mouth, a suicide. On
each occasion Poteat's response was magnificently im-
passive, and even when he watched himself burned
in effigy as an enemy of God and a slanderer—he
envisioned it as taking place at sunset by the little
round bandstand in front of the town hall—he stood

there with the firelight dancing in his face and half deafened by the caterwauling mob, but silent.

To Rooney, on the other hand, he always had something to say. She came to him in different ways, at different places. Once when he was lying in bed waiting to go to sleep, he heard her foot on the stairs, and then she stood there in the moonlight of his fancy telling him that if he would publish a retraction of his charges, she would offer him herself again, and he said sadly and kindly, "Pal, I just can't risk myself again. You almost finished me with your favors the first time. I thought I was going to die of the terrible mooning for you in my bowels, and the only thing that saved me was your legs. The time I saw you again on the street with the flowers, I noticed that your legs are a little on the heavy side, not quite as straight as they might be, and you can never imagine how that helped. I made myself forget everything about you except the legs because they were the least lovely part of you, the least hard to lose. I know it's pathetic as hell, but it worked. It was on your legs, not mine, that I finally escaped with my life."

The Epistle to the Myronians came out in the *Repository* the afternoon of the day that Rooney returned alone from Muscadine, and that evening Poteat and Metzger had supper together at Poteat's house. Metzger brought lobsters—"You know how long to boil them, don't you?" he asked as he slid them out of the bag into the sink, sluggish and glittering. "Till they stop screaming, Willy boy."—and

Poteat supplied the rest of the meal and the liquor. Metzger insisted that they drink longer than Poteat wanted; Metzger talked too much, on and on about how he had arranged with the sister he lived with a signal of knocks on the wall in case he should have a coronary, about a new heat mask that he had found for his sinus; but Poteat was willing to forgive him anything for the sake of his mere physical presence on that strange and trying day, and he was grateful that it was health that Metzger made the subject of his conversation rather than the epistle. It must have been that he had not read it yet, and for as long as he remained, Poteat was able to live as though he had not written it.

After dinner, when Metzger seemed on the point of going home, Poteat persuaded him to stay by bringing out slides of the trip that they had made to Europe together the summer before. Looking scrawny and grey in his white duck trousers and a sport jacket that was too large for him in the shoulders, Metzger sat slumped in an arm chair with his bourbon while Poteat operated the projector which lit his face from beneath as he peered out into the darkened room. The slides both soothed and saddened him as he lingered slowly through them, trying to make them last—scenes of primal, vanished innocence. Franny Nicolet had scarcely been cold in her riverside grave at that point a year ago, and Rooney Vail had been only one of a number of parish ladies vying with each other to help ease the young pastor through the newness of his grief so that although Poteat had already lost her by then, he had not yet lost her to a rival.

"You look like Socrates about to drink the hemlock," Metzger murmured through his moustache: the picture on the screen showed Poteat sitting in Paris at a marvelously littered sidewalk table—the wine glasses and bread, a carafe of red wine, Metzger's sun glasses which he must have set down there when he got up to take the photograph, all jeweled with light like a Vermeer, the colors richer than life. The camera had caught Poteat himself just as he had been leaning forward into the sun to pick up the carafe so that his face came out flat and white as a waxwork; had caught the downward flick of his eyelids so that with only the whites of his eyes showing beneath them, he looked drunk or blind as he groped for his death. In the next one, Poteat and Metzger, both in new Panama hats, stood side by side in front of Notre Dame. Then Poteat alone again, leaning against the deck rail of a channel steamer with the grey water behind him and the grey sky; and just at that point, the doorbell rang.

Poteat jolted the projector as he got up, and his image became a shadow in a blur of grey and silver. Switching on the outside light, he could see through the window that a fog had rolled in off the river, and when he opened the door, he found Rooney Vail standing there in the haze of it with a scarf tied over her hair. She held out her hand to him.

Contrary to all his earlier imaginings, he was neither silent nor eloquent but stammered out some wild banality as he let her in, unable even to control his face which refused to return her smile but waited, stunned and stupid, for some word from her to give it shape, and the word, he supposed, was meant to be one of reassurance. She said something about how she had been helping her husband take inventory at the shop nearby, as though this in itself explained why after six years or whatever it was that she had finally come, but his efforts to find some plausible response simply to her being there prevented his hearing enough of what she said to respond to that too. Then, blessedly, old Metzger appeared from the living room with his bourbon in his hand and his necktie pulled crooked. He was all grinning confusion with butter on his whiskers from the screaming lobsters, dancing around them like a child at a bonfire, while Rooney untied her scarf, saying something about the fog that hovered at the door which Poteat had left open and which he closed now not so much to keep the fog out as at all costs to keep Metzger in, the safeguard of his presence.

Metzger was drunk or playing drunk—"It's always foul weather when old bachelors get together," he said. "Beauty and the beasts."—and as Metzger babbled, Poteat found it possible to meet Rooney's glance finally, gave her a little nod that acknowledged what it must have cost her to come, promised in return at least to ease Metzger out of the house because

only a coward would hold him there to prevent her saying whatever she had in mind to say, and he was not
a coward. She even seemed to be telling him this, to
be urging him to stand up like a man if only so
that she could somehow bring him to his knees. There
could be no doubt that this was why she had come.
"The clowns have to clear out now," he said to Metzger, "so the animal act can begin," and Metzger went
gladly enough, nodding and grimacing like a fool.
But once on the front step, out of sight of Rooney, he
looked at Poteat with utter sobriety and slashed his
finger from ear to ear across his throat.

Rooney herself did not remain much longer. She
never even took her raincoat off. She refused the
drink that Poteat offered her. She sat down on a
straight chair in the hall, and Poteat leaned back almost lazily against the wall with his hands in his
pockets. They were like distant relatives meeting at
a funeral, he thought, except that in some way the
funeral was his own. It made him smile. Everything
about him suggested life, was working again now:
his face, his power of speech—he was silent but no
longer through helplessness. She could have no way
of knowing whose demise had brought them together. When he opened the door to find her there,
he had felt one last gibbering of pain, of life, but
now there was nothing. From where he stood he
could see in the living room his shadowy shape
blurred against the silver sky. So he had become.
He was old Killian yawning through Armageddon.

He was old and safe at last.

When she began to speak, he tested this. Her voice was hesitant and quiet, and she never took her eyes from his face. She told him that whatever he might believe, she and Nick were not lovers; and he knew that even if she had said that they were lovers, it would have made no difference to him. She told him that Irma Reinwasser was sick with remorse at having revealed that she and Nick were together at Muscadine; and he thought that he would have spared the woman that if he could, wished vaguely that he had not charged her with wanting to ruin Nicolet, but it stirred nothing more to life in him than that. As he waited for her to come to the point, whatever it was, he wondered whether her tone would grow angry and threatening, or pleading, hurt; but he felt in any case beyond the range of her fire. And what he marveled at more than anything was how little it mattered to him that she was actually there. For years he had dreamed her in and out of that house, every room of it, but now that she sat there with her scarf across her knees, a few ends of hair flattened out damp from the fog like sea-fern against her cheek, she could have been a shadow herself for all her presence moved him. Almost sleepily he studied her with his pale eyes. She had stopped speaking. It was as if her few words to him had been only some kind of formality. For a few moments neither of them said anything. The heat of the projector bulb might set the slide on fire, Poteat thought, and then on the screen he would see himself, the ship, the sky, go up in flames. It did not matter. She held out her hand to him, and he took it.

"I don't even know what name to call you," she said.

This was the real test; he smiled. "We've never been introduced."

"I can't stand you to hate me," she said, "if you do hate me. I can't see why else you'd have written this thing."

"Oh, it's not hate. Just an acid disposition." He wanted to release the hand, but he felt that it would be to shirk the test. "I meant no offense. That's a lot of jazz," he said. "I meant offense. But I'm not a hater. I don't have the energy."

"Don't hate," she said. "It's such a waste of something. Don't hate Nick because of me."

"You came here for his sake, didn't you?"

"No." She looked surprised by her answer. "Not for Irma's either, though I promised her I'd come. I just wanted to find out if I could look at you again." She glanced away. "At your face."

"This face?" He let her hand go and slowly, half dazed, touched his face first on one cheek and then on the other with the heel of his palm. "Old flabby?"

She nodded. In the distance, he heard a foghorn, more vibration than sound: the darkness trembling.

"Well, can you?" he asked.

"Yes, thank God." She smiled at him slightly. "But not with joy yet, I'm afraid."

"Christ almighty . . . *joy!*" he said. "Joy? The most I can manage myself when I look at it is a low belch. Joy?" He shook his head. "Jesus."

"How about when you look at me?"

Once with her thumbs she had shaped his face like clay, and he thought how easy it would be with his answer now to shape hers any way he chose. "I look at you with . . ." The sense of sheer power made him pause. There was nothing he might not do with that dreamed face leaning toward him: make it twitch with pain, burst like a dry pod. But she was in his house, sitting in his chair; he felt a curious gentleness towards her. "I look at you," he sighed, the great dimples deep in shadow, his head a little to one side as he gazed at her. "With infinite regret. With gratitude for whatever crackpot whim it was that made you once look on me with favor." Just for one instant then before she could speak, he allowed himself to think that it was not after all too late, too ludicrous, this little lurch of life in the midst of his dying; that what brimmed in her eyes as she sat there pressing her face between her hands was more than gratitude for his having said nothing worse, more that pity.

"I've got to tell you something," she said. "God knows why you of all people . . . my enemy. I haven't even said it to Clem."

Poteat squared his shoulders against the wall. Although he was looking directly at her, he could not seem to see her well. It was as if the light between them was bent, like light through a prism.

"I planned to ask you to lay off Nick," she said. "For your own sake as much as his or mine, or Irma's. Even if people believe what you wrote about him, you're the one they'll hate for it, you know. They'll lap it up, and they'll hate you for the picture they have of themselves lapping it up. But I want to say something else now." She smoothed out the damp kerchief that lay across her knees, looking down at it. "If there's really such a thing as joy on this earth, the sort religious people pray to God for, I think I've caught a little of it, God knows how, or why me, or anything. I need to say that to you. To look at you with that inside me." There was bewilderment in her eyes as she looked up at him again. "I think I'm going to be able to have a baby," she said.

There was something almost homely about her, Poteat thought, as she sat there with her heavy legs, the raincoat that was too long for her. Her mouth was too large, her eyes not large enough. Poteat found that he wanted to cause her some deep and memorable pain.

He gave the wall a thump with his fist and laughed. "Congratulations, pal," he said. "Congratulations to you and congratulations to the lucky father." He opened the front door and stood with his back to her, looking out. "Whoever you think the lucky father's going to be." He saw the fog hanging there like a curtain, behind it the cackling night.

THIRTEEN

———◆———

IRMA REINWASSER dreamed that Heinz Taffel
was dead and that the whole camp had been assembled to witness his funeral. It was snowing
lightly, and everything looked quiet and beautiful.
The prisoners were drawn up on three sides of a
great hollow square with the row of grey barracks
making the fourth side. In the center of the square
was an iron cot where the corpse had been placed.
It was dressed in black and lay on its side in such a
way that Irma could not see its face. A prisoner beside her—it was the cross-eyed little Silbermann from
Mainz—whispered, "There is worse to come. They
are going to strip us all naked and make us stand
here till we freeze to death," but she was not afraid,
and she felt that Silbermann was not afraid either in
spite of what he had said. At the head of the cot
stood Nicolet in the S.S. uniform. You could not
make out his words, but he was reciting some kind of
prayer for the dead which lasted a long time and

seemed to bore him. Every few moments he would turn his head to one side and titter stagily behind his hand. Then, slowly, the corpse began to roll over on its back until everyone could see that it was Heinz Taffel, who was smoking a long, black cigar. At first Nicolet did not seem to notice what had happened. Then with no sign of emotion, he took his pistol from the holster and started to hit Taffel again and again on the head with the butt. As the blows rained down on him, Taffel turned his face towards Irma. It was dripping with sweat, and for a moment, as their eyes met, he gave her a tortured smile. Silbermann tried to stop her, but Irma broke ranks and started running towards Taffel through the snow. *"Verzeihung, Verzeihung!"* she cried. From somewhere deep in Taffel's throat came what sounded like the clucking of a chicken.

Nicolet picked Lizard Boy up with both hands around her waist and held her at arm's length above his head where against the vast, blue sky she flapped her arms and kicked her legs. He knelt in the grass to hug Pie Face, sliding one hand under her dress to feel the warm, bare back with its delicate cage of bone, the cool little rear.

"Every night we said godbless for you," she said.

"We saw a man with a black tongue," Lizzie said.

"I missed you like crazy, pig girls."

"Did you bring us a surprise?" Lizard Boy had

taken him by the ear.

"I must have something in here." Nicolet felt in his pocket. All that he could find was the postcard from Rooney and Léon's New Testament. He handed the New Testament to Cornelia.

"That belonged to your great-grandfather," he said.

"Is he dead?"

"A long time ago."

"Probably he is in Heaven." Lizzie said.

"Will we ever see him?"

"I wouldn't be surprised." Nor would he, Nicolet thought. He laughed, pulling Lizzie's thumb out of her mouth like a cork from a bottle. Whatever it meant, the resurrection of the body must involve something like seeing, something like meeting. As a child you took the language of the faith literally; then you learned to take it symbolically before you could see that you had been more nearly right in the first place. He pictured Léon reaching out to the two children as they raced toward him across some field of miracle. In eternity, everyone became the age when he had been most truly alive; old children might dandle their babbling fathers on their knees.

"What's it about?" Cornelia held the shabby little volume in her hand. She had found that there were no pictures in it.

"The little Lord Jesus and how he grew," he said.

"Oh dear."

"The other's mine!" Lizzie pulled the postcard from his hand. "What does it say?"

" 'Thinking of you in Muscadine,' " he read.

"Where's that?"

"It's where I've been."

"Who was thinking about you there?"

"He was," Cornelia said, pointing to the picture of the dapper young man. "That's Jesus when he grew up."

Irma was asleep in a canvas deck chair where she had been sitting to watch them play. The baseball cap was down over her eyes, her mouth agape and moving.

"Pretend she's the sleeping beauty and you're the prince."

They had run over to her chair and stood at the foot of it. She could have been a great doll sprawled lifeless there with one arm spilled off to the side and trailing in the grass. Nicolet placed his finger to his lips and went up behind her. Gently he removed the baseball cap. He leaned over and touched his lips to her forehead.

When she opened her eyes, she saw only the children; the kiss was part of her dream's secret. Nicolet made a face at his daughters. Cornelia covered her mouth with both hands. Lizzie ran off all tipsy like a dead leaf blowing. Irma raised her eyes to find Nicolet looking down at her.

"*Gott* . . ." she whispered.

"I came back, you see."

"Did you read it?"

He nodded.

"It's my fault. You told me not to say anything,

but I did." She had not changed her position in the chair, her hand still dangling in the grass. Except for her eyes and mouth, she could have been totally paralyzed. "Maybe I told him on purpose, I don't think so."

"I don't think so. Anyway, it doesn't matter. I'm innocent."

"Nobody's innocent."

"Calvinist," he said. "Everybody's innocent. Even God."

"We are all trying to bury each other alive . . ." She struggled to remember how it had happened in the dream. She had run to him through the snow, but it was too late. They had rolled him into a grave and were shoveling earth in on top of him. She herself had picked up a handful or two and dropped them in. Finally all that showed above ground was the end of the cigar, glowing and fading as he breathed in and out. "I've got to help you. Some way I'm going to put things right for you. You tell me how." The small, half dreaming eyes committed him slowly to memory. "No. Even if you knew, you would never tell me."

Cornelia had untied one of Irma's gym shoes and then more or less tied it again. Now the foot was a pony, and she plumped down heavily in the saddle. At first they all thought—even Nicolet—that Irma was making a joke of it. It was hard to imagine a face screwed up like that, shriveled, for any serious purpose.

* * *

Metzger woke up feeling miserable. It was the bourbon after supper, he thought, and he knew that he should never have eaten the lobster. Twice during the night he had been awakened by heartburn—the dry, distending ache in the chest that swelled up into the neck and jaws. He had thought of the possibility of its being a coronary and toyed with the idea of testing the signal that he had arranged with his sister: three sharp raps on the wall. One or two raps might be accidental, but there could be no mistaking three; and she was to come in immediately without knocking. But the pain had subsided, and he had gone back to sleep.

Now he could hear the vacuum going in the hall. Only half awake, he thought that if misery could make a sound, that was the sound that it would make. Commencement had been last week. Except for a little tutoring, that meant no more teaching until September. He could have a long, hot shower, dress at his leisure, and walk down to Thelma's for a late breakfast. His room got no direct sun until late afternoon, but by the quality of the shade he could tell that it was a beautiful day. All of this should have cheered him up, he thought, yet he continued to feel so depressed that he could not bring himself to get out of bed. Nor could he think what it was that depressed him. It was true that old Willy had insulted him, had called him a clown in front of the young

Vail woman and had virtually thrown him out of the house, but that was their way with each other. Willy patronized him; he made fun of Willy. It all evened out. It passed the time. It was not enough to account for this sense of defeat, of bereavement almost.

After breakfast he would treat himself to a few hours at Cully's, the bookstore. That would restore him. Books were his passion. He did not even have to read them, just having them near him was enough, and bookshelves reached from floor to ceiling along two walls of his room. He loved the feel and the smell of books, the cockatoo covers of paperbacks, the austere spines of the university presses, and he arranged them on his shelves with self-conscious perversity: Havelock Ellis and Emily Dickinson, Kierkegaard and Rider Haggard, a row of Penguin mysteries dwarfed by the fat terra cotta volumes of the Variorum Shakespeare. He thought of them as a mirror of his variegated soul, hoarded by Squirrel against the coming of winter. For in this respect his nickname did not displease him, suggesting as it did a creature both nimble and prudent, a twitch and skedaddle of antic spirit through the pencil-smelling dusk of high-school corridors. To add to his shelves was to add to himself, and this thought got him to the edge of his bed where he sat with his head in his hands looking down at his bare feet.

There would be breakfast—Thelma served hash-brown potatoes with all orders, salty and crisp—the walk down McKinley Street through the morning sun, then up the hill to Cully's. He felt better already, snapped his toes against the linoleum. "Hot spit," he said to himself, a kind of doxology. "Up and at 'em, Metzger boy." Then he gave a little belch that brought up something bitter and stinging to the pit of his throat: heartburn. With it the sadness returned. Something was missing, lost to him forever, and as he arched his neck back with a skeleton's grin, he knew what it was.

When Rooney Vail had burst in mad as a wet hen at the outrageous piece in the *Repository*, he had thanked his stars that he was not old Willy. He had fled gladly. But what he had fled was just what hexed him now. It had been an ugly scene, he was sure— garbled, teary, unnecessary—but human at least, with the blood trembling and fire in the bowels. A life lacerating a life. The gust of it had blown him away like chaff. The world of men was no place for a squirrel. Willy had not even thought to introduce him. It was as if among the living he had no name.

Nicolet stared up at the snowy white church. The wooden steps mounted to the double doors which were hooked open to let the day in; the newly gilded Roman numerals glittered against the black dial, above it the spire rose sharp as a pin. The church as mother, Nicolet thought: cockeyed old sloven with her arms flung wide to embrace the world. The church as virgin: aloof and inviolate, suffering only the pure to approach. This afternoon on Congress Street she was all virgin, laced up to the chin in goose-white clapboard, Christ's maid. Nicolet scratched the flaked stair-rail with his thumbnail and read: "Pentecost: the Birthday of the Church." *Clack, clack*, he thought, and a wildness, a gaiety, stirred in him as he boarded her: the church as ark—whitewashed, barnacled, smelling of the sea.

"Betty Blackbird!" he said. Big-boned and deadpan, Betty Blackburn sat blinking at him through pixie glasses over her typewriter. She had lips painted on where she had no lips, her grey hair brushed back under a little wreath of braid. "Like the madam of a Quaker whorehouse," Rooney said once.

"You're excommunicated," Betty Blackburn said, pointing a pencil at him. "Blackballed."

"Blackbird," he said. "They're going to strip me of my prayer shawl and ephod?"

"One by one. You've had it."

"It's been great working for you. A privilege." He reached over the typewriter, and they shook hands.

"All's quiet on the western front," she said.

"You mean it?"

"The ones I've seen seem to be taking it in their stride anyway."

"Have they read the thing?"

"Everybody's read it."

"But they didn't believe it."

"At least they didn't talk that way."

"How about you?"

She gave him a long, quizzical stare. "Willy Poteat's a nut."

"You're a good chap," Nicolet said. He wanted more than anything to go upstairs into the empty sanctuary, to sit there in a back pew under the choir loft until, like sleep or some forgotten name, prayer came.

"Before you do anything else," his secretary said, "Mrs. Cusper has been phoning in all morning. She's got to see you something terrible." Betty Blackburn rolled her eyes behind her pixie glasses.

"Was she speaking in tongues?"

"I'm afraid so."

"I better go," Nicolet said although he knew well enough what he would find once he got there. Madge Cusper never explained the obscure crises that prompted her four or five times a year to summon him, and if he questioned her directly, she would not answer. She would fix him with her bulbous eyes and smile dimly. Her face was covered with orange fuzz, like a child's drawing of a lion.

The top panes of her parlor windows were of colored glass, a checkerboard of green and amber squares with the sun burning through them—a crazy little shrine with Madge its deity: head of a beast on the body of a woman. Here too a prayer might come, he thought. Her breath was fruity with the smell of gin.

"How are your two little girlies?" she asked. "I had a little girlie of my own once, but she got whiter and whiter and whiter, and one fine day she just faded out of the picture. She didn't have enough red blood. Just white blood. Like bugs. Butterflies. God's so vague." She gave a sly smile, her eyelids wavering under their own weight. "Sent me a butterfly instead of a baby. Herbert Cusper walked out on me then."

She made a purring sound. Nicolet said nothing. Silence, like a poultice, could draw the poison out. Her wide, lipless mouth was linked by a deep cleft to her nose. She belonged in *The Peaceable Kingdom* of Edward Hicks, he thought, parting the ferns with velvet paws and peering through, sleepy and fierce. The orange fuzz was a golden mane.

"I was so sad to hear about your wife, Nicky. Everybody hated hearing about it. Hated it!" She drew her paws tight on the arms of her chair and leaned forward. "Now they're crucifying that little Episcopal what's-its-name—Denbigh. What if he did run off with somebody's wife? Did you read it, Nicky?"

"It's not about Denbigh. It's about me."

She was dressed as if for a garden party in powder blue with powder blue gloves, a string of white summer beads tight about her thick neck. She turned away from him toward the window, her lion-face softening. "Will you help a lady in distress, kind sir? A lady like me. . . ."

Did you pray when you made your calls? Always the silent prayer, entering anywhere—"Peace be in this house."—and when you were asked to, of course: a grace at meals, a prayer for the bereaved, the dying. But how about when you were not asked? It was not for a prayer that Madge Cusper was pleading but for comfort, advice, reproof, all of which he had given her often before. She could not bring herself to look at him now, asking for what she knew was of no use to either of them. She was purring again, gazing out beneath the green and amber panes as out of a cave.

He stood behind her chair with his two hands on her head, seeing himself in the convex mirror as some kind of hairdresser. The carroty hair was surprisingly thin, her scalp hot and hard through it. Her skull beneath his hands. She sat stiff.

"Lie down with a plastered old lion, thou blessed lamb of God," he prayed. "Place thy hands on my hands and use my guttering love to love her through, a channel to her of thy healing grace, that she may kindle to thy dancing at the heart. . . ."

They had come through the apple trees with the sunlight flickering on them, such a fine-looking pair, Roy thought. Theo could have been a young prince with his white shirt bloused out over his trousers and open at the throat, and his friend could have been his squire, his equerry, whatever princes had—both of them fresh-shaven, vigorous, smelling of toothpaste and soap. Except for the friend's dog collar, you could never have guessed that they were priests but world-beaters, rather—crack young salesmen stuffing their faces before starting out on their routes. He wished that Zimmer had been awake at that hour to see them having breakfast with him. They included him in their conversation, treated him with such deference. It would have made her eat her words about Theo's being an undutiful son and coming only once a year to see his old dad. "Every time you have to die to get him up here, Roy, what sort of a son is that?"—he had heard that often enough—but there in the kitchen that morning what had bound them was life, not death. Even Zimmer would have seen it. Among all the clatter and fragrance of breakfast, they were boys together. He had fed them waffles with sausages and coffee that he boiled in a saucepan with a raw egg broken in to settle the grounds. It was all so rapid-fire and rollicking that it befuddled him a little, and he let them do most of the talking, just sat there with a dazed, buttery smile trying to follow.

The evening before, in the barber chair, Theo had embraced him, he thought. Theo had forgiven him for being less than a father; he had forgiven Theo for being less than a son—something like that. He did not want to think of it now but to save it until Theo was gone, but it kept coming back at him there in the kitchen; how Theo had buried his face in his old checked shirt with that crazy Zimmer pounding on the floor over their heads. He remembered seeing tears falling into his son's hair before he realized that they were his own tears, but this time Theo had not called him a cry-baby although God knows, he thought, that was the truth of it. "Have some more syrup, boys," and he poured it for them, spiraling it out from the center to fill all the squares evenly. Theo's friend told a long joke about a priest and a rabbi appearing before Saint Peter, and a jet of steam from the tea kettle tumbled up a shaft of sun towards the window. "What a breakfast, what a breakfast!" They seemed to know that it was, building it for him, block on block, to last him a long time— coffee smell, sausage smell, young men's crisp morning laughter.

Whatever had happened between himself and Theo, he was afraid to press it too far, to catch Theo's eye now for fear that neither of them would be able to sustain it. Léon had brought them together, he thought —his saga of Léon's last days—and that only added to his fears because everything that Léon touched, in death as in life, turned to dust: the Comet Fire Kindler, the crusade against Mr. Durfee, now the reconciliation between his son and the grandson whom he had never seen. "*Le bon Dieu* should be proud to have you two on his payroll," he said, "so bright-eyed and bushy-tailed. You've brightened an old man's twilight. But it's a long haul back to Myron. Maybe you ought to get started."

Then he could have bitten off his tongue. He wanted them so desperately to stay. They had not even finished their coffee yet. "But I don't mean this second. Not till you've had one of these anyway." And he fumbled for the cigars in the breast pocket of his shirt, offered them each one which they refused. His hand shook as he lit one himself, and the first puff made him so dizzy that he seemed to be looking at Theo through a swarm of bees. But at least now he was looking at him, daring doom, and Theo, his boy, God's boy, was smiling back at him through the tiny, bright wings. "Welcome home, my son . . ." He spoke with the cigar in his mouth, felt the wet of it trickling down his lower lip, but nothing mattered now, only that their eyes had met without flinching. "You've got your sleeve in the butter," Theo said. Roy heard it as a benediction.

"Who knows, in another year he may come again," Zimmer said after they had gone. They were standing in her bathroom, the medicine cabinet opened on her corn plasters, the bottles that she blued her hair with. He had fixed her toilet. Inside the water box, the plunger had just come unhooked from the handle. Probably she had done it herself to annoy him. But he could not bring himself to hate her. Fifteen years ago, he thought, he might have taken her to bed with him and punished her there; he had always had more than ordinary success with his female boarders. But this morning he contented himself with reaching out and tapping her on the collar bone with a finger still wet from his tinkering. "Matter of fact, he asked me down to Myron for the weekend," he said, "so you better quit the sabotage till I get back."

Then, even as he said it, he decided to make the lie good. Theo had asked him nothing of the kind, but he would go anyway and surprise him. There was nothing now that he did not dare, and, besides, Theo was in some sort of trouble—why else had the friend driven half the night to fetch him? Maybe he needed a father at last. But before he set off the next morning—he was sitting in his chair by the window pulling up his socks—he took a dime out of his pocket and dropped it into one of his shoes. They were old-fashioned shoes that laced up above the instep, and although it was a warm June morning, he wore his long underwear so that when he stood up to pull on his trousers, he looked like an old acrobat about to go teetering off on the high wire.

FOURTEEN

O N SUNDAY morning it rained hard in Myron, bouncing off the sidewalks, racing
down the gutters. Stiff gusts of wind from
the northeast lashed it against the church on Congress
Street, and most people arrived in cars for the eleven
o'clock service, a policeman in a yellow slicker waving
them into the parking lot, halting them at intervals to
let the ones who came on foot cross over from the far
side. Metzger came on foot, waiting with his umbrella
tilted against the wind while Grogan helped a pair of
old ladies up the steps. Irma Reinwasser splashed
across the street with an Army surplus raincoat over
her head as Roy Nicolet, hatless, followed her ma-
jestically in a poncho of his son's that billowed out
around him. Gulls blown up the river wheeled and
creaked in the low, grey sky. Inside the double doors,
among the coat racks, there was a smell of wet wool,
wet rubber—outside, the smell of the sea.

The church was the ark, Nicolet thought, with the

grey waves starting to sweep up over the beaches, scudding over the flats and meadowland until they lapped against door sills, down cellar stairs, and finally set her afloat—cumbersome old menagerie, her timbers shuddering and steeple-mast flailing back and forth as the flood took her. It was being set afloat that was the birthday of the church—being cut adrift, bound for somewhere. And the birthday of the church was only the birthday of the heart writ large: you went where the waves willed. Through the door of the vestry where he sat alone waiting for the organist's cue to enter, he could see that the center section was filled and the ushers had already started filling the side pews. Poteat had packed the place, he thought. During the night someone had scrawled THOU SHALT NOT COMMIT ADULTERY down the walk from his front door, and Irma was the first to see it. He had found her there trying to sweep it off with a broom when he came down for breakfast. "*Schwein*," she had said. "*Wir sind alle Schweine.*"

"Take my advice, son," Roy had said. "Expose him for the scoundrel he is—a bearer of false witness, a neurotic. Put on the armor of righteousness. Denounce him from the pulpit!" His scorched eyes were aghast as he chopped at the air with his fist; then suddenly, lowering his voice, he looked away. "There's hot blood in the Nicolets, Theo. I of all people should know. And she's passing fair, Theo. There's no doubt of that. You can speak to your dad." The children were fascinated by their grandfather, built wonderful new games around him. "You bleed," Cornelia instructed him, "and we'll be the doctors." He let his head loll back in his chair, groaning extravagantly, while they struggled to undo the top buttons of his shirt.

"He's pathetic, pathetic, Nick," Rooney said over the telephone. "Pray like Hell for him, please. For my sake."

"I'll do better than that," he said. "I'll go see him."

"Is that better?"

"It's harder."

"Clem says there's talk about the merchants withdrawing their ads from the paper."

"How is Clem?"

"He has great, bright wings. Wherever he walks, you find little white flowers growing afterwards. He's sitting beside me now, throwing up."

"Then you're O.K.?" he said. "No sweat?"

"None."

"Just one question then." Betty Blackburn came into his office bringing the mail. He waited until she had left. "Was Willy the one . . . the stranger?"

"Bless the memories, Nick. Everybody's," she said.

He had tried to see Poteat later that day. At the newspaper they said that he was probably at home, but at his house there was no answer to the doorbell. The door was ajar, and Nicolet walked in, calling his name up the stairs, but again there was no answer.

Standing in a man's empty house was like watching a man while he slept; even compassion became espionage. Yet he could not bring himself to leave immediately. A window curtain swelled, then sucked flat against the screen. He stepped into the living room where there was a slide projector set up on a table. He switched it on and saw Willy Poteat standing against a silvery sky on what might have been a bridge. "Willy," he called again, less now from any hope of being heard than from the desire to justify his presence there if only to himself. "Willy?"

What would he have said if he had found him there, he wondered. Less and less he seemed to know in advance what he would say to anyone. He had probably frightened Madge Cusper half to death, had certainly frightened himself; prayers came unbidden. "Do you love her, Willy? Is that the secret your house keeps?" He spoke to the picture on the screen. "Is that the secret of every house? Love bangs on the wall trying to be heard. Sometimes it sounds like hate, sometimes like a shutter flapping. Sometimes it sounds like two branches clacking." He switched off the projector and turned to go but stopped at the door. "Peace be in this house," he called up the stairs.

Rain beat against the vestry window, and he felt his pulse quicken. It was nearly eleven. He could hear the prelude drawing to an end, then there would be the introduction to the opening hymn and he would step through into the chancel and take his place at the high-backed chair behind the pulpit. When he stood up, his black preacher's robe nearly touched the floor, the broad, black velvet band running down the front and the two Geneva tabs jutting crisp and white from his collar. He opened his hymnal to make sure that the sermon was there. His mouth was dry. "I was glad when they said unto me, 'Let us go into the house of the Lord.' " No preacher had written that, he thought. "I was sick to my stomach when they said unto me . . ." That was more like it. The madness of presuming to speak for God; better, if you had the courage, to stand up there and be silent for God or to say, as he had dreamed by Roy's barn of saying, just "Yes. It is true about God. Whoever would have believed it? But it is true." And then the silence, he thought. No organ hamming it up. Just the slap and rattle of the rain at the tall windows.

The organist's hand must have slipped. He had been modulating the prelude to a close, to the moment's pause before the first hymn, when there was a burst of treble pipes like a scream of astonishment, and he lurched immediately into the hymn before anyone was quite ready for it. The effect was oddly terrifying. Then as the choir started to sing and the congregation rose to its feet, Nicolet stepped through the little door, crossed the chancel, and stood by the oak chair.

Joyful, joyful, all adore Thee,
God of glory, Lord of love.

Hearts unfold like flowers before Thee,
Opening to the sun above.

He read the opening words without singing them, then closed his eyes for a moment, prayed. "Be with me in thy house."

Melt the clouds of sin and sadness,
Drive the dark of doubt away.

Faster, faster, he thought, starting to sing himself; each verse should leave the lungs aching for breath.

Giver of immortal gladness,
Fill us with the light of day.

He spotted Rooney and Clem. They had taken places much farther front than usual, and instead of her broad-brimmed black hat, Rooney wore only a dark band in her hair: let them all see that she was there, unabashed, with her husband beside her. Nicolet wondered if she was adding up the hymn numbers to find if they came out even. He hoped that they did. In the front pew sat three boys in their late teens, two of whom were strangers to him but one of whom he knew that he had seen somewhere although it was several moments before he could remember where. It was the boy who had picked him up on the road to Muscadine—still chewing something, it seemed, but with his hair slicked back now, uncomfortable in shirt and tie. Nicolet wondered if the rumors of scandal had brought him or possibly just curiosity to see in action a man whom he had every reason to think was out of his mind. Nicolet tried to catch his eye and nod to him, but the boy did not notice, his smooth jaws working as though he was trying to crack a seed between his front teeth.

They were his people, his ark—the ones who had come to gawk at a priestly philanderer no less than the old ladies—and if he had had to go by way of Muscadine to reach that knowledge, it had not been too far to go, he thought, although he had returned with little enough to give them: like the sprig of olive in the beak of Noah's dove, only a scrap of splendor from a derelict orchard to bear witness to the presence of a land, a hope, beyond the grey sea-swells. Half way through the last stanza, he stepped up to the lectern where he opened the large Bible in the middle and placed his notes on it, then leaned forward into the fresh silence that came with the end of the singing.

"The Lord is nigh unto all them that call to him," he called out to them, holding on to the sides of the lectern. "To all that call upon him in truth. He will fulfil the desires of them that fear him. He will also hear their cry and save them." As he paused, the silence deepened, and he wondered how long he could hold them with it before the first clearing of throats, creaking of pew and floor board. "Ask, and it shall be given unto you. Seek, and ye shall find. Knock, and it shall be opened unto you," he said. Then, "Let us pray," and a great shuffling and rustling came as they bowed their heads.

"We knock fists against the walls that wall us off from brothers. Give them to hear us. Give us to hear the terrible needs that beat like hearts behind brothers' walls.

"We knock fists against the walls that wall us off from you. Hear us and know the loneliness of lives walled up in flesh and rib."

As he looked up, Nicolet avoided the eyes of those who had not bowed their heads, glancing past them to the windows where he could see the trees that grew along Congress Street tossing in the wet wind.

"Holy Spirit that set fire to the saints on Pentecost and fans flames among us still, blow back the curtains of the air and show the glory forth . . ."

It was the prayer that he had written but not the prayer that he felt now—something wilder now, he wanted, a Lillian Flagg prayer, old rugged cross of a Jesus prayer in that sane and stately place—but he was bound to the words before him and hurried through them to the General Confession.

"Let us confess our sins unto Almighty God," he said.

He thought at first that someone had fainted. There was a stir in the pews at his right toward the back of the church. Two or three people seemed to half rise, then sit again. Several voices were murmuring at once, and Nicolet hesitated on the brink of his praying. A woman stood up.

"I confess my sins to you, *Herr Pastor*," she called

out, Irma Reinwasser waving a hymnal above her head as though she needed to catch his eye in that place where already all eyes had turned toward her save for a few of the old ones glazed with dread— had fire broken out, someone suffered a stroke right there on Congress Street?

"I am going to confess to you and to the people of this town," she cried. "It is the only God I got."

"Let her alone!" His voice rang harsh and metallic through the public address system as, leaning forward, he almost touched the microphone with his lips and the feedback whined to a shrill needle of sound. He raised his hand to stop the usher who had hurried to her from his station by the side door and was reaching for her now across the laps of the three or four who sat as if paralyzed between her and the aisle. As Nicolet spoke, the usher drew back as though he had touched fire. For a moment it seemed to him that Irma herself was on the verge of drawing back. Then she began to speak again.

It was less like a dream than as if all the churchery that had gone before it was a dream,—the death-size cross of gilded wood above his head, the black priest's robe he wore with the starched white tablets of the law at his throat, all were symbols of what only now was gathering to a madness of truth: Irma telling wild, holy lies to save him, offering herself up to the slaughtering eyes of Congress Street for him. Separated by wave on wave of turned heads, their faces almost touched now, hers in the devouring storm-light drifting, swelling, like a cloud as he watched it. He whispered "No," and the sound rolled out like distant thunder from the high speakers, but no one noticed. The church was hers.

"They are my fault," she said, "the things they are telling about the pastor. I myself started the rumors. All the bad seeds, I planted them. Ask the newspaper man. I, Reinwasser, was the one that told him the pastor was with a woman. Sure the pastor was with a woman. He went in mercy, bringing God to her in the town of Muscadine. He went to her like a pastor, but Reinwasser told the newspaper man he went like her lover. He wrote down in the newspaper the lies I told him. Only now I am confessing it."

The organist had left his bench to peer down at her from the choir loft, his pince-nez revolving slowly on their black cord as he leaned way out. In the front of the church, people were kneeling on their pews to get a better view of what was taking place behind them; the boy who had given Nicolet a ride had come as far as the lowest chancel step to look back over them, his jaws finally at rest. She had no form or comeliness that they should look at her, Nicolet thought, no beauty that they should desire her, hunched up there in her soldier's raincoat, a gnome of sorrows, acquainted with God only knew what.

"Now I am also going to confess why I wanted to hurt him so then you will know everything," she said. "I wanted to hurt him because I was jealous. Because he would not look at me, an ugly woman. Because he has eyes only for God. Do you understand it? I made up the lies to hurt him because I had crazy love for him, a young man, and he had nothing for me except maybe he was sorry for an old beat-up Jew woman. Now I am the one who is sorry. It is too much. So you know the truth now, and you are going to forget all the lies I made. You are going to be good to this pastor again now and not write filth on his sidewalk for children to read."

She had squeezed herself past the knees of the people beside her as she finished and stood for a moment in the empty center aisle. The church was silent as if snow was falling in it and they were all prisoners of the silence and the snowing. Nicolet cupped both hands over his mouth as though trying to warm them. An ancient female voice quavered, "What did she say? What did she say?" as a companion shushed her. But again, like paper crackling, "What did she say . . . ?" Irma Reinwasser had gone. There was the sound of her heavy shoes creaking down the stairs.

Nicolet came down from the pulpit as far as where the boy was standing, put his hands on his shoulders and softly shoved him back towards his seat. The organist mounted his bench again. Breathing heavily, Roy Nicolet leaned his head back until it rested on the back of the pew, and sitting behind him, Madge Cusper had a nearly irresistible impulse to seize his candy-white hair in her teeth. Metzger kept his eyes fixed on the Vails. They looked expensive, he thought. People said the money was hers.

Nicolet did not return to the pulpit but remained on the steps, face and hands of wood. Two hundred, three hundred, sat there waiting for him to say something, to make it all right again, and he waited with them, his curiosity no less than theirs: now they would see. Sometimes, making a fool of himself with the children—sticking his thumbs in his ears and waggling his fingers at them, ruffling up his hair and gibbering like a troll under a bridge—he had speculated with Franny about what would happen if he got up some Sunday and did such a thing in the pulpit, stuck a flower from the communion table behind his ear and whirled around like a top with his black skirts flying. The chances were, he had decided, that they would choose to doubt their own senses rather than so fundamental a part of their faith as that nothing untoward ever happened at the eleven o'clock service. A minister, like the God that he served, was a gentleman, after all, so what they were waiting for him to say now, Nicolet thought, was in one way or another that nothing had happened, that the wiry little apparition who had disturbed the grey peace that did not pass their understanding was just something that the Junior Sunday School had put together out of papier maché to top their Fourth of July bonfire with the next week. The best that he could do in their eyes would be to continue from where she had interrupted him with the General Confession. They could bow their heads, and when they lifted them again, all would be well. But other words rose in his throat, his eyes asking their forgiveness as he spoke.

"These rumors you've heard about my sins of the flesh are only rumors, that's the truth," he said, "but that's about the only truth there was in what she told you. It's not true she started the rumors, of course. It's also not true I went to Muscadine to bring God to anybody. As much as anything, I went to get away from God. To get away from you."

Without the microphone, his voice sounded flat and muffled in the great room. He could see some of them cupping their ears—old eyes glazed, old jaws clamped tight—in their effort to listen.

"I wanted to get away from you," he repeated more loudly, spacing his words. "But away from God too," he added, a sudden queer rush of tenderness for them making him smile, smile and almost shout at the same time. "So don't be sad—at least you were in good company. And anyway, it didn't work. You can see I didn't make it. 'If I take the wings of the morning and dwell in the uttermost parts of the sea, even there shall thy hand lead me.' It led me back to you again."

Holding a knot of his robe to keep from tripping on it as he went up the steps, he turned to go back to the pulpit. He had said all that he had to say, he thought. Now he could go on with the service. He had come back to them, his people, his ark. He had not known until now how much he wanted to preach to them again, just now, with the rain drumming at the windows, drawing them close. For the first time

in his life he felt that he had something to tell them
—like the rain, it comes down, the power from on
high, wells up like a secret spring, the deep magic
and laughter of God—and for the first time in their
lives, perhaps, they would actually listen to him because they had come to listen. Always before they
had thought, and with reason, that they knew what to
expect from him, but now, thanks to Poteat, they did
not know what to expect him either to say or to be.
The time was ripe.

But then, as he looked down from the lectern at
their faces, grey in the rain-light, he knew that the
time had passed. It was Irma's church still with
Irma's ghost haunting them, Irma's voice still ringing
in their ears. What would a sermon on Pentecost
mean to them now who wanted to hear only what the
filth was that had been written on his walk and who
had written it there. She had said that she loved him,
waving her hymnal in the air. Whatever else they
might doubt of her confession, they would not doubt
that. To his horror, he realized that he did not doubt
it himself. Why else would she have tried to save
him, to take upon herself the chastisement that would
make him whole? The Suffering Servant of the Lord,
he thought; was it always like this to be suffered for
by another, to be given at such sickening cost a gift
that you did not want? Had he for years preached the
sacrifice of the cross only in the end to be revolted
by it? He felt the self-mutilation of Irma Reinwasser hanging at his neck like a dead cat as he stood

there in the pulpit while the congregation waited in silence with their faces uptilted as if to see a man perform a dangerous trick in the air.

The trick was to hide his anger from them, if possible to hide it from himself—this sudden idiot anger at Irma for the pain that he had caused her without knowing or wanting to cause it, for her having ruined by her outburst this one irrecoverable moment when he might have preached and been heard. Nicolet saw in his mind the muddy face and flailing hand as she had debased herself for his sake, and for a moment of great ugliness and great peace he hated her. "Let us confess our sins unto Almighty God," he said, not bowing his head but staring out at them with his turquoise eyes round and surprised as a child's.

When it came time for the sermon, he read it rather than preached it, ran his thumb from line to line to guide his reading. The words that he had written with excitement fell from his mouth dead. Ordinarily when he preached, he needed only an occasional glance at his manuscript, typed out by Betty Blackbird on small half-sheets, but now he felt lashed to it, hardly dared lose touch with it for an instant for fear that he would lose everything then and drown. In Jerusalem there came a sound from heaven as of a rushing, mighty wind. Faces burst into flames. An apple tree stammered joy through wooden lips. This was the sermon. But on Congress Street, the old ark foundered, its decks awash, and between pulpit and pews Nicolet could feel the sea rising.

Then he stood just inside the open door shaking hands with them as the rain spattered on the glistening steps. No one lingered to chat with him—just the touch of the hands, the murmuring, eyes lowered and uneasy. It could have been a funeral. "Nice sermon . . . we're all behind you . . . sorry about the ruckus . . ." More of them than usual went out the side doors to avoid him. The air felt cool to his perspiring face. Voices in the rain, the slap of windshield wipers, Denbigh's chimes ringing from Whittier Street—it all revived him a little. He crouched down to shake hands with a child who curtsied precariously. Farther back in the line, he could see Roy, his face puffed, pursed, to say something enormous, but by the time that he reached his son at the door, it seemed to have spent itself and he said nothing, just stood there for a moment in silence with Nicolet's hand clasped in both of his, smelling of bay rum, then moved unsteadily off into the wet like a victim of assassination. The policeman blew his whistle, and the slow procession of cars stopped as umbrellas bobbed across the street. Out of the corner of his eye, Nicolet could see that the church was almost empty, only a few more left in line. Then, suddenly, he felt his hand seized in a cold, hard grip.

"That old bitch!" It was the boy who had given him a ride, his voice a fierce half-whisper. There was something cat-like about him, his pale eyes set wide apart, a faint feathering of blond whiskers at the corners of his mouth. "They ought to ride her out of this town on a rail." Then before Nicolet had time to answer, the boy sprang down the stairs followed by his two friends and went jogging off with his hands in his pockets, his head ducked against the rain.

Nicolet had followed him out onto the top step, and the last look that many of his departing parishioners had of him that morning was standing there with the starched lappets fluttering at his throat and his eyes narrowed against the rain. He loved the rain, alone would have tipped his face and opened his mouth to it. The sermon had been a failure, but it no longer much mattered because he knew in the rain again that the truth of it was true; there was no part of the world untouched by joy. Even behind the boy's queer violence a kind of wild joy had trembled. All that troubled Nicolet now was the suspicion that the violence was somehow his own doing, that the hate that for a moment he himself had felt for poor old Irma had shot out burning into the tinder of the boy's heart.

FIFTEEN

<hr/>

IT'S MAGIC. That's why you have to sit on it. Otherwise it might go flying away without us." In the middle of the red and white checkered table-cloth that was spread out on the grass, Roy had placed the picnic basket upside down with the children's sandwiches and their cups of milk spread out on its flat bottom. He wanted them to use it as a table so that they would not spill so much and get grass stains on their shorts. They wanted to sit on the grass with everything in their laps. "This way, if it starts flying away," he said, "it will take us with it. Won't that be dandy?"

"What's dandy?" Lizzie asked. "You talk funny."

It was Monday, Nicolet's day off, and he had driven them to a meadow on the heights not far from the Vails' house where behind them the land sloped up to where it looked like the outermost green edge of the world with the blue sky huge and cloudless behind it, in front of them sloped down to a barn and

outbuildings beyond which you could see patches of
sea. Nicolet had said that he would drive back and
pick them up after the picnic.

With Irma gone, Roy had made the sandwiches
himself, taking the greatest pains with them. Ruining
and throwing away a good deal of bread in the process, he had sliced each piece into two thin slices, cut
off the crusts, and spread them with what seemed
right to him for small children in springtime—quince
jelly and cream cheese, deviled ham, watercress. Now
he wanted them eaten right, he said, and picking Lizzie up under her arms, he set her down on the table-
cloth beside the overturned basket. He was afraid
for a moment that she was going to cry—her great
unblinking eyes followed him slowly around to where
Cornelia was picking a bouquet of yellow mustard
and campion—but she did not cry. Seeing her grandfather approach, Cornelia went of her own accord and
sat down beside her sister.

"What does the magic table-cloth do?" she asked.

Roy used the full weight of his arm to press down
on his beer can until finally with a crack and a hiss
the puncture came, shooting him with a delicate,
beery mist. He wiped his face on his shirt sleeve and
smiled. The second hole always came easier for some
reason.

"Oh, magic . . . You never know what it's going
to do or what's going to do it or who it's going to do
it to." He waved his beer can vaguely through the
air, then took a long swallow from it. Cool and bitter,

it stung his throat faintly and made his eyes water. "Sometimes the most everyday kinds of things turn out to have some magic in them. Old lamps. A rabbit's little hind foot with the fuzz on it."

"Maybe it will fly us away," Cornelia said.

"Maybe. There is never any sure way of telling. Eat up." He lay down on his side with one elbow in the grass, his chin in his hand, and watched them.

"Your teeth look like pits," Lizzie said, her mouth full of watercress.

"Maybe it will fly us up even higher than the birds can fly. Just think of that for a while," he said, thinking of it himself. "Two little girls with yellow, hair floating through the sky with their granddad as nice as you please and going up higher and higher and higher till the world doesn't look any bigger than a nut."

"Tell us a story," Cornelia said.

"I am telling you a story."

"Pretend we're flying now."

When they returned from church the day before, they had found Irma's room empty. Her clothes were all gone. The bed was stripped. All that remained of her was the miniature pair of Indian moccasins hanging by the dresser mirror. She had left no message. Theo had called the few of her friends that he knew, but none of them had been able to tell him anything. Neither Grogan, nor Grogan's stout, silent son who helped him out on weekends, had driven her anywhere. Theo was off now checking the bus station and the train station, whatever he could think of, but it was unlikely, Roy thought, that he would find anything. It was probably for the best.

"Where are we flying to, then?" Lizzie asked.

He glanced at his youngest grandchild with curiosity. Towheaded, button-faced, she could not look less like a Nicolet yet the blood was in her, his blood, Léon's blood, all the fox-like French faces in Léon's plum-colored album; what a rendezvous of ghosts a child was. Her upper lip was white with milk.

"Some wonderful magic place," he said. "The land of heart's desire. The blessed isles. The happy hunting ground."

"What's it like?"

The sun felt so hot on the top of his head that taking his handkerchief out of his pocket, he tied knots at each of the four corners and put it on like a cap. This was so much more interesting than a story that the children stopped asking questions and watched him in silence. He wore it pulled down much farther in front than in back so that it gave him an oddly rakish air. Once more he raised the beer can to his lips.

"Well," he said, "it's a lot like this place where we are, I shouldn't wonder. There are green meadows and buttercups like this. The birds are always singing, and there are never any clouds except the pink ones and the golden ones that come when the sun starts going down. It's the place where all the lost things are found. That's the magic of it. Never-never land. Everything that was ever lost since the world began turns up there in the end. And all the people who were ever lost turn up there in the end." He felt a little light-headed; beer on an empty stomach, he thought, and reached for a sandwich.

"Pretend we're there now," Cornelia said.

"First I've got to get something on my stomach." They watched him bite into the white bread. The handkerchief on his head was white, and except for the withery skin around his eyes, his face was white. Lying on one elbow, he had his face tilted sideways so that the sagging lower cheek seemed twice the size of the other. Cornelia wondered if she could achieve the same effect by tilting her head sideways but did not try because her grandfather was looking straight at her while he chewed.

"We *are* there," he said finally, having trouble swallowing so that his eyes bulged for an instant's panic, then went back to dreaming as he finished off the last of the beer. "The magic table-cloth has landed, and here we are. Oh, children, children!" He suddenly flung his arm out wide. "Isn't it beautiful? The land of heart's desire. You see it? Avalon. Watch them all come running over the hill through the green grass—all the lost children, the lost years!"

He pointed up to the swelling green brink of the world behind them, half-blinded by the sun, and as they turned around, a figure rose up over it and paused against the empty sky. It was Léon, his short military cape fluttering as he raised his good arm to wave down to them. From the way he stood, from the

pitch of his shoulders, Roy could see the disappoint-
ment heavy upon him, and after all, Roy thought, it
was no wonder that he should be disappointed to find
this old barber to be his only son, cringing in the
grass with children and giddy on a single can of beer.
But "Oh, you also disappointed me, Papa," Roy
thought. "You also disappointed me." And although
he did not want to smile, once he started he found
that it was very hard indeed to stop.

"Bluebeard!" Cornelia shouted and ran up the slope
toward her father, who picked her up and carried her
down again as she undid the sweater that he had
tied around his neck by the sleeves and hid her face
in it.

"Nobody's seen her leave," Nicolet said. "She must
still be in town somewhere."

"I wish I could have a hankie on my head like
that," Lizzie said wistfully to her grandfather.

Lillian Flagg was in her back yard painting a picture when Rooney telephoned, and as soon as their
conversation was finished, she returned to it. She
meant simply to put it away for the day, take her
canvas in out of the sun and close up her paints, but
she found this impossible. She could not leave it as it
was. Standing there in her bathing suit with her
hair up in curlers, she stared at it through half-closed
eyes. She moved a few steps farther away and bent
over to see it upside down through her legs. She took

up her brush and with the point of its handle picked off an insect that had gotten gummed up in the wet, green pigment that she had used for the lawn.

There was nothing wrong with the perspective that she could see, and by and large the colors seemed true enough although the shingles of the house were perhaps not quite so chocolate a brown. With a little white on the tip of her brush, she modified this. The sky was better than her skies usually were. One plume of cloud came down too far and made it look as though it was coming out of the chimney, but she fixed that easily. It was only after she had stood there staring at it for some time longer that she decided that she knew what the trouble was. It was not that it did not look enough like what it was supposed to be but that it looked so much like nothing else. The house that she had done was only the house, her sky and trees were hopelessly sky and trees. The sharp slap of her hand to her bare shoulder was partly for the bug that had bitten her there, drawing blood, but more for this tediously accurate lie that she had told with her tidy little brushes.

Mixing some lavender and thinning it to a wash, she swept it back and forth above the clouds, then ribbons of indigo that streamed together to make a jagged hole in one corner of the sky where she put in what might have been a star or a white bird. Marvelous things happened to the pine that rose above the roof from behind, the branches folding down like dark wings, and with her palette knife she spread cadmium yellow thick and glistening across the windows and in a long swath that fanned out from the back door. The house exploded with light.

By the time that she had finished, it was nearly time for lunch, and she realized that she had altogether forgotten about what she had promised over the phone to do immediately. The picture had been her only miracle that morning, she thought, a wild mess of a miracle. She sat down on the back steps and closing her eyes tried to see again the skinny young minister and the girl that any fool could tell he was in love with. Only colors came; lavender, indigo, gold. Anyway, it was a woman that she had never seen that Rooney Vail had asked her to pray for. She struggled to keep her eyes closed, tried to see a face-that-might-have-been beneath a face-that-was. "Come forth," she said. "Don't be afraid any more." It was not easy with someone you had never seen.

In khaki shorts and T-shirt, Clem kneeled at the back of the shop to open the large cardboard box that he had picked up at the station on his way to work. It contained a consignment of hats from the West Indies. They were floppy, shapeless hats of loosely plaited straw with high crowns and wide brims, dwarves' hats, and they smelled of fresh cut hay. He thought that he had never seen such fine colors—purple, burnt orange, yellow, lime. He set a radish-colored one on the back of his head as he unpacked the rest and placed them in several nested stacks on the counter. They made everything else in the shop look dead. He took the Help Wanted sign down from the door and on the blank side printed in red letters, "Zowie! Only one per customer," and leaned it up against one of the stacks.

Rooney had finally sent him out of the house. "Go help Nick look. Go tend shop. You make me feel like some kind of natural wonder the way you keep watching. Please get the Hell out of here, darling." Anyway, she said, it was probably all a false alarm, and alarm was just the word for it—panic almost, with the muscles of his stomach tightening when she had first told him. Then a crazy exuberance that made him afraid that if he stayed, he was in danger of somehow wrecking them both. Her own calm astounded him--the way she could talk to Lillian Flagg over the kitchen telephone in her ordinary morning voice while he sat there with his coffee cup rattling in the saucer.

Help Nick look for what? He remembered then. How she had stood there in the dim church begging them to hate her, and he had thought at the time that she was all Jews standing there begging to be hated wherever they were not loved. What could Rooney's miracle woman do for her now? As Rooney talked to Lillian Flagg over the telephone, Clem had reached out and touched her. She lifted his hand away. He decided that he had better take her advice and get the Hell out of there.

Through the store window, he looked out onto Mc-
Kinley Street. Sunday's rain had washed the pavement clean, and people kept to the shadow of the shop
awning as they passed. The windshield of a truck
flashed the sun at him as he ran his hand up under
his shirt and felt his own flesh, the pliant shield of his
ribs. Down from the direction of the parochial
school, a group of children came with a nun. They
were all bare legs and sneakers, and the nun was a
pair of great black wings that beat the air all around
them. He grabbed up a stack of the hats and with the
radish-colored one still on his head stepped out of the
shop just as they were passing. He handed hats out to
all of them and himself placed a yellow one on the
nun. She asked no questions but blushed like a girl
and hurried off in her undertaker's shoes after the children who had raced ahead half blinded by the flimsy,
bright brims. It was the one that she caught by the
shirt-tail and folded away in her black wings that
Clem saw with something like terror as his unborn
child.

When she was sure that no one was watching,
Miss Zimmer slipped into Roy's bedroom and closed
the door behind her, leaning back against it with both
hands on the knob. Evers, the Railway Express man,
had long since gone to work on his bicycle. She had
seen Mrs. Doyle feeding the goldfish in her room as
she passed, and old Taylor, who smelled of feet, was

not even awake yet. If anyone should happen in upon her, she could always say that she was looking for a book that Roy had borrowed.

Nearly everything that she saw irritated her. The room was not really neat but old-man fussy. On the medicine tray hooked over the radiator he had all his bottles and jars lined up according to height, but the tray itself was sticky with dribblings. The brass bed was sloppily pulled together with the extra blanket rolled at the foot like a soldier's. She opened the drawer of the bedside table. There were several cigars, a cracked magnifying glass, and a black grease-crayon that she had seen him use to mark the date of purchase on the canned goods that he stored in quantity on shelves in the cellar. She took the crayon out of the drawer and touched things with it as she moved about the room, tapped the red glass mug with his name on it that sat on the window sill, ran it across the brass railing at the foot of the bed. She used it to flip over the brochure that lay on his dresser. It was a catalogue of barber equipment—scalp vibrators, sterilizers, razor strops. Her eye was caught by a framed photograph that stood on the bedside table. She knew that it was his father—there was little that she did not know about Roy—and she picked it up for closer scrutiny. He wore his cape thrown back over one shoulder, a close-cropped, fluffy beard, and there were little welts under his eyes. She tapped the glass with her crayon and found that it left a black mark on the bridge of his nose.

Laying the picture flat, she continued the mark around the eye, then around the other, so that he wore a pair of owlish spectacles. Then she darkened and enlarged the moustache and drew in heavy eyebrows. It was only when she had added a black cigar jutting out of the corner of his mouth that she realized that she had transformed the old bore's Christ into a remarkable likeness of Groucho Marx.

They were both in hiding; if either of them had happened to look out of the right window at the right time, they might even have caught sight of each other. Poteat's house stood on high ground just the other side of the McKinley Street bridge, and from his second floor you could see back over the low, flat roof of the elementary school and across the playground to where Irma's friend Hilda lived with her husband in a narrow box of a house at the dead end of Auburn Street. It was here that Irma had come in the rain when she left the church on Sunday. She slept there Sunday night, and her original plan was to leave Myron for good on Monday, but Hilda persuaded her to stay a few days longer, arguing that she needed a rest and that it would give her time to think about where she was going to go next and what she was going to do when she got there. Actually, it was less for these reasons that Irma decided to stay than in the hope that another day or so might give her a chance to find some way of seeing the children again and saying goodbye to them without being seen by anyone else. Hilda told her that at the Old Myron what she had done at Nicolet's church was the principal topic of all conversations and that if she ever showed her face outside, she would be mobbed.

So on Monday morning she remained out of sight in the house, and when Nicolet telephoned to see if Hilda might know her whereabouts, Hilda lied and said that she knew nothing. Irma spent most of her time trying to keep out of the way of Hilda's husband, who worked as nightwatchman at the shoe factory and went wandering around the house in his undershirt complaining that he could not sleep. Hilda said that she had known him to go on this way for three or four days without sleep until there were times, he had told her, when he started having dreams with his eyes wide open, and rooms that he knew intimately turned queer and unfamiliar and walls had a way of disappearing altogether.

For Irma, walls multiplied as she explored Hilda's stuffy little rooms—thin, papered walls that kept her turning sharp right, sharp left, to pass through doors to other rooms, other walls, until the geometry of her pacing made her think of the puzzles that she had sometimes come across in the children's picture books where with a pencil you were supposed to trace your way through a maze until you came at last to the hollow square in the middle marked Home.

Poteat, nearby, had a terrible cold. The inside of his head felt charred. Both nostrils were packed tight although from time to time with an audible clicking in his sinuses one of them would come temporarily clear. His mind moved very slowly, and it was as if he saw and heard everything through plate glass. In a strange, slow way he enjoyed the cold. It gave him an excuse for staying in the house where he would have chosen to stay anyway. But he also enjoyed it for itself. He enjoyed slopping around the upstairs in his bathrobe—dozing, reading, looking out the window. He enjoyed not answering the telephone; and when the doorbell rang, he would look out of the bathroom window to see who was there, and only the time that Metzger came had he gone downstairs to answer it. Metzger had come in the downpour Sunday to tell him about Irma. Earlier, Nicolet had come. Standing behind his closet door, Poteat had heard him call up the stairs, "Peace be in this house."

Peace was already there, had come on the foggy night of Rooney's visit. Whatever had bound him to her was severed then; he felt free of her at last. He felt free and old and remote as he padded around with his eyes swollen and his nose red from blowing. He went through the ritual of bicarbonate of soda and aspirin. He drank lots of fruit juice, and he gargled. But he knew well enough that a cure was the last thing that he wanted. Not to be able to smell the world or to taste it, to hear everything as if it came from another room with the door closed—this was his peace, and it was enough.

"You and your Myronian epistles, Willy boy!

You've even got that poor old Israelite playing Joan of Arc." Metzger had been unable to wait even until his coat was off but stood there dripping rain all over the carpet as he delivered his report. "When she said she'd been nursing a guilty passion for him all these months, you should have seen his face. It cracked right down the middle like a plate. The deacons and deaconesses fell bleeding to the ground."

"Shut the door, pal," Poteat had said. "I've got a filthy cold." And except when it was opened again to let Metzger leave, it had remained shut ever since. Unlike Irma, he was not sure what he was hiding from—from people like Metzger, he supposed, who moved about too fast and spoke too excitedly about matters that seemed a long way off—but the hiding itself, like the cold, he found not unpleasant.

SIXTEEN

———◆———

THERE was a hiss as the rocket cut up through the night, then a little thud as it burst into a fountain of glittering embers that came softly down toward the river. Then another and another until it looked as if the darkness itself had burst apart and Myron was being inundated by fire from beyond the darkness. People sat crowded along the banks of the river, on blankets, the hoods of cars. It was a warm night. The cupola of the town hall was lit up and, behind it, the white spire of the Congress Street church. The instruments of the high school band glinted in the falling light. The tide was in, and black water lapped against the concrete embankment that ran along behind the McKinley Street shops.

The three boys clattered, laughing, down the hill past Poteat's house which, like most of the other houses, looked empty and dark with almost everybody gone to the river to watch the fireworks. The boys stopped under a street light near the bridge and locked their arms around each other's shoulders to make a kind of swaying huddle with their heads bowed forward and talking down into the little tent of dark that was sweet with the spearmint and beer of their breathing, the brothy smell of sweat.

"You mean we got to find enough to fill this whole stinking bag?"

"If we weren't looking for it, we'd be wiping it off our feet. This town's full of it."

"You're full of it."

"Christ, we only need a bag."

"I still say you're full of it."

"We're all full of it," said the boy who had given Nicolet the ride. "Give you any ideas?"

"Jesus!" They leaned in against each other, helpless with laughter as another group of rockets shot up. They crossed the bridge single-file and kept peering down into the gutter, their shadows stretching out thin behind them.

They had almost reached the Something Shop when the Vails' red station wagon drew up to the curb and Rooney got out followed by Clem. The boys hung back as the two of them cut through the alley that led down past the side of the shop to the embankment behind it. It was lined with people sitting along the edge with their feet hanging down and their faces tilted toward the sky. No one took any particular notice of the Vails as they hesitated there for a moment before moving on. Rooney wore a trench coat over her shoulders, and Clem came after her carrying a blanket. When they reached the place where Roy Nicolet and the children were sitting, Rooney crouched down behind them.

"We've been looking for you," she whispered.

"Dear lady . . ." Roy spoke before he had seen who she was; the night was a dear lady. "Everybody is looking for somebody. I have been looking for Theo."

"Where is he?"

"Still looking for you know who, I imagine."

They moved over to make room, and Rooney sat down beside them. She lifted Lizzie onto her lap; the child's hair smelled warm, like grass, and she put her thumb in her mouth.

"I'm sure she's left town by now," Rooney said.

"The children say they saw her today."

"Look," Cornelia said. She held out a small kewpie doll with plumes glued to it and one cheek pushed in. "Irma gave it to me."

"What did she say, sweetie?" Clem knelt down on the blanket.

"I don't remember."

"She said goodbye," Lizzie said without removing her thumb.

"Glob, glob," Clem imitated her. "Now say it," he told her, pulling out her thumb.

"Watch there, watch there!" Roy warned, pointing to the sky. High above them in a shower of golden sparks from the latest rocket, the largest and loudest yet, a tissue paper parachute came floating slowly down. A breeze caught it and carried it farther out over the river. A manikin in a frock coat and white beard dangled from it with one arm twisted in the strings so that it could have been trying to signal them.

"What will Heaven disgorge next?" Roy said.

"Makes me think of Nick's sermon." Clem whispered it to no one in particular. He slipped his arm around Rooney's waist. "Power from on high."

Cornelia gave a little sigh of passionate tenderness and regret. "It's a tiny, old angel."

"It's only Uncle Sam," Rooney said, "but I can't bear him just to fall into the river."

"What she said was goodbye," Lizzie murmured sleepily. None of them heard her.

She had said a good deal more than that, but it was at least half in German so that of course they had not understood. For almost a week she had seen no one but Hilda and her husband with whom she spoke only German, and consequently she had found it difficult to keep to English with the children. She told them to take good care of their teeth and to try to keep their room in order. She told them not to bedevil their father by doing things like putting sand in his shoes because he had troubles enough and there would be nobody to help him now. She said that she was going away, and she tried to tell them a fanciful story to explain it, but the story was not successful. At first the children did not even seem to be sure who she was, and that was not surprising, considering her

disguise. She had borrowed from Hilda some clothes
—a navy blue spring coat, white gloves, a little straw
hat with a veil—and she was also wearing a pair of
dark glasses. She had had Hilda call first the house
and then the church to make sure that Nicolet was at
neither, and from that she rightly guessed that, as on
her days off, he had left the children to play on the
lawn with Betty Blackburn to keep an eye on them
from the window of her office across the street. She
counted on Betty Blackburn's thinking that there was
nothing amiss about a respectable looking woman in
white gloves stopping to talk to them, and in this too
she turned out to be right. But her fear of being
found out made her speak too rapidly, and the borrowed clothes made her feel strange and awkward,
and even as she was making up her story, she wished
that she had not come.

She said that across the ocean there was somebody
who needed her to take care of him. He was sick because years before bad people had fed him poison.
She had not seen him for a long time, but recently he
had started coming to her at night-time in her dreams
and telling her that he wanted to see her again. He
was all alone with no one to cook for him and make
his bed so she would bring him fresh eggs and milk,
and then he would soon get well again. She did not
know just where he was living or how to find out, but
she would have to go back across the ocean to start
looking, and she would send them picture postcards
along the way. In the meanwhile, she would leave

them certain things to remember her by, and it was here that she gave the kewpie from the Palisades to Cornelia and the red, white and blue rabbit's foot to Lizzie.

As she sat on the edge of their sandbox in Hilda's stylish spring outfit, she came to believe for a few moments that what she had been telling them was true and that, lacking any other plan, she might indeed devote herself to just such a search as she had described to them. She did not know what purpose it would serve. She did not know what she would do if she ever found him. But it felt to her as if the whole absurd tangle of years since the war would somehow rearrange itself, if only she were to see him again, into a circle, and for all these months and years of her life she would turn out to have been traveling not just anywhere, nowhere, but in a great, inscrutable arc that would finally close back upon itself.

She could picture him grinning at her, his little eyes bright with some kind of crazy pride, while she denounced him in court as a war criminal and the prosecutor came over to her and not without embarrassment requested her to take off her shoes so that it could be seen what was there and what was no longer there, and Heinz Taffel would see too, and, who could tell, perhaps he would be sick again like the time when old Maxl had come waddling in upon them.

Or she could as well picture something else. The children had finally decided that it must be Irma after all behind the glasses and the veil, and Lizzie leaned with her cheek against her while Cornelia played with the kewpie in the sand. She could picture him sick as she had already told them that he was, could see herself climbing several flights of dingy stairs to get to his room where she would find him sallow and grey on a cot, and he would have no idea at all who she was until perhaps she might give one cackle, one little flop of her wings, and then she would take his head in her lap, and they would weep together like old war comrades or old lovers. But perhaps the dream about his funeral meant that he was dead. Then she would take a flower to his grave—*Ich vergebe, Heinz Taffel . . . vergebe, vergesse.* Or she would go by night and on his moonlit grave would place a single egg in memory of how she had once been forced to amuse him and his brothers-in-arms.

Whatever she did, punish him or forgive him—in either case free him from the past and free herself— it would be to bring symmetry out of disorder, to draw clean into one great circle the snarled rope of the years. But even as she dreamed all this, smoothing the hair back from Lizzie's temples with a gloved finger, she had the sense that the circle had already been drawn. She knew suddenly that in the church on Sunday it was as much about Taffel as about Nicolet that she had spoken—"You are going to be good to this pastor again now" . . . you are going to be good to all now in this world who suffer and who cause to suffer.

Then she had noticed Betty Blackburn peering out of her open window across the street, and giving them each a kiss on top of the head, she had said, "Goodbye, children. Tell your father goodbye," and hurried away with the little veil fluttering at the great bridge of her nose. It was just as she was approaching Hilda's house that the boy who knew Nicolet had seen and recognized her.

The manikin with his parachute fell into the river where it floated, spreadeagled, on the dark water. At the end of the pier that jutted out from the embankment, a high wooden lattice had been erected, and this was ignited now. With a sputter of pinwheels and showering of sparks, it blazed up into a great American flag and, underneath it in fiery letters, GIVE ME LIBERTY OR GIVE ME DEATH. The high school band struck up a march, the warm breeze carrying most of it down-river except for the throbbing of the bass drum. Girls in short, white skirts fired Roman candles into the night.

"She's in there, all right," the boy whispered. There was a woodshed built against the back of the house, and standing on top of it, he could see through the window. It was a small room that looked as if it was used partly as a workshop, partly for storage. There were piles of old newspapers along one wall and above them crude shelves cluttered with paint cans, jars of nails, turpentine. Woodworking tools hung on nails with their outlines painted in black on the unfinished walls. In the center of the room was a bench

saw and close to it a drill press. The only light came
from a shaded bulb that hung from the ceiling near
where Irma Reinwasser sat; the rest of the house
was dark. It was a high-backed rocking-chair facing
into the room so that all that the boy could see was
the top of her head with her scalp showing faintly
pink where the hair grew thin. The chair was tipped
back toward the window, and her legs were stretched
out with her heels resting on the edge of a packing
case, the toes flopped out to either side. The boy
sprang down lightly from the top of the shed and
squatted on the grass by his two friends.

"Where'd I leave it?" he asked.

"By the bush." One of them pointed.

"Get it."

It was a brown paper bag, and the boy went over
and started lifting it gingerly by the top.

"Watch it, for God's sake," the boy said. "Lift it
from the bottom or it'll rip. That stuff weighs a ton."

"You ought to know. Most of it's yours."

"Christ almighty!" The third boy had stood up but
bent double now with stifled laughter. "What a way
to spend the Fourth." He could barely get the words
out.

"Does that stuff ever stink!" The boy stepped back
from the bag. "You lift it from the bottom yourself."

"Shut the hell up, or she'll hear us." His whisper
was fierce, but as he leaned over to pick it up, his voice
cracked in spite of himself. "Man!" he said, holding
his nose in his fist.

"You sure got it in for her."

"Just shake her up a little, the horny old Yid. She asked for it." With his knees bent deep, he crept along close to the wall of the house, holding the bag as low as he could and his head tipped all the way back. The moon had risen, and his revolted young cat-face looked milky in the light of it. Kneeling on the lowest step just beyond the woodshed, he set the bag down carefully in front of the back door, then with both hands on the back of his neck, he pressed his forehead down against his knees for a moment, his shoulders heaving. The two friends stood side by side behind him; it could have been young priests offering sacrifice.

"Who's got the juice?" he asked when he had recovered himself. One of them handed him a can of lighter fluid which in a series of long squirts he emptied on the bag. "Soon as I touch it off, start yelling like crazy and then beat it. She comes out to see what the hell's up. She finds this thing on fire on her stoop. So what does she do? She starts stomping hell out of it to put it out." Once more his voice broke. "Before she's through, she's got it all over her up to her knees." In the silence they could hear the faint boom-booming of the drum by the river.

Irma slept in her chair. Through snowy, grey air a great circle revolved slowly. Around the circumference, wild beasts pursued each other but with a kind of ritual stateliness, dragons and unicorns, long-necked birds with their wings outstretched and open beaks, all richly colored like an Indian carpet. Nearer to the center, the colors grew cooler, blues and lavenders, and there were fewer figures, only a scattering of stylized suns, moons, stars. The snowflakes floated all around but did not enter the circle itself which seemed to generate stillness and deep peace. Inside the hoop formed by a serpent with its tail in its mouth, four pale, filmy petals pulsed dreamily in and out like a sea flower, and here the circle barely turned. At the very center, there was no movement at all. It was emptiness, a vortex.

Hilda had tried to persuade her to go with her to the fireworks—no one would recognize her in the dark, she said—but she had refused. That afternoon she had seen the children, the next morning she would leave Myron, and she looked forward to an evening alone in between. She had eaten a cold supper of sausage and potato salad with Hilda and her husband, and then they had left her—the husband for the factory, Hilda for the riverside. She chose the workshop to sit in because it was at the back of the house and no lights would show from the street. After trying for a while to read the newspaper, she had closed her eyes and hovered for she could not tell how long on the border of sleep. Then the grey snow had begun to fall, and she had thought that it was going to be the square of the prison yard again, but instead, like an eye opening, it was the circle, and this was less a dream than it was herself, the dreamer, the eye beholding at last the eye.

The caterwauling of the boys failed to wake her. They whooped and pounded on the back porch before running off, but she heard nothing. A thick vine of smoke twisted in through the door from the kitchen, tendrils slipping in under the baseboard and up the walls. At one end of the lintel, a rose of fire blossomed, then another and another until the whole door was framed in roses. They spread out along the shelves where jars cracked, shooting brilliant roots down into the newspapers. Scarlet and lilac, gold, green, coral, the floor was thick with flowers. By the time that Irma opened her eyes, the little room had become a bower.

SEVENTEEN

THE afternoon was humid and overcast. It had looked all morning as though it might rain, but then there would be a break in the clouds and the sun would shine through for a while instead. Myron seemed emptier than it had. People had gone away on vacations, or they spent more time at the beach. There were more gulls than usual on the river, attracted by the debris left by the Fourth of July crowds. They sat along the embankment with their grey wings tucked tight to their sides, dropping cumbersomely over the edge if anything floated by on the glassy water to entice them. It was a lethargic, in-between kind of time—no longer spring but not yet quite summer—and the news that Irma Reinwasser had died in the Auburn Street fire had occasioned little stir. The cause of the fire was not known, but there was little speculation about it. It had been an old house with old wiring, and there had been no one around to see it start.

When Franny died, there had of course been almost immediately an endless number of things for
Nicolet to attend to—relatives to notify, letters of
condolence to acknowledge, her belongings to dispose
of. There were scraps of food that she had cooked left
over in the refrigerator to be eaten or thrown away.
Mail addressed to her continued to arrive. On the
kitchen blackboard that they used for shopping lists
and telephone messages, her handwriting remained
for days before he finally had the heart to erase it. So
for all its suddenness, there had been also a degree of
gradualness about her death or, in another way, she
had died for him again with each new thing to be
done, and if this had made it no easier to bear, it had
at least made it easier to believe. It had given him
time to choose between ways of believing. But with
Irma there was none of this. If she had relatives, he
had no idea who they were—there were no letters left,
no addresses, and except for the little souvenir moccasins, all her possessions had been destroyed in the
fire. So as he drove Roy and the children to the cemetery, it was not so difficult to believe that she had
died as it was to believe that for more than a year she
had lived with them under circumstances of the greatest intimacy, almost that she had lived at all. And yet
he knew that his children mourned for her as they
had probably not mourned even for their own mother.
He had found Lizzie that morning crouched on the
floor between their beds with her hands over her face
trying not to let anyone hear her, and it had been

her trying more than what he had heard that had by contrast made him feel cold and inhuman as he picked her up and placed her on the carrousel horse where she still would not take her hands from her face. He remembered, as he drove, the time that he had telephoned Irma from Muscadine and how he had suddenly called her his own true love or some such nonsense, swearing that he would never be unfaithful to her with Rooney. And to his surprise, this was the picture of her that came clearest in his mind now although it was a picture that in life he had never seen —Irma standing at the kitchen telephone that late afternoon with the receiver touching her mouth as she listened to him inanely mock her the way a husband might mock his wife, and he remembered how for an improbable moment it was as his wife that he had thought of her.

When they arrived at the cemetery, there were others already waiting there. Hilda and her husband still had on the clothes they had been wearing the night of the fire because those were all they had left, but from the neighbors who had taken them in Hilda had borrowed a raincoat to cover the unfuneral pink of her summer dress. A little apart, her husband in his grey work clothes leaned back on the crook of his umbrella and gazed out over the river below while Hilda whispered to Nicolet that it had been days since his last decent sleep and she was afraid that he was beginning to see things again because when they had first arrived, the breeze had blown over some of

the flowers and he had turned white as a sheet and
almost jumped out of his skin. She apologized for
having lied to Nicolet when he had called to ask about
Irma, but it was Irma herself who had told her to, she
said, and it was the faint edge of resentment in her
voice as she said it that more than anything else gave
Irma some reality for him again. Grogan was also
there sitting in his cab with the two-way radio
turned down low, but he switched it off as he saw
Nicolet approach and got out of the cab with his bad
eye wavering off in the wrong direction as they shook
hands. Irma had always called him a crazy schlemiel,
and Nicolet smiled at his being there now: *wie man's
macht, ist's falsch.*

He did not plan to begin the service until the Vails
arrived, but he stepped behind his car to put on his
black gown, to reach into the front seat where he had
left the prayer book and put it in his pocket. Franny's
grave was nearby, and he thought of stepping over to
look at it but did not. One wife at a time. There was a
rumble of distant thunder, and the children ran over
to their grandfather who took them each by the hand
and turned them to face the river. The water and
the sky were both the grey of gulls' wings. He fastened his gown all the way down the front, hiking it
up to do the last few buttons, then letting it fall as
he folded his arms and rested them on the roof of
the car.

He watched the handful of people who stood mo-
tionless in the silvery air, waiting, as he found him-

self waiting, and for more than the Vails, for more
than the time when he would step up with his ancient
words to the neat, square hole where a mat of artificial
grass covered the raw earth and the urn had already
been placed down inside by the undertaker and his
assistant who stood at a tactful distance now, also
waiting. Waiting for it to rain perhaps, waiting for
it to be time at last to go home and forget about Irma
Reinwasser. *Waiting for you,* he thought, *always you,
though half the time we hardly know it's you or that
we're waiting. Come be with the living here and the
dead and the ones it's hard to tell about.*

Across the river, Clem waited in the car for Rooney to come out of their house. In the middle of the
night he had felt her climb out of bed and go padding barefoot across the floor. After a while he had
gotten up and followed her, standing there in the dark
to talk to her through the closed door, shivering
though it was a warm night. Had anything gone
wrong? Had it been just another false alarm after
all? Her answer was finally to open the door where
she paused in her nightdress for a moment with the
light streaking out past her and not saying anything,
then turned him around and with her hands on his
bare shoulders steered him back to bed and climbing in beside him told him that sometimes people had to get up in the night and there was nothing
wrong about it except when other people made asses
of themselves by following; and then he had closed
his eyes and with his lips touching her hair slept like

a child until morning. He tapped the horn lightly now, and in a few moments she came out in a black linen dress with an armful of day lilies and glanced up at the sky to see about the rain before hurrying to the car, dropping a lily on the gravel drive as she came. "Let's not talk till this is all over, O.K.?" she said, and he obeyed her. Among the things that, with effort, he did not talk about was how he had given away the wonderful hats, how when she had come out just now in her black dress, he had remembered the day that he had found her waiting for the train at Princeton Junction and he had gone up to her as much in terror as in longing and how of these two, finally now, only the longing was left. As they drove in silence up the long hill, to the cemetery, they passed a man climbing it on foot, but neither of them recognized him as Poteat.

He walked with his head down, kicking a white stone before him, and several times when the stone went skipping off the tar road into the grass, he cut out into the grass to kick it back again. His cold was better, but he was clammy with perspiration and there was still the smell of menthol in his nostrils, the feel of menthol at his throat so that even the warm air stung. Although he walked slowly, his breathing was heavy and his seersucker pants clung to his legs unpleasantly. He had had no intention, when he left his house, of making this trip. After lunch he had wandered down to the newspaper office where he sat at his desk for a while glancing through the mail without really reading it. There was an unsigned letter to the editor that caught his eye, saying something about how the Epistle to the Myronians was the work of a communist atheist, misspelled, and he had slipped it into the out basket marked "Print as is." He read the short piece on the fire and Irma and noted the time and place of the burial. The woman who handled subscriptions asked him if he felt better, to which he replied that he did not really feel much of anything, but otherwise no one paid any particular attention to his return. When he left after about an hour, his plan, as much as he had one, was to walk as far as where McKinley Street turned up the hill, then go back around to Auburn Street past the scene of the fire, across the playground and home again. He had no wish to see anybody, but he felt a need to be seen, verified somehow.

When he reached the remains of Hilda's house, he stopped. The air still smelled burnt, acrid, and as he turned up the cement walk to the front door, broken glass crunched beneath him. A white cat sat in the grass licking the inside of her paw, and when he reached out with one foot to rub her neck, she licked his shoe. The house was in ruins, but the front door was still intact in its frame. Its inside was charred, but the outside looked untouched. It was half open, leading nowhere.

He had been asleep when the fire occurred, but the noise of the sirens woke him, and he had opened his eyes to the sight of firelight flickering dimly on

his bedroom wall. He had sat at the window with his
inhaler in his hand watching it—fountains of sparks
jetting up into the air, then falling like fireflies on
the dark houses. Seeing it by daylight—the tram-
pled grass and shrubs, the back wall bared where the
roof had fallen in so that by the different kinds of
paper you could guess at where the rooms had been
—he thought of the words that Nicolet had called up
the stairs when he had been hiding behind the closet
door; and after the fire, he thought, maybe there was
finally peace in this house and for this woman, the
peace of dereliction. He had found it so himself. He
felt suddenly a deep kinship with Irma Reinwasser.
She, as no one else, would understand what it was to
be beyond burning. Both ineptly, comically almost,
she had loved in her queer way where he in his queer
way had hated or tried for a while to hate; and it
made of them all a kind of slapstick family: he and
Irma, Rooney Vail, Nicolet. If he belonged anywhere, he belonged somehow with them. Only with
them was he likely to find proof that he existed, if
there was such proof. The smoke in the air made him
sneeze several times so violently that it brought tears
to his eyes and frightened away the cat. He would go
help them bury her, he decided, the eccentric, pink-
nosed uncle, the family ghost.

There were about a dozen people there when the
Vails arrived, several whom they had never seen before. Denbigh had come, and he looked curiously out
of place standing in his clericals with the others

rather than out front as the officiating priest. He acknowledged their coming with a modified little smile but did not speak. Rooney crouched down to lay her flowers with the others. There seemed to be too many of them for the small, cubical grave—yellow roses, red roses, two bunches of field flowers that the children had gathered. With a few harried sweeps of her hands, she tried to bring them into some kind of order, but they seemed more of a hodgepodge to her than ever, and she finally just left them and went back to Clem.

When Nicolet stepped out from behind the car where he had been waiting and took his place by the grave, he motioned for them all to come nearer, and they stood in a rough semi-circle facing him. He was about to begin when he saw someone coming up the path and paused again. Glancing down at the children, he found their eyes fixed on him with a look of dazed fascination, and he gave them a barely perceptible wink. They were standing in front of Roy, who had a hand on each of them.

It seemed to Nicolet that the spit of land where they were all waiting was the prow of a ship, and that the clouds, the river, the far shore of the river where Myron stood, were a grey sea. Only a few scattered raindrops had started to fall, one of them spreading out dark on the page of the prayer book that he held open in front of him, another striking his cheek, but the air was heavy with the smell of rain to come. He felt a surge of excitement as though something more

than this was about to come but this at least, a great
cloudburst to drench them to their skins and wash
down the sloping deck. Nothing that he could see
was as real to him as the sense of sailing on a ship
that he could not see, and he could feel the earth
tilt beneath his feet with the grey swells, the raindrops flicking his hands and face like sea-spray.
When he saw that it was Poteat who had arrived to
join them, staying behind the others with his thin hair
blown across his forehead, the fact did not surprise
him just because it was a fact. Only what he could not
see seemed capable now of surprising him, whatever
it might be, whatever secret the voyage held. He
found that he was glad that Poteat had come—not
Poteat as he actually saw him there, dabbing under
his chin with his white handkerchief, but Poteat as no
one saw him, Poteat as he was not and as he might
become or might never become. The thunder sounded
farther away, but the sky darkened.

"And I saw heaven opened," Nicolet began to read,
"and behold a white horse, and he that sat upon him
was called Faithful and True, and in righteousness
he doth judge and make war." And *I wish you well*,
he thought, as if this itself was the secret, *I wish
you well, I wish you well*. Nicolet glanced up at
them, squinted at them, voyagers with him, through
the drizzle.

"His eyes were as a flame of fire, and on his head
were many crowns," he read. "And I saw an angel
standing in the sun, and he cried with a loud voice,

saying, to all the fowls that fly in the midst of heaven,
'Come, gather yourselves together unto the supper of
the great God.' " He sheltered the little book with his
hand. All his wives, children, fathers and brothers
were gathered with him there on the prow of the
world with the smell of the rain in the air, the smell
of the sea, and Myron a mariner's grey dream in the
distance. They were all of them more than they were,
angels standing in the rain.

"And the beast was taken, and with him them
that had received the mark of the beast, and these
both they cast alive into a lake of fire."

Hilda's husband stepped around the flowers and
stood behind him, opening the umbrella and holding
it out over his head with the rain delicately pattering
down on it. He could smell the newly turned soil and
the wet flowers. They were standing on solid earth
again. They were burying what was left of Irma
Reinwasser. Poteat sneezed into his handkerchief.
Clem took off his jacket and put it around his wife's
shoulders. There were wisps of cloud that drifted like
smoke beneath the great quilt of higher clouds. Nicolet
looked back at his book.

"And God shall wipe away all tears, and there
shall be no more death, neither sorrow, nor crying,
neither shall there be any more pain, for the former
things have passed away."

Toward the end of the short service, he hurried a
little as the rain, which at one point seemed to have
been stopping, increased again. After the sentences

of commital and the benediction, most of them turned quickly to go, and only Roy and the Vails were left, with the children, lingering there with him as he unbuttoned his black gown.

It was then that Poteat, who had started off with the others, turned around and came back. He did not even seem to see the others but went straight up to Nick and placed a hand on his shoulder.

"Good show, pal," he said. The dimples were like black slits in his face, like gills, as he smiled. "Just one little thing. This supper of the great God . . . no more death, no more pain. Ask her." He pointed down to the ground. "The Hell you say, pal. The Hell you say." He made a quick jab with one finger to tickle the stomach of Lizzie, who had come close with her sister to watch. They both darted back, giggling, and then they did an unexpected thing.

They grabbed up some of the flowers that they had brought and started pelting him with them—orange hawkweed, daisies, clover—and stooping over like a great, pale bear in his baggy seersucker suit, he kept on lunging at them with his finger. Nicolet, Bluebeard, threw back his head and laughed. Even old Roy had to smile as Poteat went lumbering off with the little girls after him. When he got as far as Nicolet's car, he turned around for a moment, and it was only then that they could see that he was more or less laughing himself.